Lady of Intrigue

A GROUP OF EIGHT NOVEL

Lady of Intrigue

A GROUP OF EIGHT NOVEL

SABRINA DARBY

Entangled Publishing, LLC
2614 South Timberline Road
Suite 109
Fort Collins, CO 80525
Visit our website at www.entangledpublishing.com.

Scandalous is an imprint of Entangled Publishing, LLC.

Edited by Alethea Spiridon Hopson
Cover Design by Heidi Stryker
Cover Art by Shutterstock

ISBN 978-1-943892-90-7

Manufactured in the United States of America

First Edition November 2015

Chapter One

"Asked for milk," Lady Jane Langley said, stifling a yawn as they began another round of The Minister's Cat. They had already gone through the entire alphabet once using adjectives as per the rules of the simple game and thus had moved on to verbs.

"Batted yarn," Lady Powell said. "And he's asleep." Lord Powell punctuated his wife's observation with an indelicate snore.

As a child accompanying her father on his frequent travels around England, Jane would bring stacks of books and happily pass hours immersed in some work by Voltaire or Davy's *Elements of Chemical Philosophy*. In recent years she had lost the fortitude of those early days and could no longer read in a moving vehicle without suffering from nausea, which was why Jane had jumped at the opportunity at the last inn to switch carriages and leave Mr. and Mrs. Brumble and Sir Joseph Grimsby behind for a few hours in order to travel with two of London's wittiest members of society. However, there had been the weight of tension in the air all morning, as if she had caught the couple mid-argument. And it was clear from the way Lady Powell leaned forward, her eyes sharp and her smile sly, that she was happy her husband was no longer listening.

"What do you think of Alistair Whitley?"

The tall, thin, red-headed man, the third son of Baron Sloane, was a clerk with the foreign office and, as best as Jane knew, was already in Vienna with the British delegation. She'd met him at dinner parties and soirees, but as a junior clerk he worked long hours and was not as much in society as others.

"Serious, keeps his opinions to himself," Jane said. She thought the tactic a wise one, gave the man a chance to get his footing in the political world and gain supporters before seeking greater positions in government, as he surely would.

"Yes, he has a very attractive silence," Lady Powell said. "And all that red hair. I've always been partial to men with red hair. Or hair, for that matter." She slid a scathing look at her husband who had lost much of his hair at least a decade ago, despite being not more than forty. "His height is appealing as well. When men are that tall, they tend to do the most adorable knock-legged thing in order to kiss."

Jane raised an eyebrow. She hadn't yet observed that particular phenomenon.

"I think he shall make a very good lover. Mark my words, Lady Jane. Young men are the best. They can be trained."

Jane coughed and then gave in to her shocked laughter. "Very kind advice."

"Do not judge me too fast," Lady Powell said. "My

husband's current mistress will be in Vienna, and his mistress before that as well. He thinks I am unaware but it isn't as if I care. I am happy to have my own delicious pursuits."

Jane glanced at Lord Powell. Still sleeping. "Your marriage is hardly my concern."

"No, it is not. I assume you plan to marry soon. If you do not, let me impart another bit of advice. Do not let yourself become a spinster assisting your father forever. When he dies and you are old, then you shall have wasted your life."

Jane couldn't speak, couldn't force any sort of laughter. She was traveling to Vienna to join her father and act as his factotum, as she had for years. He trusted her far more than he trusted his secretary, or any man he employed. She would have accompanied him a week earlier when he traveled with the initial British delegation, but as a female there were social obligations one must attend to that men could so easily put aside. Her cousin's wife had requested her company for her lying in and Jane could hardly refuse a direct plea in favor of matters of state. No one would ever allow such an excuse to a female.

Jane was no Mary Wollstonecraft, chafing against the bit of a male-dominated society. She had enough of a grasp of history to understand that the rights and freedoms of women in civilization had had its ups and downs and that this period was neither the most liberating nor the most constricted. If anything, Jane was fundamentally practical. She prided herself on that quality. It was what made her the most useful to her father. Yet, Lady Powell's bits of advice all pointed to the unfairness of a society in which a woman's value was dependent nearly entirely on her usefulness or attractiveness to a man.

The carriage listed and Jane fell to the side, slamming into the door. Her stomach and heart lurched as well.

"What the—?" Lord Powell sputtered from the floor where he'd fallen upon her legs. Lady Powell, too, lay sprawled across the carriage in a tangle of limbs. As the carriage righted itself, so did its occupants.

Powell rapped on the roof. "If that damn driver fell asleep at the reins, I'll have his neck."

The carriage picked up speed, charging over the road in uncomfortable jolts.

"Perhaps he's dead already," Lady Powell said acerbically, even as she tried to stay in her seat.

Asleep, dead or drunk, Jane didn't care. She simply wanted the carriage to stop or she'd soon be sick all over it.

It stopped with an explosion of wood and fabric, and Jane's head slammed back against her seat. She looked up at the blue sky, at flying pieces of wood, and then, fear coursing through her, she fell forward, hands flailing, reaching for purchase, finding wood that collapsed beneath her hands as she collapsed. She breathed in the heavy scent of earth and varnish and horse before something fell on top of her and her world turned to black. She wasn't dead; there was far too much pain for this to be death. As she struggled to open her eyes, she heard voices and opened her mouth to cry for help, but she choked on the sound as her vision focused.

On the angel of death bending over Lord Powell, whose face was frozen into a mask of fear.

Was she next? Nausea clenched her stomach and she struggled to swallow down the acrid taste of her fear. With the sickening crack of Lord Powell's neck, Jane realized two things. One, surviving the carriage accident might not mean she would survive this. Two, the accident was no accident. She did not want to die like Lord Powell. She did not want to die at all. With effort, her gaze swept the area, searching for help, and then lingered on a horse that huffed and squealed as it struggled to stand, and beside it the soles of Lady Powell's green brocade shoes. The woman's body was eerily still.

The carriage carrying their servants and luggage was far ahead of them but the carriage carrying Mr. and Mrs. Brumble and Sir Joseph Grimsby was perhaps only an hour or two behind, if they had not stopped again. Not close enough to save her if she was marked for death. Desperation welled up in her strongly, froth upon the waves of pain and nausea. She could not give in to weakness. If ever she had needed clarity of mind, it was now.

Think.

If she were already dead, there would be no one to kill. She shut her eyes and slowed her breath as best as she could, but there was a raspy, rattling quality to each inhale that felt as loud as thunder in the perfect September day. *Do not look at Death. Do not look at him. Do not move.* She thought the commandments in the precise enunciations of her last governess. Perhaps if she had kept to her original seatmates, instead of leaping to join the Powells at the first chance, she would then be the one to soon gasp over the wreckage of the carriage, to cry over the lost friends, to think it all such a horrible accident.

Her breath sounded so loud that she almost missed the whisper of cloth against cloth, the scruff of boots treading upon packed earth. He was coming for her. But why? This shadow of a man could steal her valuables without murder.

"I know you are conscious," that rough voice said, first in French, then in crisp English.

His words gave her hope. Why speak to her if he intended to kill her? She opened her eyes and the brilliantly clear blue sky pained her. She parted her lips to speak, to say anything that would fight off this murderer. She fluttered the fingers of her right hand but could not move the appendage more than that. Something pinned her arm down. Then he was over her, suffocating her nearly with his body looming so, his dark hair a curtain against the sun. He looked familiar, but she was certain she had never before seen this man. A shadow of hair lined his jaw in a swarthy streak. The darkest eyes she had ever seen met hers. He took her breath away. The pain ebbed under the force of his gaze.

"What is your name?"

Perhaps this was death, or the moment before death, this floating, this being held up by one man's eyes, one man's will. She blinked, found it within herself to remember the pain. Where there was pain, there was life. She had learned that truth at a much younger age. But Lady Jane Langley lived in stately homes, intellectual salons, and crowded ballrooms. In this moment there was nothing to tie her to that girl. She was simply a woman struggling to stay alive. Shakily, she asked, "What name should I give you so you won't kill me, too?"

That look in her eyes—it made Gerard uncomfortable in a way he hadn't been in years, not since his first kill. This woman with her too pale face, her long English nose, even as she lay there bleeding and trapped under the wreckage of the carriage, stared at him with such an awareness of him. The way a lover looked after months, not moments.

That knowing cut him to the quick, made him wish she hadn't witnessed this final act of murder, because he would remember this look. Perhaps he could leave death behind, but still her eyes would haunt him. She was not Lady Powell—he had spotted her moments ago. This was an unexpected occupant, a slight wrinkle in the plans. Was she embroiled in Powell's secret life or was she as ignorant of it as he suspected Lady Powell to be? To make certain that Powell's death would not create an international incident, at least publicly, beyond the scope of Gerard's job, he carefully chose the manner of death and its location, on the border of Nassau and Hesse. But this unknown woman's disappearance... all his research and planning was undone by her existence. She had witnessed him ensure Powell was no more.

Gerard reached for the woman's face, grasping her neck in one hand, her cheek, and the curve of her jaw in the other. Strands of fine, light brown hair slid over his fingers. With one firm movement she would be gone, that wary, challenging expression in her shockingly light, clear blue eyes extinguished forever. Under his fingers the skin was silky, soft, delicate. But she still watched him steadily, and he knew beneath the exterior, she was not delicate.

Her blood was seeping onto his trousers.

Nausea roiled through his stomach. That sensation, too, was one he hadn't experienced in years. He had become inured to death. Yet here he was quailing at the act when it was the only reasonable solution to an unexpected wrinkle in his plans. But he no longer wished to be the servant of death, especially not on a distasteful job he felt obligated to do.

When he had found Lady Powell lying several lengths away, assessed her injuries and determined that she was unconscious, he had felt a glimmer of satisfaction. She had witnessed nothing, and as far as he knew was not involved in the matter that had imperiled her husband. As a result, he had no wish to kill her if he need not, and her lack of consciousness allowed him to offer her mercy.

It was not the same for this unknown woman before him. She knew the wreck was no accident and thus there were only two options: he could kill her or take her with him.

And that last option didn't make any sense.

He removed his hands from her neck, pushed aside the wood that kept her pinned down, the glass that had cut her legs, arms, and cheek. He lifted her then, felt her muscles tense with pain, knew the moment that she passed out in his arms and that the burden of her unconscious body was completely his. He was a fool for what he was about to do.

Chapter Two

She was cold. She turned to her side to curl up. Pain flared at the attempt. It was everywhere, like the licking flames of hell. But she was still alive, and the pain that seemed to be all consuming was not. Mostly, there was a bone-crushing ache in her shoulder, a stinging in the vicinity of her chest, and a deep, aching pain in her leg.

She had been in an accident. She shuddered, reliving the jarring force of the crash of the carriage. The screams of the horses, of her companions. Her own screams.

The sound of death.

Her eyes snapped open as fear made her body rigid. Where was she and where was *he*? In the flickering candlelight, she could see the outline of a male form leaning against the wall, knees drawn up to his chest. Recognition knifed through her at the silhouette of his profile. She breathed in deeply and pushed the useless fear back, forced herself to take stock.

She was alive. She was naked but for a blanket and though her entire body ached and stung, she had the sense that not only had he let her live, he had tended to her. In the darkness she could not make out much of her surroundings, but there was a wall to her left and a bed beneath her.

He had taken her prisoner.

Had this all been about her? Was she being held for ransom? And if so, why?

His head turned and fear coursed through her body as his dark gaze met hers.

"You are awake." He pushed himself up off the floor and stood up. He grew larger in her vision and then, half illuminated by the candle, loomed over her. The shadow of hair at the line of his jaw was more pronounced. How long had she lain there?

"Who—" Jane stopped, swallowed, and tried to wet the desert of her throat. "Who are you?"

He pulled back the blanket to study her body, and though it was her body he bared, she felt infinitely more naked, as if he were stripping away from her everything she had ever known. His hands pressed lightly here and there, and each place where he touched flared to life with renewed pain.

"How badly am I injured?" She forced the words out between her swollen, cracked lips.

He pulled the cover back up and, perversely, she started to shiver.

"Your arm was dislocated. I reset it. It has started to swell but should heal. The rest of your body is mottled with bruises from collarbone to knee." Each word seemed to pierce the corresponding wound with fresh pain. "There is a deep gash on your leg that is stitched shut and, as yet, heals well. Inside? I cannot tell." He finished his litany, his eyes never once straying from her face.

He had tended to her injuries. Was that the action of a man who intended to kill her? Ransom, then. But again, why? Lord and Lady Powell were worth as much as the Langleys. Political secrets, then? Was there some information about the congress at Vienna that he wanted from her father?

Who are you? That question he had not yet answered, but he didn't need to answer for her to understand that he was an assassin.

She closed her eyes against his gaze, against dark eyes that revealed nothing even as they seemed to see into her, to know her in a way no one else had ever come close. Yet that was impossible, a fancy born of pain. How could an assassin look at her that way?

"Perhaps you will be able to give more information."

Was that why he had let her live? He wished to interrogate her? Should she admit she could not have any knowledge he sought? What answer would keep her alive? She opened her eyes again, met his curious gaze.

"Do you feel pain inside?"

Shock warred with relief as she realized he referred to her body. "I cannot distinguish between the sensations yet."

He made a small sound of acknowledgment.

"Come. Let me help you sit, and you may drink some water."

She watched him cross the room—the remnants of a rough, peasant sort of dwelling—and retrieve a full leather water bag. She struggled to move but found her limbs ridiculously weak. But he was at her side again, sitting beside her and lifting her with shocking gentleness. Pain and his heat burned through her. Cradled in his arms, she opened her mouth at the touch of the sweet water against her lips. She swallowed the liquid down, her thirst reborn with each new taste.

"Thank you," she said when she'd had her fill. She frowned at the grateful words that had come unconsciously. She was nearly certain that her injuries were due to an accident he had somehow instigated. She could not forget that even though he was now acting as healer, too.

"Why did you sabotage our carriage?" His body tensed and she tilted her head to look up at him, but even that small movement flared into agony. Tears blurred her vision. She was physically helpless. She couldn't move so much as to study his face and gain what little information she could from his impassive visage. Instead, he held the water gourd close to her mouth again, but she turned her head away angrily.

"Don't you have anything to say? Why did you kill Lord Powell?"

He shifted so that he held her up with one arm only. As he bent to place the bag on the ground their eyes met. His gaze was sharp as he studied her, and she realized she had just admitted that she knew nothing. She fought the desire to look away, to hide in whichever way she could.

"You want to live," he said. There was a threat behind the words and yet he was laying her down on the bed so gently. If he had wanted to kill her, surely he would have already, unless his plan was more nefarious and he intended to hold her hostage. Or he still thought she possessed some information he needed. But in that case, why not interrogate her already? She breathed deeply again, her ribs, shoulder, and muscles protesting at the movement.

This exchange mattered more than any she had ever had and yet it felt outside of anything she knew. Despite the pain, she managed to speak. "If you intend to kill me, then you might as well satisfy my curiosity. And if you do not... what does it matter if I know the reason why? Isn't it enough that I know it happened?"

"You like questions."

"I like answers better," she said, teeth chattering and her whole body shivering, which hurt even more. Exhaustion overwhelmed her.

As he leaned over her, his lips curved and the embryonic smile made him less sinister. He pulled the blanket tighter around her, shrugged out of his coat, and placed that over her too. Then he brushed the hair back from her cheek with a gentleness that made her swallow hard. His hand was warm and she was so cold. "I cannot please you then."

Please you.

She closed her eyes, the oddness of the phrase sticking with her even as she drifted back into sleep.

When she next woke daylight filtered down, diffused by a layer of grayish clouds. The air smelled acrid with impending rain. These ruins would be little shelter in a storm, but that was not her concern. Not now. That was *his* concern. Now her only concern was to rest. To heal. To stay alive.

Nausea tumbled through her stomach, rose in her chest, as the sickening crack of a neck being broken shuddered through her memory.

"Good, you are awake."

A neck broken by *this* man. The low timbre of his voice had become familiar to her. She turned her head to him, found him standing in silhouette by the door. This stranger who had touched her body more intimately than any since her nurse.

"What is your name?" she asked, as if it mattered. He was a villain who, for some odd reason of his own, had happened to let her live for now. And who acted as her nurse.

"Do you begin every conversation with a question?" He laughed as he moved toward her, his features visible, another day's growth on his jaw.

"This is unlike any other conversation I have ever had."

He sat down beside her. "You do not need to know anything but that you must rest." He touched her hair again, brushed it from her face. In another time and another place, it would have been the gesture of a lover.

But she had had no lovers. There had been a handful of courtiers, men who wished to tie themselves to her father or avail themselves of her dowry. Never had there been a man who had stolen a kiss, pulled her into a shadowy corner for a passionate embrace. Nor would Lady Jane Langley have wished for such a thing. But that life was so very far away and his touch was warm and pleasurable.

Beneath the sheet she was naked. Tending to her, this stranger had seen her body in its most vulnerable state. She should have felt shame or embarrassment at the thought. There was none.

She lifted her hand to her pendant, the gold medallion of Lady Justice with her blindfold, holding her scales and her double-edged sword. It had been a gift from her father, and Jane had always taken comfort in the reminder of the power of reason and the righteousness of the law. The pommel of the sword was a ruby. On one scale was a diamond and the other a sapphire. This man was a murderer but not a thief. She slotted that into her mind as if it were a piece of one of the jigsaw puzzles she liked to complete.

"What happened to the coachman?"

That dark gaze met hers with amusement. "I think you know."

Nausea rolled through her but she did not look away. She was not a coward and she need not fear. If he had meant to kill her, surely he would have already.

"A casualty of war?" Who had been the target of this incident? Lord Powell? Lady Powell? Jane? She did not know what role Lord Powell played in the upcoming negotiations between countries, but Lady Powell had almost certainly planned to attend for the excitement of the unprecedented event.

"The war is over, no? Napoleon tucked away on his little island?"

"War comes in many forms." Though Napoleon had been vanquished and banished to Elba, that did not mean all his cohorts and admirers had been vanquished as well.

He shrugged. "True, but irrelevant. And you have distracted me from my purpose." He held out a package. The scent of warm yeast hit her as he opened the paper. Hunger flared again.

Just as he had hours before, he helped her to sit up, wrapped in that scratchy wool blanket, his arm around her supporting her. Oddly, it was…comforting…to be taken care of, to give up her volition to someone else for a temporary time.

He smelled of horse, as if he'd ridden recently. Yet she had neither seen nor heard a horse. Where had he stabled the animal, if indeed he had? She had a faint recollection of being on one during a brief moment of consciousness. A horse trained to bear the scent of blood.

Blood. She could take no comfort in this half embrace.

She ate, wondering how far they were from other dwellings and where he had procured the simple ham, bread, and rich wine that helped to warm her from the inside. Her right arm lay useless by her side and her left ached as she lifted each bite to her mouth. She was in no condition to attempt an escape, but at some point she would be, if an escape were needed.

She looked about their shelter. On the far side, rain trickled in through the gaping holes in the roof.

"Will it hold?" she asked.

"The roof is sturdy enough in this corner." The accent that was not quite recognizable gave his voice into a musical lilt. A rich violoncello.

She picked up the half-eaten round of bread and took another bite. Then exhaustion took precedence over the needs of her stomach. She leaned against him more fully, again trusting in his strength. She stared at the rain-filled sky as if it held answers to all the mysteries. All the mysteries but one. The one only he could reveal.

"Why did you let me live?"

As single drops evolved into a curtain of water flowing over the edge of the ragged roof, puddling in pools on the earthen floor, he repeated the question in his mind. Why had he let her live?

If there were a search, and certainly for a woman as clearly well born as this one, there would be, he had not traveled far enough from the wreckage of the carriage to ensure no discovery. A risk, but how much of a risk would be determined by how persistently those who loved or needed her searched. Her identity was the key to that. It was time for some questions of his own. "What is your name?"

"What is yours?"

He laughed at the obstinate challenge in her gaze.

"So we are back to my question," she said, her tone light. "Why did you let me live? That you act as if you do not know my identity suggests you either are steeped in intrigue or that I was not your target."

Her succinct summation made it even clearer to him that this woman was a danger. While he did not believe her to be involved in any intrigue that concerned him, she thought it possible that he had always intended to take her captive. He could press her, use her injuries to torture the information from her that he wished, but the compulsion to tend to this woman, to care for her, bewildered him. He could no more help himself than he would go against the finely honed instinct that had saved his life countless times.

Yet it was wrong, in the way everything had been wrong since last winter, when he'd received the command from his grandfather to pick up a package from his half brother, Marcus Templeton. The legitimate brother he had never before met, heir to a title and lands in England. The contrast between Gerard's life and that of his soft brother made it pointedly clear how much an "accident of birth" defined the course of his life. That difference had…angered him. For the first time, he questioned everything he had taken for granted.

"Instinct," he said, half surprised that he spoke and that he did so truthfully. But as he needed to keep her fearing him, his next words were less truthful. "Instinct is a whimsical thing. I might very well decide to kill you in the morning."

She shifted against him, letting out a soft moan as she did. He was relieved that the sound lacked the intensity of acute agony. She was healing. This tenderness toward her… He had not felt such a thing in years. Not since…not since Badeau's death.

Anger flared. His muscles tensed, as they always did with the thought of Badeau's final days, his tutor's body skeletal from illness, frail and helpless as he had never before been. She shifted again, turned her head up to look at him, her gaze questioning. *Always questioning.* That made him smile. He breathed deep, willed his muscles to relax.

"It disturbs you that you let me live," she said.

It did. Because it felt right and yet letting her live went against all of his training. Because he felt clearly at a point of inflection, the curve of life shifting to something new.

But to reveal that was far too much. She was already too unafraid. Her strength fascinated him, but there was danger here.

"You should be quiet, rest and moan. Not interrogate your captor."

"Is that how you see yourself? Am I a prisoner?"

Yes, by default, she was his prisoner. After all, even if she were healed, he could not let her go. That she could identify him endangered him. He could deflect or ignore each question. Yet did he wish to?

"For now," he said. So he had managed to silence her with that. He studied her pale face. She looked shocked and scared, and well she should be scared, enough to stop questioning him.

When her body finally relaxed into sleep, he lay next to her. The bed was narrow and his leg pressed against hers. He imagined that beneath the dust and sweat and hay that he could discern the scent she had used in her bathwater. Long hair tickled his nose. Hair that was tangled now but was fine and straight. The last time he had lain next to a woman thus the circumstances had been vastly different: the bed firm, the linens luxurious and scented with lavender, and the scent of passions well spent in the air. He had not lingered in that bed, as he did not linger in that of any woman, whether he knew her as Gerard Badeau or by any other name.

There was no passion here. Not with the dampness of the rain in the air, the knowledge that he had compromised his work uneasy in his gut.

Why had he let her live?

Yes, there were the surface details—her forthright gaze, the youthful beauty, and the slim figure—none of which were disguised by her injuries. But it wasn't desire that had inspired him to spare her life. It was something a bit more... domestic. She was a woman and a man's instinct was to take care of the fairer sex. It was an instinct that had not troubled him in a long time. Women were as treacherous and foolish as men. They were spies and manipulators, assassins and leaders of crime. Not that he thought this woman any of the sort. She had been raised softly. That she was well born was clear not only from her clothes and the company she had kept, but also from the way she spoke. Her small reticule had held no passport, no letters of introduction or letters of credit, but somewhere in the wreckage of luggage, those items would be found. He had had no time to tarry and search.

He had let her change the conversation, but in the quiet of night, it was easier to think. He needed to know her identity before they were found. Someone would miss her. Her own suggestion that he had planned the carriage wreck in order to kidnap her implied as much. And even if she possessed no knowledge of import, those who would suspect Powell's death to be other than an accident—Gerard did not fool himself that no one would suspect such a thing—might think her disappearance of more import than it was.

Might think that she could lead them to him. Or to the secrets behind Powell's death. Whether or not she actually had any information, and he was inclined to believe she did not, he had made her important. She knew enough to make others think she knew more. He might have spared her a quick death only to sentence her to a future tortured and prolonged one. When she woke, he would discover her identity.

His body tensed against the future threat, he stared into the falling rain. Actions had consequences and like a stone thrown into a pond, ripples were made again and again.

Why had he let her live?

Chapter Three

When she next woke, rain still spattered down through the hole in the roof and she was shivering beneath the blanket again, his solid warmth gone. She wanted it back, to sink once more into sleep cocooned in his warmth. *His.* She didn't even know what to call this man who kept her warm while she slept and tended to her wounds. Who had been the cause of those wounds.

Her chest tightened and her stomach clenched. Any kind emotion toward him was like the Sabine women defending their new husbands, men who had abducted them, to their fathers. Minus the husbands and fathers. She laughed, pressing her face down into the fold of blanket protecting her from the prickly mattress.

Her father didn't even know she was missing. Would not think anything amiss until the Brumbles or Sir Joseph sent him word or called upon him. *Her father…* She imagined him in his rented rooms, with only his valet and his secretary, and a mere handful of servants. He would be devastated when he learned of her disappearance.

Her insides twisted at the thought. They had been each other's only family for so long. He *needed* her. Not that he couldn't manage without her, but everything went far more smoothly when she was at his side. He had even expressed such a thing when he'd learned she would attend her cousin first.

How many days had it been since the wreck? One? Two? Surely not more than that? Long enough that someone would realize she was missing. Someone would be searching. And she could not be far from the site of the carriage wreck. Not with her injuries, not two to a horse. Yet, no one had found them. Now the rain would wash away what trail there might have been, creating a divide between the outside world and this strange one in which only she and this man existed.

She was cold and each shiver made her keenly aware of all the ways in which she hurt. Her body still ached acutely and her arm resisted movement. A whisper of leather against earth, cloth against cloth, a breath louder than silence, alerted her to his presence.

She opened her eyes. The room was cast in a dim bluish light. Late afternoon perhaps, which meant she had slept through the day, as if her body had decided sleep was the best medicine. Here in the wild, away from modern medicine, it likely was.

The relative wilds. Their shelter had once been a sturdy house but looked to be the bare remnants of a fire. The ravages of war? As her carriage had traversed from Calais to Paris and then across the border into Nassau, she had seen some of the effects of war on the French people. Not nearly as bad, she had been told, as those of the countries France had invaded. England, that fortress of an island, had been spared such a fate.

Her gaze caught his form once again made dark by silhouette as he stood staring out into the rain. Sinister and yet beautiful. He had lain beside her, pressed against her. Her stomach tightened again, her chest as well. Too much emotion welled up inside her, emotion she couldn't begin to examine because she sensed it would go against that very reason upon which she prided herself.

Who was he?

An assassin, yes, but beyond that? For whom did he work? For what country? What power? In the days when he was not laying traps for carriages and English noblemen, or tending to the injuries of women he had taken captive, where did he live?

A house in the crowded warrens of a city, one more anonymous man amid a metropolis of unknown men? Or perhaps, even a bucolic estate, with happy cows and sheep, a waiting wife and children... Neither extreme was easy to imagine.

Was he married? Could such a man of violence be a husband?

She blinked at the stupidity of her question. History was littered with such men. Women, as well. The acts perpetrated in the name of duty had little bearing on one's domestic life. Unless, of course, one's duty was solely to marry, to forge bonds between families. Cold relationships. With each year that passed, her hope for finding a match based on mutual intellectual respect and possibly affection was subsumed by the greater likelihood of settling for social and dynastic advancement alone.

She was eminently practical and the reality had not bothered her. Additionally, she had found intellectual satisfaction in the work for her father. Yet, Lady Powell's last words had been a warning to Jane that if she continued to live her life as it was, she would become irrelevant.

There were too many thoughts in her head, images of the past creeping in, of wanting love, of wanting approval, wanting her father's respect. Because respect was what he had to offer instead of love. But it was entirely possible that she was now in this predicament because of some intrigue that involved her father and the little political games he and his friends liked to play. Her father included her in so much of his work, and yet there were still secrets he would not entrust to her.

A cold awareness seeped under her skin, made her shiver again from more than just the cold. There was so much beneath the surface. She had always taken everything emotional at face value. Life was easier that way. People like her father, men in politics and trade, were Machiavellian. The logic of business and manipulation was quite easy to understand. Emotion was not. It was messy and weak, and she had always thought that wanting something one did not have and had no way to attain was impractical and the road to dissatisfaction. But here, where she existed without past or future, only in the present with the desire and aim to survive, there were things she wanted.

Odd things. Things she shouldn't even acknowledge to herself: the comfort of this stranger's touch, even though he was her captor and threatened her life, and his conversation, even though they threw questions at each other and withheld answers. It was so strange to be living moment to moment, acting on needs more than cold reason. To have the pain of her injuries unearth trembling emotions she couldn't yet name. Perhaps it was weakness, but it felt more like a door opened to a different way of living life, to all the feelings that brimmed beneath the surface. To how much she craved tenderness and comfort. How much she craved love. And it had taken the shadow of death to bring her to the edge of revelation. Perhaps her father loved her, but he had never said so much, had never shown her as much tenderness as this strange man who had upended her life.

Surely an assassin was a cold, emotionless creature. Surely the tenderness of his touch was a figment of her imagination. A question formed inside her head and for a moment she dismissed it as too personal. Then anger surged. At him. At herself.

He was the one who had pulled her from a different life. She could ask what she wished. It was strange to have this silent intimacy without any knowledge of him, and if he wouldn't answer any questions that revealed his purpose, who or where they were, he could at least answer this.

"Have you ever loved?" Her voice croaked around the words. He did not move and she coughed to clear her throat so that she could speak more loudly.

She focused on the back of his dark head, on the hair that curled around the smooth skin of his neck above his coat, and repeated herself.

"**H**ave you ever loved?"

He had heard her the first time, but the question was so unexpected from a woman who was essentially his prisoner that he thought at first to ignore it.

This time he turned and surveyed her with amusement. She lay on her back, her head turned to the side, her light brown hair pillowed beneath. Even in the ignominious position of being clothed only in a blanket, of being injured and helpless, she looked composed, certain of her right to ask intimate, probing questions.

Though by birth he was an outsider to society, he knew such a question would not ever be asked in the parquet-lined floors of ballrooms and sitting rooms. It was a question that could only be asked here, apart from the world, from time even. That she was asking of *him*.

They had tossed questions back and forth at each other, and as she had suggested, had reached an impasse. Unless he wished to use harsher means, he was unlikely to get the information he desired from her by direct questioning. As for him, he could not reveal anything that might compromise his identity at a later date. But this question had little to do with names and identities, and there was something tantalizing about indulging in the past, in those luscious days of his youth when women were a mystery and flesh a bountiful faire.

He stalled for time as he warred within himself.

"I heard you, but there are many types of love. Which do you mean? Agape, Eros, Philia or Storge?"

She laughed, as if he had intended to be witty. "I see your tutor made you learn Greek."

Not wit then. The laughter was surprise that a man

she considered beneath her was educated as a gentleman, as if he had been attempting to impress her when what he had intended was to deflect out of habit. But hers was such an innocuous question. Yet no question, and certainly no answer, was ever harmless.

"Among other things," he said simply.

"Eros then."

Of course. It was what his mind had turned to first as well.

"Thus your question is have I ever loved a woman?"

She nodded, her gaze even, expectant. The tension he had felt dissipated. He could fall into that gaze, study the light blue irises, the dark pupils, try to discern what lay behind. To anyone else he would continue to deflect the question or would obfuscate, speaking of his wife, a fabrication he often used to confuse his identity. But to this woman who stared at him, *into* him, with such knowing, he felt compelled to speak the truth. As if speaking that truth to her might set him free, a beguiling idea that manifested inside him with a buzzing intensity, an energy that hummed inside him, which meant he needed to be even more careful.

"Yes, of course. I was once a boy and boys…love passionately."

She tilted her head to the side. He laughed, half surprised at an odd buoyancy, the delight in her silent challenge. She would not let him leave it at that, not this woman who wished to know the world.

"I was fifteen. I was supposed to be studying but I had taken my book down to sit by the water. The air was thick that day, the sort of thick that sticks to one's skin."

He never indulged in reminiscing about the past. If he thought on past events it was to analyze them for information and insight. But now, letting himself fall into the flow of those long ago moments, it was odd the details that he remembered, though he hadn't thought of that day in years. He could almost smell the air, the sense of anticipation that had come with life each day all those years ago. All of it tinged with an odd sadness, as if watching someone he knew vaguely, but who was nearly a stranger now.

"Not England. Not France."

He laughed again in surprise, enjoying the speed with which her mind worked despite the pain she surely felt. For a moment it was as if the past and the present were all entangled, and this woman before him was the one he had stumbled upon all those years ago, the first and only recipient of a youthful infatuation. But Jane was far different than the young girl he had romanced in the summer heat. There had been very little of the intellectual in that affair.

"Venice," he said, and Jane leaped on that information. He could see the wheels of her mind turning, as if it were the clue to his identity. But the information should be useless to her, as safe as any information could be. It was why he had allowed her to have it.

His only mistake thus far had been in letting her live. And…he was no longer convinced that had been a mistake. Certainly not a permanent one as, if she ever did present to be a danger, he could still rectify the situation. But turning to death would be a shame. There was something about her that called to him, that cut through every social veneer and touched the part of himself he most thought of as him, as Gerard. Since Badeau's death, only Gerard's valet, his grandfather, and perhaps his half brother, Templeton, had ever come close to bridging the chasm that separated him from society, from an honest conversation. Each conversational exchange with Jane created an intimacy so oddly based in truth, and he wanted more. He wanted to be surprised by what she said next and then to delve deeper.

He had always subscribed more to the deism of the philosophes, but her presence in his life was perhaps the active hand of a higher power. If his half brother's appearance just a few months earlier had been the herald of change to come, this woman could be that change: his salvation.

Salvation. When had he decided he needed such a thing? That his life was that of a sinner? Yes, there were times when his work required him to be judge and jury over another human's life, but during a time of war many men did as much, and then simply because they wore different color clothes. Not that his work was anything as dubiously noble as war. But salvation? Such an odd concept, even if he accepted the premise of his errant thought, how could this woman offer such a thing?

Letting her live was not some magic key. One life allowed could not negate the ones he had extinguished. But he would not count his sins, would not linger on the past if it were simply to flagellate himself.

"What ended the affair?" she asked, piercing his thoughts.

"Naturally, the dramatic. But you jump ahead. Do you not wish to know of the girl? How it all progressed? The stolen kisses and secret meetings?"

"A story of your love would bore me. It is the meeting and its end that are the most interesting and revealing."

He contemplated that. At length, he nodded. "My tutor discovered it."

"Aha! You did have a tutor. And he did not approve?"

Gerard laughed, disliking that his laugh was tinged with

a revealing edge. Badeau had been much slyer than that. The wily man had known that to forbid a fifteen-year-old boy anything was to ensure its triumph. Instead, Badeau had planted the seeds of doubt, told cautionary tales of dangerous love in the guise of lessons. Gerard's bitterness was cut with amusement. The poison had done its work well. It was only later, after Badeau's death, that Gerard understood what had occurred. But by then it did not matter. His tutor had done his best to prepare his charge for his profession. Gerard's reason and intellect had dismissed any notion of resentment. Until six months ago when he'd been confronted with the oldest of his half siblings, the only one who carried their father's name.

Until the deepest dark of night when his troubled mind matched his troubled soul.

Yes, *soul*. That he even countenanced the existence of such an ephemeral thing illuminated his struggle. His chest ached with emotion he would not acknowledge.

"You are very far away."

He let out the breath he had unknowingly held. "I am contemplating my life."

Her eyes widened. She looked as surprised as he was at the honesty with which he answered. Yet something like relief or release came with the admission. Into the midst of this struggle had stepped this additional complication.

Salvation.

As if he regretted his life thus far and wished to be something other. How weak and pitiful an idea.

"And?"

"And nothing," he said, cutting her probing short. "The past is what it is." He studied her face. She was watching him equally intently, those pale blue eyes searching. She had a beauty that came together with each new expression, but when her face was still, objectively he could see she had plain features, nothing that would make her stand out. Except that she did. If he saw that, so would other men. "What of you?"

She quirked an eyebrow in that supercilious way of hers, but she did not pretend to misunderstand his question. "The past is what it is."

A flippant answer but she was his captive. He should be the interrogator, the one unearthing answers.

"Have *you* ever loved?" It was not a question he had ever imagined himself asking of anyone, and yet he waited for her answer with something bordering on breathless anticipation.

"My life began pinned beneath a carriage."

He frowned. Flippant again. A dismissal. But he shrugged and turned from her as if he didn't care. Why should he? He had not shared a fragment of his own story out of any wish to act on the promise of her knowing eyes, to forge a... *connection.*

"I was answering you honestly," she said. "I see now how you misunderstood but I mean that my life until that point...I was sleep-walking." He turned back again to cautiously study her, to parse the words she offered so freely. She had struggled up to her elbows and the blanket gaped about her, revealing the mottled bruises where the carriage had pinned her. His stomach clenched and he swallowed back the unwanted, foreign sensation of guilt. "No, that's not right. I was...in ignorance. And then, everything I knew took shape with stunning clarity."

"You were bleeding to death. Hallucinating," he said,

his voice cold. She was being fanciful and ridiculous, as was every word exchanged between them.

"Yet I had never been more alive."

"Why are you telling me this?" It was too much to share, so much more than a careless story of the past. Perhaps she didn't realize that this was the revelation of a woman who wished to be reborn. But he felt that desire deep inside his chest, an aching that needed to be set free. Like recognizing like. God, yes, he understood.

Salvation.

"Why did you let me live?"

The words punched him, robbed him of his breath as his own moment of stunning clarity struck. Not only had he let her live but he had every intention of continuing to do so, come what may.

"Instinct," she whispered before he could speak, repeating his previous answer back to him.

The air was thick, the intensity of the moment too sharp, and he looked away, to the stone walls of the ruined house. Struggling for breath, he turned back to the rain, which pounded more heavily, as if it knew it should underscore the tension between them—the tension within Gerard, whose skin tingled everywhere with anticipation.

He was silent and in that yawning space, Jane's thoughts churned. There was room for instinct in the world of logic and reason. She fully believed humans were able to pick up on clues and data imperceptible to their usual facilities. Clues that existed, not the fraud perpetrated by false prophets.

She, too, had been acting on instinct. Was it wise to challenge him? To risk his ire and that he might decide she was less trouble to him dead? But the threat of death seemed very far away, and despite the shadows of his eyes, the darkness of his life, he was infinitely gentle with her. He had laughed, smiled, and met her honest conversation with truths of his own. Perhaps it was a grand trick, to gain her confidence for some unknown reason, but there were moments she thought he was as affected by her presence as deeply as he had already affected her life. She felt *instinctively* that she could say anything to this man.

Despite that, she was nearly silent as he fed her, offered her his coat and took her out into the rain to tend to her needs. Later he examined the wound he had apparently sewn shut with small neat stitches while she was unconscious. An assassin and a surgeon.

Jane loved the rain, loved the way it played with perception. A mist softened, a downpour blurred, and when a storm finally passed, everything clarified in its wake. Before her kidnapping she had always had the choice of remaining cozily indoors, by a fire, with a hot cup of tea. Now she felt the cold damp that seeped into the bones, chilled one from the inside out. She wasn't certain anything would be clarified when this rain ended.

"Keep me warm," she said softly. Instinct, again. Instinct was perilously close to being ruled by emotion and yet…and yet it was irrational not to heed it in certain circumstances. When under threat…humans did what they needed to survive. She needed warmth now, but there was more to it than that. This was not purely a medicinal desire.

He lay behind her, pulled the bundle of blanket and body close to his chest and she closed her eyes. Breathed him in. Listened to his breath, his heartbeat. Shivered as his warmth started to penetrate her. Shivered again when his hand stroked idly up and down her arm through the blanket. Pleasure unfurled within her and she gathered it up inside. It was wrong, most likely, to enjoy his touch, to feel safe in the embrace of a dangerous man, and yet she did. Executioner and nurse. But for her the threat was not bodily death, no longer.

"We are spending too much time together to remain nameless," she said as she grew drowsy. "For now, I shall call you François."

"What's in a name?" he quipped, and she silently filled in the rest of the Shakespeare quote by rote: *that which we call a rose by any other name would smell as sweet.* But his next words were less sweet. "A sword is still a sword."

The implied threat jarred with the sweetness of his touch. Her exhaustion deepened. "Then François it is."

The progress of his hand stilled and he was silent. The silence lengthened and the edges of her consciousness softened.

"Not François," he said at length. His voice sounded deep and much further away. "Gerard will do."

Gerard. He said it the way a Frenchman would, and briefly she wondered if he realized that slip. Then, with the weight of the name repeating in her mind, she gave in to the insistence of his warmth and his soothing touch, and waking thought turned to slumber.

Chapter Four

The water was cold and just deep enough to reach her hips. She wanted to sink down to immerse herself completely. She leaned her head back to soak her hair and then reached for the bar of soap and found that the act of washing her hair was one that was beyond her current abilities.

The sky might have cleared, he may have thought her strong enough for a bath—and yes, she could withstand the cold river water for the chance to no longer smell herself—but he did not have hair that fell past his waist.

She eyed him where he lay, staring at the sky, ostensibly not looking at her, despite the fact that he had already seen her body in its entirety. It was different now, somehow, with her standing outside, on the path to healing. Embarrassment and something else, some desire to taunt propriety even more now that she was so far from civilization, warred within her.

"Gerard," she called. The name felt foreign, awkward, on her tongue. Calling him by any name at all made things more concrete, but she wanted to taunt him. He was staring at her, his expression a question. "Would you…assist me?"

For a moment he didn't move, and then in one nimble motion he was on his feet, divesting himself of his clothes. Shocked, she looked away, then looked back. He had looked at her body dispassionately. She would view his much the same. After all, she had seen men nude before. Sculptures and drawings of men, at least. Real men were never as perfect as the imaginings of artists.

Except…this man was.

His clothes concealed a body that was tall, lithe and strong. Muscles cleanly defined and yet not the bulky strength of the peasants in the field, or of the men who frequented Gentleman Jackson's. He left his drawers on but as he stepped into the water, her gaze was drawn to the rest of his body, to the puckering of his nipples, the goose bumps on his skin.

She tensed in embarrassment. She was naked and he was practically so. As he stepped closer, the plan no longer seemed like a good idea. Breath came with more difficulty and she was all too aware that he was going to touch her, and touching her this time would be different. For her, but not for him. She clung to that, repeated it in her mind. It was only Jane with these wayward thoughts. Perhaps it was the danger that made him more fascinating to her, to this new version of her that was so susceptible to emotion.

"I wished to give you some privacy but I should have realized you would need help," he said, moving behind her, placing one warm palm on the damp curve of her head. He threaded his fingers through her hair and her scalp tingled with the sensation.

Then the scent of caraway and lemon. She was inordinately grateful that this strange man had an item of such luxury.

"Have you done this before?"

"Whenever I take a bath."

She let out a soft huff. "You know very well that isn't what I mean."

"This is another of your questions. Have I ever been in love? Have I ever washed a woman's hair? No. You are the first."

She liked the way he cared for her, the way he touched her so gently. There had never been anyone in her life to treat her this way and it was…beguiling.

"You are doing quite well for a beginner," she managed to say. His fingers kneaded her head, her neck, and she fell into that touch, into that and the water, her eyes drifting shut, warm pleasure radiating down her body.

Her legs started to buckle and then she was in his arms. She let him take over. He leaned her back over one of his arms so that her hair was under water, and as he raked his fingers through the strands, washing the soap away, she opened her eyes again.

His face was inches from hers and her breath caught in her throat as she admired him, admired the different textures of his skin, the jaw roughened by a day's growth, the neck smooth, his shoulders—

Her fingers itched and she lifted her arm a half inch to feel that juxtaposition of rough and smooth before the acute pain of her injuries stopped her. He must have shaved at some point. The soap, the shaving, the clean scent of him…

He was a man who attended to details.

"Did I hurt you?" he asked as he straightened her. She stumbled on the rocky bottom of the stream and he caught her against him. Their bodies were both wet and cold, and hers was now screaming with renewed agony, and yet she wanted to stay there, pressed against him, nakedness to nakedness, as if they were Adam and Eve.

If only this were a dream. If only she could enjoy this fantasy and know that it would be gone come morning. But each time she woke, despite this world apart, despite saying that here she had been born anew, somewhere Lady Jane Langley waited.

He had bathed her body before, with a cloth, stripped away her torn and bloodstained clothes, both for access to her wounds and to make an escape impossible for her before he had decided on a course of action. He had felt nothing but curiosity and frustration at the compulsion to let her live. This, bathing the soap from her hair, supporting her naked body against his naked chest—it had seemed an intelligent idea at first to peel away the majority of his clothes so that he did not soak them. But skin against skin, even if wet and slippery—in the fresh air of a post rain autumn day—was an unexpected aphrodisiac.

He should not have been surprised by his desire. She was a female and he a male. Attraction was natural. And danger tantalizingly tinged their encounter with that of the forbidden. But there was dangerous and then there was stupid. Never before had Gerard been stupid. He would not be now.

And she was injured, her body mottled in bruises turned purple. Still…warmth unfurled within him, as did a growing tightness, a need. But her hair was clean, as was her body. He could stop touching her, and with that thought he lifted her up, carried her out of the water to the blanket, which was hardly clean, but better to ruin this one than the other blanket he had procured.

He wrapped her up, rubbed her down, and her eyes fluttered open. She watched him and he struggled to ignore that gaze. He was all too aware of her now. The body he had assessed dispassionately was achingly feminine, covered only by his blanket. In the past twenty-four hours he had been drawn in by the suspicion of a sharp intellect, by a certain quality about this woman that was irresistible. It was inevitable that attraction to the physical would follow.

He had not missed her glances, the expression of pleasure on her face. Whether she would acknowledge it or not, she was as affected by him as he was by her. Not only in the ineffable way that made them say things to each other no stranger would ever say to another, but physically.

He helped her into the spare shirt he kept in his saddlebag, watched as the snowy cloth obscured her form. He knew what lay beneath, but he did not know what lay beneath her skin.

"What was your relationship to Powell?" The question was abrupt, designed to remind him of the seriousness of this endeavor. Remind himself that the job was not complete until he had received the second half of his payment, that he could not indulge in frivolous thoughts such as desire. It was time for answers. There were other threats to her life and to his.

"Ah, I see now. You soften me with a bath, with a clean garment, and then you interrogate me. Is this some new method to ensure that information is true? I have heard that those who are tortured will often say anything to make the agony end."

He shook his head. She had laid out a good strategy but it had not been his aim. It should have been.

He waited for her answer. The silence between them grew, turned uncomfortable.

"Acquaintances traveling to the same destination. I thought to gain a few hours of amusement by joining him and his wife for the day."

He laughed again, though there was little of humor in it.

Her sidelong gaze was full of irony. "This was not exactly the entertainment I imagined."

"And who were your original companions?" He lifted her up, started the short walk back to their shelter. She smelled clean against him, and beneath the edge of the shirt, her bare legs hung over his arm.

"So you can establish my identity?" He liked the way she looked, eyes glittering, face animated. "I am increasingly confident that my presence was not in your plans. Why should you know any more about me than I know about you?"

Because it was his job to know everything. He should have known who she was, and that she had switched carriages. Knowledge in his line of work was power. Withholding knowledge was also power, but he had admitted enough to let her know that she was right. She had been a surprise and continued to be one.

"You know my name," he said. "What is yours?"

"Your Christian name, if that is actually yours," she returned quickly. He said nothing. Better that she thought it untrue. But Gerard was the one thing he had been given at birth that he retained.

Her silence bothered him. It would be easy enough to discover who she was; surely by now people were searching for her, her name dropped at every local inn. However, an insidious part of him wanted her to offer up the information of her own free will. As if that would mean something.

She rested against his chest and with the gentle pressure of her head on his skin, the energetic tension turned to something else, something intimate and overwhelming. His chest ached with an unfamiliar protectiveness.

"Jane," she said softly.

His arms tightened about her, triumph surging inside, which he tamped down as quickly as it came. *Jane*. Quite common in England. A sensible, economical name, one that fit her. A name that gained a sensual appeal by simply being hers. She imbued everything about her with that appeal. He had to resist burying his nose against her skin to breathe in that scent that was distinctly hers beneath the lemon and grass.

He carried her back to the bed, laid her down and stood, at a loss, hands empty. He had pressed his body against hers for warmth all through the night. Yet now, now that he was acutely aware of her, he didn't know what to do with himself. Despite the fact that one wall of this structure was nearly gone and half the roof missing, he felt trapped.

There were things he should be doing. He needed to secure the area and they needed food. He also needed to listen to the local gossip, discover what talk about the carriage "accident" might be circulating. He had traveled with Jane as far away from the site as he could with her injuries, but every minute that they lingered here increased the risk of being discovered. Before first light they would move on. She was strong enough.

After that…at some point he would need to decide what to do with her.

"Rest. I will return soon."

"You don't worry that I'll flee now that I have this voluminous garment?"

She was not a small woman and yet his shirt swamped her. Everywhere but the long legs it revealed. Shapely legs. Legs he could part with his hands as he ran them over her silken skin.

"And no shoes. You won't get far."

"I am quite inventive if need be."

He studied her. She was healing, but she was in no condition to travel on her own. Even with shoes. He suspected her of trying to rile him, to argue for the sake of arguing, but…

"Do you intend to flee?"

She smiled. "Will I have to? I can't imagine you would want to keep me here forever."

Of course not. The idea was ridiculous. At least, the part that included staying in their present location. He was used to planning far in advance and for every eventuality, so that usually his spontaneous actions were in truth merely the execution of a back-up plan.

There was little of the usual about this situation, and he had no answer for her. Instead, he laughed and settled for the only truth he could give. "I'll be back."

Chapter Five

Tension thrummed through him as Gerard dismounted his horse. He had made the necessary excursion primarily for food and to send a letter to his servant in Paris.

The sleepy town that had been briefly thrilled by the excitement of the carriage accident: an Englishman dead, a lady injured and another missing. There had been a hue and cry for several days when their friends discovered the tragedy. All was quiet now, but that did not mean no one was searching for Jane. Or would return to do so once news of her disappearance reached Vienna or England. Every day that he stayed in this mountain hideaway increased the danger of discovery. Thus he'd purchased other goods as well, all the items necessary for travel, and sent another letter to his office in Berlin, where, as Friedrich Amsel, he owned a store dealing in rare books.

There was an alias for each alias, a facade for a facade. If someone suspected and were diligent enough—if there were another man as skilled as Gerard pursuing him—he could indeed be tracked. But there were few who focused to that detail, who assured they knew the entire story of any job before taking action. It was a risk, in fact, to send letters to both Paris and Berlin from the same town. A risk he did not take. It was a small matter to travel another dozen miles to another town, and another posting house.

It was a risk as well to even send the Berlin letter at all. His client would not be pleased to be refused, not at such a late date. Gerard, or in this case, his pseudonym, had made his fortune on being dependable and accurate. He was no longer either.

He did not bother to stable his horse far away. Instead, he led the animal inside. At first glance the rough shelter was empty. Sharply alert, he scanned the room. A shifting of the shadows behind the bed caught his eye a moment before she stood, stepped forward. Her face was pale and tight with pain.

"I was worried it would be…someone else," she said.

Of course, she had been afraid. Injured, she was nearly defenseless. He had left her alone in a country that had not fully healed from war. This would be the last time he left her in harm's way, although that promise was ridiculous.

"You need to rest," he said gruffly, frustrated at his own weak emotions.

"I'm fine. I've been in that bed for days and it looks as if you had a much more eventful day than I," she said with a laugh.

He wanted to force her back into the bed; instead, he nodded in acknowledgment of her words and turned to unload the packages, aware she watched his every move. He heard her light footstep, smelled the citrus of his soap on her skin as she neared, wanted her with an acute need.

"We will leave here in the morning. We need supplies."

"Where are we going?" She laughed again. "For that matter, where are we now? The last place I know for certain being is on the road to Vienna."

He glanced at her and she met his gaze, sliced deep into him with a painful sort of pleasure. Clear, pale blue eyes opened fully to him, hiding nothing, demanding everything.

"You were bored."

"Out of my mind!" Her exclamation made him laugh too. "I know you will tell me nothing. It doesn't matter, as I will know soon enough."

There was no rancor in her voice, no fear of him anymore. That pleased him though it was a danger. As dangerous as the way she swayed toward him, unconsciously, he would wager. He liked her this way, flirtatious and forward, as if she could accept this strange new life. What if she could?

"So what supplies? Clothes for me? Or do I get to ride as Lady Godiva?"

"Lady Godiva did not have my shirt."

"Details."

"An important detail, I assure you." His gaze raked over her and it was all too easy to envision what she looked like beneath. Warm desire settled low in his body. Knowing her form well was an unusual aphrodisiac. Usually the discovery and the exploration was part of arousal and seduction.

Seduction. Was that what this was? Was she attempting to use flirtation as a way to control him? He did not think so but he was trusting too much to his instinct. A man could die that way. He pushed the parcel that was her clothes toward her and she descended upon it eagerly.

"Do you know I've purchased dresses from the finest dressmakers in London and yet I have never been more eager to see a frock than now? Please say it is a dress and not some boy's pants."

But even as she finished speaking she shook a petticoat out, and then reached for another length of cloth. She pulled the brown dress up against her and fitted it to her frame.

"So I am to be a farmer's daughter or some such. But it looks to fit. Thank you."

The outfit itself presented a risk that Jane would flee, not that he thought she would try. Not yet. She knew she would not get far in her condition. More than that, there was something that had grown between them in the last few days, something to be explored.

"Come, I've brought supper. We can sit outside before day ends."

The air was brisk, stung his lungs a bit when he breathed in deep, but it matched the stark beauty of the mountains, the wasteland of this small valley with its burnt-out trees and outbuildings. Beautiful land. Perhaps its owners had fled or died. At some point, someone would reclaim this land, but for now, for this last night, it was his. His and Jane's.

There were people missing her and searching for her, people who knew and loved her. Yet, here, with empty hemp bags making a carpet for them to sit on over the cold earth, she was the woman who pierced through the barrier of his loneliness.

Loneliness. How odd that what he had thought was independence and strength turned to weakness when placed in contrast with companionship. He pulled her close to him, offered her his warmth, his strength, reveled secretly in the softness of her body against his, the need that lingered almost uncomfortably full. As they sat there in the twilight, the knowledge of their mutual lust hung between them. But beyond desire, he wanted to penetrate her defenses, know who this woman was beneath her collected exterior.

"Tell me something about your life before."

She laughed. "You won't allow me my fantasies."

That she had been born in the wreckage of the carriage. He would accept the metaphor, but it was not everything. "Rebirth is a metaphor."

"I do not believe the church would agree."

Impatiently, he grabbed her chin, forced her to meet his gaze. "Jane, don't hide from me."

"Jane." She shivered. "No names," she said, blinking.

"Names are part of our identity." He intended to have hers in its entirety, before ignorance could do more harm than he had already let it.

"Identity?" She turned her head sharply and he let his hand fall. "Before this week I would not have considered it, but it is such a malleable thing," she scoffed with a laugh. "You cannot tell me you do not take them on and discard them with ease. Not in your profession."

"And what profession is that?"

"Assassin."

The word was burning cold, like a knife slicing through muscle.

"I am not."

"You are a murderer then? Or perhaps a lunatic?"

"My only choices?"

"What other reason for killing a man in cold blood?"

"Perhaps I acted the assassin that day, but that is not my profession. Death is merely one tool to reach an end."

He caught her shiver. He swallowed back the sudden nausea. He was growing soft.

"You may answer your own question, then. Have you ever loved?"

For a moment he thought she would persist, not follow his lead to the new, safer topic. Then she shrugged.

"A passionate love? No."

He could show her passion. He had never been one to care about being the first, had no need to mark his territory via the purity of a woman's body and yet, satisfaction at her words was a knife edge.

"As a child, I wanted too much to prove myself. My mother died early and, aside from governesses, I was raised in a world of men. I had infatuations, to be sure, but for much older men who were hardly eligible," she said. "But they were intelligent men who spoke eloquently about whatever the issue of the day was, from war to tariffs to crop rotation to parliamentary reform. And at night, I'd tear down that childish admiration for persuasive rhetoric by silently taking apart their arguments, thinking for myself in the privacy of my room. Then...my first season..."

Her first season. He had gathered already that she was the daughter of a political man, but that phrase, *her first season*, was a telling one, revealed more about her than she likely realized.

"I did not make my debut with any sort of flair or drama," she said. "I had been living in London for several years already. I was present at many events it would be unusual for a girl still in leading strings to attend"—she caught his look and laughed—"metaphorically, that is. My governess cared deeply about fashion if she did not care deeply about me."

His parentage had defined his life as hers had. He had been raised without his father and she without a mother, but he'd had a surrogate for whom he'd cared.

"Yet you remained unmarried."

"Are you truly surprised?"

"Too forthright?"

"And too well versed in politics and history."

"I would think some aspiring politician would have seen that as of value. Perhaps one of these men you admired." She didn't answer right away and his mind strayed to the clues of her identity. "Your father is a politician, then. House of Lords?" He watched her carefully, as much as for what she would not reveal as for what she would. But she slanted him a mocking glance.

"And *your* father was?"

He admired the way that she turned everything back to him, but he was done playing. As much as he wanted to know her identity, he wanted to know what lay beneath more. He wanted everything.

"I will have all of your secrets, Jane."

She looked down. Then she looked up and her eyes were large and moist. "I think you already have the only one that matters."

He puzzled over that for a moment, trying to discern which secret she referred to. Faced with her tears, she was an enigma.

"Now it is completely dark," she said. "I'd best rest if we are to travel tomorrow."

He stood before she could finish struggling to her feet, swept her up into his arms. She was right. Any journey would be taxing to her.

The distinction between outside and inside was so slight, but now there was his horse to walk around, the packages on the floor, and their presence made the pitiful nature of this hideaway even more obvious. If she had been more gravely hurt, here was where she would have died. He laid her down on the bed. She closed her eyes and rolled toward the wall. He sat down by the hearth, leaned his back against the cold bricks. The nights were growing colder. Whatever shelter he sought next would need to truly protect them from the elements, protect them from the danger he knew would come.

He could not lose himself in this woman.

Since the moment he had first found her she had intrigued him because she was brave, honest, and vibrant in the face of death. Despite fear, she put rational thought ahead of unbridled emotion. She was softer than he and her life had been soft, but she was like him. Yet turned away from him, he could not identify her expression or its cause. She was a mystery. He did not know this woman, but he wanted to, and that desire was making *him* softer, endangering both of them. The thought was as sobering now as it had been tickling the back of his mind for the last days. When he let Jane live, he had instigated change. How much, he could not guess. A wise man would recognize that now was the time to cut his losses.

He was beyond wealthy. He could leave Amsel and Gori, and all the other versions of himself behind, be the man of leisure Gerard Badeau was known to be. *Assassin.* She had used that word to describe him and though he had never thought himself in such a way, to an extent she was right. He knew the origin of the word, knew the history of the art of death. Understood the importance of executioners, whether they stood in their black masks by the chopping block or guillotine, or whether they worked in the shadows. But he had spoken truly. He had not yet lied to Jane, hardly even the lies of omission. He made no secret of the secrets he kept.

Badeau, perhaps, had been an assassin. Certainly he had explained the intricacies of poisons in an underground workroom, the stench of oils and herbs so strong Gerard could still smell them, feel the sting of them in his nostrils. Badeau had instructed him in swords, pistols, and fists. He had imparted the importance of knowing the limits of one's own body, from the most dynamic to the most still, the agility needed to move silently through an old, creaky house, or to step across leaf-strewn grass without anyone the wiser. But those were not the only lessons. There had been the classical English education, the study of politics and strategy, the focus on draftsmanship and language. The drills in social etiquette so that he could blend in on a farm and in a ballroom. He had been trained to take on any identity, if needed.

This history had been his own; he had never spoken of it with anyone, not even those who shared it—the English grandfather, the legitimate half brother, and the tutor who was more of a father than his own father could ever have been. He was proud of his abilities, without doubt about his choices—at least, he *had* been.

At the shuffle of skin against fabric, he looked to Jane. Her bright gaze was trained on him intently.

"The year the revolution began a man showed up at our door." He was speaking before he realized he had intended to. Instinct again. Or need. "Until that point I lived with my mother and grandmother." He watched Jane's expression, which was a mask of polite curiosity. He had not wanted to be known and understood in a very long time, but here and now he did. By *this* woman. "I thought at first it was her newest lover and then I realized he wore no jewels. An elegant man, but one meant to be forgettable. I did not until later realize that was a skill one learned."

He had taught Gerard what a shadow moves like, a shadow that no one sees. He had imparted the art of disguise. Illusion. A sleight of hand here, a bit of padding there. Dye for the hair, kohl and ashes for new angles to the face.

She laughed. "There are many young ladies in London who would love to shed their natural talent."

"He claimed to be from my grandfather," Gerard said, now compelled to finish this narrative. "That he had been sent to take me to safety. I did not wish to leave my mother, even though she insisted. I went to bed in my home and the next morning awoke in a carriage far from Paris, this stranger staring at me over his book."

"You ran away from him."

It was his turn to laugh. "Of course I did."

Her lips turned up.

"But only because he let me." Gerard's humor faded as he considered that time, the desperation, loss and rage at being sent away. "He let me so he could catch me. It was the way he taught lessons. A loose but firm rein."

"You sound fond of him."

Something twisted inside of him, ached. Every moment of Badeau was touched with the bittersweet, tinged with what Gerard had later perceived as betrayal, and with the despair of the man's death. "Fond enough to have taken his name as my own," he said simply, at a loss to explain the complexity without revealing too much.

"So he was your tutor."

"My tutor…my father." The man who had groomed him for a life in the shadows, at his grandfather's request. He had never blamed Badeau for that. The earl, however, had put Gerard into Badeau's care.

"Where is your real father?"

"Deceased now. At the time, I did not know. Somewhere begetting more bastards. Spreading the pox in his wake."

She winced. "You are illegitimate."

"Yes." Which had never bothered him before. Many men were born such. It was simply the way of the world. It had never stopped him from going where he wished, doing as he wished, obtaining anything at all that he desired. But this woman thrust these words in his face: assassin, illegitimate. For the first time, they threatened him because his choice to let her live, her presence in his life, changed everything. He could not just step back into his world.

"So from Paris he took you to Venice."

He nodded, drawn back into telling his story.

"Among other places, but that was home." A home different from the rooms he had shared with his mother. When he returned years later to see her, those rooms had been occupied by someone else. An inquiry had revealed that she had passed over a year earlier. He had never been informed. By then he had learned to put emotions away as if they were foreign relics to be studied objectively. The rooms had no longer looked like the home he had remembered, just as the Venice house had changed with Badeau's death.

Home. He had not had a home in years.

His stomach felt hollow and that odd twist inside his chest intensified. *Sentiment is the harbinger of death*, he could hear Badeau say as if the man were still alive. A man in a dangerous position could not afford the luxury of insipid emotions.

"So your grandfather put you into the care of a man who would teach you to be an assassin and a spy?"

He laughed, her question breaking his solemn reverie. How easily she added that new aspect to his interrogation, hoping to catch him in an inadvertent truth. If she had not been trained in the art of subtle inquiry, she certainly had natural technique.

Her face was lit only by moonlight, and yet he could see the shape of her mouth. If she had been closer he would have kissed her then, taken her face in his hands and claimed those lips, that cunning mind, for his own. It was good then, that four feet of dusty, earth-covered stone separated them.

"Neither of those words describe…" Gerard stopped. Yes, he had at times acted as both spy and assassin, but there had been more to the work as well. Negotiator, peacekeeper, courier. "Death is one means to an end."

"Death is *the* end."

He nodded in acknowledgment of the quip, and then stood, restless, frustrated.

He was wrenched inside by his weakness. *An assassin*, he wished to say, to frighten her into silent submission, *would have killed you and would at the very least do so now*. But the childishness of the threat disturbed him. Such an action would be a sign that he had lost control.

"You are the one who wished to forgo names," he said roughly. "What I do, that does not need a name."

Chapter Six

His dark form paced the confines of the room, such as it was. He was bothered by the title of assassin, as if he were troubled that she knew, but also, as if he were ashamed.

If his actions were for good—not that good was ever such a simple thing—then he had no need for that shame. But clearly it bothered him that she distilled his employment down to one facet. Yet, he refused to admit to anything else and this she had witnessed.

"I cannot even bear to hunt," she said softly, "but I understand it must be done. I do not have enough information to know if…this…if Lord Powell was something that must be done. Or if the casualties, Lady Powell and myself, were worth it."

"You are alive."

"That was not your intention." She sat up, leaned forward toward him. "Why? Why do you let me live? What does your instinct say?"

He was at her side before she could form a thought, his expression full of furious emotion. He pulled her up toward him, his left hand grasping her injured arm too tightly, and she gasped. He loosened his grip instantly, and the thunder left his expression. What was left looked oddly like remorse. Then his mouth flattened into a harsh line. "My instinct is that I would be better off with you dead."

"Perhaps you would," she said, "but let's not pretend anymore. You have no intention of killing me."

She studied his expression for something, searched his dark gaze.

"You are breaking me," he whispered, each word sounding as if it were being pulled from him by force.

She shook her head mutely, even though inside joy surged. For one instant, she knew him utterly, and then his lips were on hers.

His lips were dry and cool against her closed mouth, but then his hand tugged at her chin. She parted her lips and everything changed. Desire shot through her broken body and made it whole, made pain disappear. All that mattered were his lips tugging, nibbling, urging her own. Then she was sitting on the bed, cool air rushing in, and through blurred vision she could see Gerard leaning against his horse, could hear his labored breath. Or was that hers?

She blinked, lifting her fingers to her lips. Had Lady Jane Langley truly died in the crash the way she insisted? Certainly that respectable, reasonable woman would not now be having fanciful emotions about her captor. But was Jane so much less reasonable? Was this distilled, freer version of herself so different? So…weak and womanly?

"Jane." He turned and crossed the room back to her,

knelt at her feet. Still, his face was only slightly below hers and she could see without a doubt that now his expression *was* remorse. For kissing her?

"I should not have taken advantage of you in such a way."

She laughed in disbelief, even though it was no more than she had come to expect from this strange, contradictory man. "You have no qualms about taking a man's life and yet you balk at a stolen kiss?" Heat filled her face and she wanted to cry.

She had almost died a few days ago. Certainly that was reason enough for her emotions to vacillate so, for her nerves to be fraught, and tears ready to her eyes. Still, her watery emotions frustrated her, even more because if she were alone, she might examine them and come to fully understand what now only teased at the edges of her mind.

But one thing she did know, she leaped so quickly upon each sign of compassion and humanity from this man that it was clear she was in danger. If not her life, then certainly her sanity, certainly everything she had ever known about herself and her world.

"You are under my protection, Jane." His voice was low and intent and it reverberated through her body, gaining weight and meaning with each moment that passed.

Under his protection.

He had kissed her, he had bathed her naked body, and yet, the mere inches between them were a tense barrier she could not abide. She lifted her hand, all too aware of her daring, aware that she was touching *him*, and pressed it to his cheek. His skin was smooth and rough and warm. He was utterly still—she thought he held even his breath—and she moved the pad of her thumb slightly over his skin.

Then she grew more daring, ran that thumb over his lips, slipped her hand over his jaw, down his neck. He didn't object and that tacit permission made her brave, made her feel as if he were hers to do with as she would. To kiss again, perhaps.

He caught her hand in his, gently placed it down on the bed.

"What am I to do with you?"

Kiss me, she thought. She fell back upon the bed and closed her eyes, closed them against her own stupid desire. "Take me to Vienna and leave me there," she said. "Or take me to the nearest coaching house and pay for my fare. I shan't speak of you. It is simple enough to say that I stumbled from the wreck looking for help."

"You're not a fool," he chided. "You know that will not be enough."

Perhaps she was a fool, because she didn't understand why not. She would not speak of him. Yes, he had no reason to trust her discretion, but surely he understood already that she had every reason not to wish to admit to having been alone with a man for days, for having had her every need tended to by him. Essentially, if she admitted this story, even though she was a victim, she had been compromised as far as society would see it.

"When I was a girl, my father would send me and my nanny to visit my cousins' estate. I hated those months. Felt that I had been exiled. Worse, my cousins were three girls, all a year apart in age and each one more lovely and feminine than the rest. Our interests crossed in music and art, but otherwise there was little that we shared then."

He rocked back on his heels, an eyebrow quirked. "That is more than many share."

"Perhaps, but remember, I had been taught to think those things necessary for society but superfluous to the concerns of people who mattered."

"Your father is a member of parliament. House of Lords?"

"My father's actual power and his desire for power are two different things," Jane said, avoiding a direct answer. And it was true. Her father had taken his seat in parliament years ago, but as a member of the unofficial "Group of Eight," men who predicted and plotted out the future of the world in order to best protect and design England's path forward, he intended to have far more of an impact. To some extent, he was succeeding in his ambitions. After all, he would never have been invited to join Castlereagh et al. in Vienna were his opinions and understanding of history not of use. "But that is only to explain how and why I had very little interest in music and art. I have since recognized that early error.

"They had a tutor," she continued, itching to finish telling this story of a long ago incident that she had never revealed to another soul. "A man who then seemed much older, but in truth had just finished his studies. He taught the harpsichord and the pianoforte and the elder two girls liked to go on and on about how handsome and skilled he was. How elegant his fingers." She shivered. "How well he understood passion and matters of the soul."

"They were seduced by Mozart and Bach," Gerard suggested and she nodded in agreement.

"He was very popular among the local society. Did good works when he was not conducting lessons. Played concerts at the church. Everyone admired him."

Gerard shifted, settled down, one arm resting on his

raised knee and his chin resting on that. His hands were long, his fingers elegant and skillful and deadly. Yet so different from the pale, elongated hands of the music master that now, years later, she could remember down to the bluish veins.

Suddenly she couldn't bear to keep thinking about the story. She finished the tale in a rush, the words running together. "I walked in on him compromising Alice, my oldest cousin, by force. He had been careless. Locked the door to the hall but forgot that the music room shared a door with the library, where I had been sitting when I heard Alice's brief muffled cry. I assumed she'd found a mouse or some other sort of thing.

"He didn't realize I was there until I hit him on his arm with the bow of the violoncello, and then he grabbed me"— she could still see his shirt hanging down over his sagging breeches, his forehead beaded in sweat—"twisted my arm until I dropped the bow, and told me that he and my cousin were in love and I wasn't to speak of what I had seen to anyone. But Alice did not look as if she was in love and the force he used on me did not inspire me to believe him. To Alice, he said in what I perceived as a menacing voice although he had a smile on his face, 'I shall leave you to handle your cousin, my dear.'"

"He thought to convince you of your mistake."

"He had threatened her, convinced her that if she told anyone of the incident, she would forever be ruined. After he left the room, she threatened me in turn. She picked up a letter opener, waving it around as she gesticulated. I know she didn't intend to hurt me, but in the altercation, I fell on it." She rubbed idly at her stomach, over the scar that remained. "I didn't tell anyone how the injury occurred, but

I forced him to leave our town, told him I would keep silent only for Alice's sake and only if he left immediately."

"A brave act for a young girl."

She snorted. She was glad of the scar. It served as a reminder that beneath a pleasant exterior could lie evil intent. "I was angry at myself for not doing more, but Alice was devastated. Why did I tell you this?" She wiped at her forehead, trying to remember the point she had intended to make but caught up in emotions that had long been dormant.

"That is not the end of the story," Gerard said, and startled she met his intent gaze. "What did you do?"

She laughed nervously. He was right, and a part of her was pleased that he understood. "Years later, in London, I hired a man to inquire about the music teacher's whereabouts. He still taught young women and who knew how many others he had hurt. I knew what I wished to do, to ruin him and force him into exile. He is in New South Wales the last I heard."

She'd sold her soul to do so. The elderly Earl of Landsdowne had seemed diabolical enough to know how to enact a financial ruin. As she had expected, he never questioned the why of her request nor revealed that request to her father or anyone else. Alice's secret remained her own.

"A woman after my own heart," Gerard said with a laugh, unfolding himself.

His words did a funny thing inside of her, as if someone had tickled her. Even more, she remembered the purpose of her story.

"All of that is simply to say that I know what it is for a woman to be taken advantage of and *you* did not take advantage of me. Perhaps I did not wish to be here with you, would never have considered such a thing if it were asked of me, but I do not regret that kiss." She studied his face, the lips that had claimed hers parted, his laugh stalled. "And yes," she added, before she could formulate any more Lady Jane Langley style unfortunate thoughts, "I want you to kiss me again."

He shook his head. "All that strength, all that wisdom… You think you are in control of the world."

She didn't understand what he meant but at the first caress of his hand on her cheek, she leaned into his warmth. Wakefulness and sleep blurred. Perhaps the kiss could wait. Perhaps, just now, to simply be touched was enough, as she fell back upon the bed, eyes drifting closed with a deep, overwhelming exhaustion.

When she stirred against him, the first light of day was breaking in the sky. Over the hours he'd watched her shiver under the thin blanket, then again under the double layer of a blanket and his coat. Only when he'd lain next to her and pulled her body close to his, did she finally relax into a deep sleep. In those hours that he'd been awake, he'd sat against the cold hearth, waiting. Thinking.

The rain of the day before had likely erased any tracks he had inadvertently made and yet discovery was still a threat. Descending from the shelter of this mountain with Jane held its own dangers. However, they could not stay here. Even if he wanted to linger, to watch the early light reveal the curve of her neck, her earlobe. Wanted to lick each place the light touched.

He was hard against the soft roundness of her bottom, his trousers the only barrier between them, as the cloth of his shirt that she wore had risen up between them. With each passing moment it was easier to accept his desire and fascination for her, to accept that in these few short days something had kindled between them, something that transcended the prevailing codes of morality and society. Not that he adhered to those codes in the usual course of things.

The gray light brightened to yellow, illuminating them both, and her eyelashes fluttered, then parted. She shifted, turned toward him, and for one moment, he had a glimpse beneath the loose shirt of the bruised, distended skin of her injured shoulder.

His arousal fled and unease settled in his gut instead. It was easier to hide from truths in the darkness.

"You look very fierce," she whispered and he met her questioning gaze. Of course she was questioning, wishing to know his very thoughts. The bed was no proper bed and distinctly uncomfortable, and yet he wished to laze here longer, to enjoy the challenge of her conversation and the intimacy of the space.

Such a domestic desire. What was it he wanted from her? What was it that he thought she could bring him? He watched her arm move and he was still stunned by her hand on his cheek, the pads of her fingers running over the rougher texture of his jaw.

"In half an hour we will begin our way down the mountain to the main road," he said, catching her hand in his and holding it there against his skin. "Each step will bring us closer to the rest of the world. You will think of how you can escape, with whom you can beg shelter and protection—it is only natural. But remember this. You are drawn to me as much as I am to you. Your life, for now, is with me."

"For now," she said.

He turned his head to press his lips to her palm. The skin was so soft. It was the hand of a woman who was protected and cosseted, even if her upbringing and education were slightly more unusual than the average young lady of society.

As they dressed, he said more. The story he had concocted as he first tended to her. She was his wife, Beatrix, and had suffered a fall from her horse. The horse had not survived. They were traveling to see family in Hesse because his father was on his deathbed and thus they needed to travel with the swiftest speed possible, made slower by her injuries. He was tempting fate by trusting her to stick to the story. Once they were traveling, he would not be able to control all the variables. But remaining here was a greater risk.

It was clear within the first half an hour of traveling that Jane's pain was magnified by the movements of the horse. Instead, they walked side by side, and as they did, with the dust of the road and the sound of the horse's breath heavy in their ears, words flowed.

"Thanks to my father, I have seven half siblings of which I know," Gerard said. "I met the legitimate heir this past winter."

"You envy him."

He laughed at her statement. "I am far richer than he is. I have land in Venice, in the Alps, Paris. I want for nothing."

"But your life is in the shadows. I assume his is not."

She had so easily named what Gerard could not. Yes,

his life was in the shadows, but he had always taken pride in it, understood that he was skilled and necessary, that there were few who could do the work that he did. While death was sometimes required, more often than not his work was the gathering of information and the couriering of documents across borders.

"There was this night in Florence when my brother thought he was saving a man's life and instead he put both of ours in danger."

"He thought you intended to kill a man and you did not?" Jane asked.

Gerard nodded. That night Gerard's work had not been simply about acquiring information. Rather, he had needed to keep information from reaching other hands. As a result of his brother's interference he had had to hunt down the thief once more.

"What a fool he was," Jane said, and Gerard smiled. This woman would never do anything so foolish. She was cool and collected, even under duress.

"What of your other siblings?"

"What of them?"

"Are they, too, trained as you?"

"I should not know. My grandfather told me of them as a cautionary tale against the excesses of my father. I hunted them down."

Of course he had.

"Three still live. Marie, she is married, her life settled. Giana, I found her in Florence working in a brothel as a maid. I placed her in a convent. She was not grateful." He laughed. "Thomas is not grateful for my interference either. I am told he runs away from his school regularly. But I pay well for them to hunt him down and drag him back."

"Thomas…"

"Born to an English mother, yes."

"Then your grandfather—"

"As best I know cares nothing for him. I was the fortunate one."

*F*ortunate. Raised to be a man's lackey, his dagger. His poison. But Gerard seemed so confident in his power. Though he had power over her life for now, there were men who made laws, strategized, planned…and then used men such as Gerard to further their purpose. She had spent her life amongst these men.

"Once I became my father's unofficial factotum, a new world opened up to me," she said. "Instead of reading about politics in the daily papers, or waiting months after the fact for a decent analysis, I listened and conversed with the men who were making the important decisions and were manipulating events in order to achieve the outcomes they desired. There were women, too, of course. The occasional wife or mistress who hosted a dinner or a salon. But more often these were gatherings for men only. If I was quiet and spoke only when spoken to, I was forgiven my female nature."

Gerard laughed. "Women have as much an interest in politics as men. Some day they shall have an equal say."

"How radical of you." And it was. His statement was more in line with Mary Wollstonecraft and women of her ilk, women with whom Jane had never identified. Hearing him speak in such a way unnerved her.

"What? An intelligent woman such as yourself does not believe you could govern your nation as well as a man? I will admit to superior strength, and perhaps I would not place the fate of a nation in that of most women, as poorly educated as they are, but you…"

He said nothing she would not admit to without a blush, and yet, the words felt like a compliment.

"I am practical," she said with a shrug. "Certainly a woman can govern, as did our Elizabeth, but…" She trailed off. Perhaps it was simply that she had been surrounded by men for most of her life, had been molded by their points of view. Men who were conservative in their approach to governance.

Gerard was different. He had nothing to lose.

She shook her head. As much as she could try to dismiss his point of view because it made her uncomfortable, she was being closed-minded and unreasonable. In this matter, had outside forces other than her own reason shaped her vaunted practicality? By inertia rather than momentum? Exhaustion struck her and she stumbled over a pebble. Ridiculous, she thought, even as she caught herself.

His hand on her upper arm startled her, and though its intent was to steady her, she wavered where she stood. Her vision wavered as well before she realized that the movement she saw was of a cart pulled by a lone horse, rumbling over the road toward them. Exhaustion fled as every sense focused. She had not seen another person other than Gerard since the wreck.

"A farmer transporting his wares," Gerard murmured. "Don't risk his life because you feel you must make some futile attempt to escape."

Jane's stomach twisted and cold dread slid down her back at his casual threat. One moment they were exchanging intimacies as if they were friends but then the outside world intruded. How could she have forgotten for a moment that assassin was not some word to describe a man with a tragic past? Gerard was a man who had and would kill.

The farmer rumbled past with the briefest of nods. She looked over her shoulder to watch him disappear down the road. Had her silence been practicality or cowardice?

"You made the right choice," Gerard said quietly.

Anger flared within her, making her forget her exhaustion. "I made the choice you wanted me to make. This may be your life but I wish to return to mine."

"*This* is your life now," he said, before sweeping her up off her feet. He had done such so many times over the past few days that it almost felt normal and natural. Yet, she wanted her own strength; she needed to rely only on herself.

"For now," she said, as she had earlier that morning. Soon she would be recovered, and an escape would not require endangering anyone else.

"For now," he said, and with that tacit acknowledgment that someday she would leave, tension fled from Jane's body and she curled against his body in relief.

Chapter Seven

They traveled in small stages, alternating between companionable silence and conversation. She didn't try to escape the first night they took a room at an inn, pretending to be husband and wife on the way to visit relatives, or the next night, or the next after that. Jane's injuries were not so visible if one did not watch how carefully she walked, how she barely moved her arm. Gerard conversed easily with nearly everyone they met, and she understood much of what they said, but the subtleties of the different dialects and variations of the German tongue eluded her. She had studied the language from books, supplemented by an Austrian tutor. With England at war for much of her adult life, she had rarely traveled beyond England's shores.

Gerard, however, had traveled as far east as Moscow and as far west as Dublin.

"At sixteen, I was sent for my first employment from Venice to Berlin to collect a parcel, a locked box. It was easy to discover its hidden contents. I avoided the trap of attempting to open its lock and instead dismantled it from the bottom, revealing the hidden compartment. However, the papers within were relatively unimportant."

"It was a test," Jane said, shaking her head at the world in which he had grown up, one in which intellectual games were translated into physical tasks, in which wit was a matter of life and death.

"Yes."

"And did you pass? Was it a test of your loyalty and discretion or of your skill?"

Gerard laughed. "Both, I believe. I was roundly scolded, but imagine I would have been equally scolded if I had not successfully opened it."

The stories overlapped sometimes, so that she'd heard parts of one then folded up with other years of his life, and so she found herself doing the same. She understood what they were doing, recounting their histories, forging them for each other. Histories were more real when told, shaped through current perspectives. This story of his life he was molding just for her, leaving out the smallest details that would reveal his identity. She did the same. But despite the small omissions, this room, the burnt out cottage and the other shelters they had found in the last days had become wellsprings of truths. She knew deeply that here they were their most open and their most fragile. That he was to her the most deadly, and she to him. They could entrust only so much.

By most accounts, Jane's life had been easy. She had her father's hard won respect and society beamed upon her. There had been the slight tremble when she had befriended the slightly scandalous new Lady Templeton, but even then few had judged Jane. After all, Lady Jane Langley would never act outside of reason, would never debase herself for love, and her weakness in championing a once courtesan was chalked up to her mannish upbringing.

She would never do anything as shocking as chase after a man, demand he love her after he had made clear to all society that he scorned her. Equally, she would never admire a man who did the same to her.

"It is very important to you that no one think you weak," Gerard said one afternoon.

The words troubled her, as if Gerard were pointing out just how weak she was. "I don't care what people..." *A lie.* She would not lie to him. Or to herself.

"You care what your father thinks."

She nodded. "But society? Whose opinion should I consider?"

"No one's."

She met his gaze. Of course, this man with his shadowy life would care for nothing. Except...

"Your grandfather."

He raised an eyebrow.

"You try to please him."

Gerard laughed, and Jane's stomach tumbled. Apparently she cared about Gerard's opinion as well. She swallowed hard.

"You do," she insisted, standing her ground despite his dismissive laugh. "In your stories, he stands as this mysterious benefactor. He's the reason you do anything you do."

"Ah, yes. As a boy, I suppose I did try to please him. As I tried to please my tutor." He rubbed his chin and then dropped his hand, shaking his head. "But a man learns that he can only please himself. None other matters. Your father, he does not matter. And, as you say, society's opinion is insignificant. All that matters is you."

That night, at yet another inn, she lay a hand's breadth away, warm enough between the clean sheets but craving his heat. In that shared bed, they returned again to his grandfather, to his past.

"I grew up in Paris," he repeated, starting the story again. "I was raised the first few years by my mother, but then on my sixth birthday a man showed up. I thought he was my father at first, but I found out that he was to be my tutor, sent by a distant grandfather. Father to my own father."

He had said as much already, but he linked it together now, thawing, the way she was thawing, discovering how she felt about the simple facts she knew.

The curtain was open to let the moonlight stream in, and she could see her arm, bare beneath the short shoulder of her rough chemise. She could see him, too, lying on his side next to her in a foreign bed, talking companionably as if there were nothing strange about any of this at all.

"In many ways," he said, "my tutor *was* my father and I took his name when I came of age to do such a thing."

The first name he had taken for himself. Then he created numerous identities, but not one satisfied the void of birth: he could not take his father's name as his brother had done. The message beneath his words was clear, yet Jane suspected Gerard was still unaware of that significance.

"I was flattered at first that my grandfather took notice of me. I longed to meet him. Dreamed of a day he would bring me to live with him. I dreamed of fields and open space and horses."

She listened to his words, but even more she listened to his voice, to the rhythmic cadence of his speech, the way it slipped every so often from the clipped English to the hint of an accent, and then, on very rare occasions, into French.

"You are half English, then?"

His lips twisted.

"Your accent," she said with a shrug that then made her gasp from the pain.

"I never knew my father, but I knew of him, and I knew how he died. This noble father of mine died like any other rutting fool—ill of disease."

"You said the pox."

"Syphilis."

He looked at her, waiting for shock or judgment, and then it didn't come, just as he should have known it wouldn't, because this woman was unusual. Was as perfectly chosen for him as much as the tutor who had appeared on his birthday, only this time, it wasn't his grandfather who had arranged the gift. It was almost enough to make Gerard believe in a god.

"I had a very different childhood than you," Jane said softly. "My mother died at my birth. I was raised by my nanny, well, by a succession of nannies until finally I made my father realize I wasn't just a girl. I was his child and his heir, at least, of whatever will not go to my cousin, James, who stands to inherit..." She stopped herself. There were only so many earls in England. She coughed to try and cover the mistake but he was watching her so intently and from the way his lips thinned, she knew he knew and was displeased. Her own lips twisted before she continued in a bit of a rush. "And when I was fourteen, finally he treated me that way. We've been inseparable ever since. I've learned so much from following him, listening to his friends."

"The men you admired."

She laughed. Of course, he would remember that. "Are you jealous of them?"

"Yes."

He grabbed her face as he admitted to it. She was surprised at his honest vehemence and her pulse raced at his sudden proximity, at the heat that grew between them. In the dim light, his eyes were dark pools.

"I would be jealous of any man who came before me," he said.

His lips claimed hers. The way he had said he wouldn't, that he hadn't for some four nights, even as he slept beside her, often with her head on his shoulder as they drifted to sleep. But this was the opposite of sleep. Firm and demanding, he awakened her skin. Sensation radiated, vibrated throughout her. His body pressed against hers, pinning her against the mattress and between his hot mouth and the wonder of what he would do next, her breath caught. If he moved his hand lower, what would she do? If he moved his lips?

She would stop him, because her virginity would go with her to the marriage bed, but there were many points between a kiss and a deflowering, and inexperienced as Jane was, she was not ignorant.

With her left hand, she grasped the bare skin of his upper arm, ran her fingers over the flexed muscles. She parted her legs and his hips settled between hers, his weight welcome, the stiffness of his arousal fascinating and hot, separated only by her chemise. His hips rocked against her and then with a groan he pulled away, rolled onto his back and rested his forearm against his head. Cold and empty, she reached for him, and he pushed her hand away.

"Not yet," he said.

"Not ever," she corrected with a nervous laugh.

"Not *yet*," he returned, lowering his arm and turning his head to look at her. "This is inevitable."

Deep down in her body she understood him, knew his words to be true. But only true in this strange world they had created between them. Once she left, once she was back in England, the spell would be broken.

"You would ruin me? What is it you intend to do with me?"

He was not ready to answer that question because he did not yet know what he would do with her. What would come of his foolish intuition?

He was still wondering when they arrived at his small apartment in Frankfurt on Main. It was one he knew well. Owned under an alias, he stopped there several times a year as he crisscrossed the continent. Over the years he had discovered that there were benefits and dangers to inns just as there were to private residences, but at least at a residence he would find a change of clothes, his own belongings, even if he arrived in the dead of night with no valise or trunk. In fact, the only trunk within had been sent shortly after he acquired the flat, along with simple furniture befitting a man of business who traveled frequently.

The woman who lived below him opened her door and

greeted him, stared pointedly at Jane until Gerard introduced her as his wife. Jane chatted with the elderly woman as if she were not traveling under duress and Gerard was only able to break the conversation by agreeing that Jane and he would join his neighbor for dinner that night.

"Think of it as a test," Jane said when they were alone.

Of her loyalty or of her stealthiness. Would she be able to unlock the chains with which he had bound her?

"You frighten me." Yet he was pleased, and he looked forward to seeing what Jane would do. The last several times that they had stayed at inns she had been exhausted by the time they arrived. Yes, she could have sounded the alarm at any time but he trusted in Jane's good sense not to put herself in a potentially more dangerous situation when she was at her weakest.

Trust.

That he had any sort of trust in her was nothing short of miraculous. That he used a word such as miraculous to describe it was even more confounding. But as tired as she was, the dark circles under her eyes pronounced, her lips thin with barely concealed pain, it was as yet early afternoon. She would have time to rest, to formulate her thoughts or a plan.

A test, she had said. Just as she had guessed he would make an attempt to run when he described his first day with Badeau, so he knew she would not be satisfied unless she had as well. Unless he could convince her to stay. If that was what he wanted.

She kept asking what he intended and he kept refusing to say, but that was because he was uneasy with the answer bubbling at the edges of his thoughts. That he liked her company. That he liked being able to share parts of himself, share the shadows. That he wanted to drag her into them fully and make her his own. Yet she was almost surely the daughter of some nobleman or someone else of some importance in English society. What would make her satisfied to stay with him?

Next to him, Jane looked around the barren rooms. It was a modest apartment—he saw no reason to keep the dozen some homes he had all at the same level of ornate furnishings.

"I know enough to be the death of you," she said softly. He stiffened, tension coiling in his muscles. He would have to leave these rooms, this identity behind, and clean up everywhere else he used this identity as well, but she could make no connection to Badeau. And yet, he knew she was right. Deep down in his bones he knew, as he had known when he first spared her life. More than anything, he was no longer the immovable fortress he had been. She had seen his weaknesses. He had been the one to make them visible to her.

"Come sit," he said, brushing the warning of her words aside. "We shall freeze in here sooner than that."

He moved to the cold, empty fireplace, pulled wood from the stack beside the mantle and set about coaxing out the warmth-giving flames. The tinder crackled as he worked. He could hear the creaking of wood as she shifted, settling more fully on the sofa.

"Why did you first kill?"

He hissed and pulled his thumb back from the hot ember that had scalded him.

"The first time I killed a man," he repeated slowly. "Why do you wish to know that?"

This was the story he would not tell her. Not yet, perhaps not ever. He could not share the numbness that had made him see the world coolly, logically. That had made him impervious to the work that needed to be done.

"Because I need to know if I should hate you."

The statement hit him in the gut. He was shocked that she cared, and not shocked at all.

"Don't you?" It would only be natural for her to do so. Yet, he wanted—the words all whispered in his brain, competing for precedence—*salvation, love, desire, hope, joy…this woman.*

The embers blossomed into flame. He added another log and then sat back, brushing his hands on his trousers. She looked troubled, and her usually forthright gaze did not meet his.

"You are exactly who I thought you were in the moment I first saw you. But I did not realize I would also come to… admire you."

Nausea struck him again, low and thick. He wanted to void himself of everything he was that was not worthy of this woman, that she would not accept. And he wanted her in a way he had never desired anything before in his life. With a sense of permanence. Of future. A sense that he did indeed have something to lose.

"And why did you kill Powell?"

"Why is any man targeted for death?" he shot back. "Greed, money, power. Love, lust, faith, have your pick."

"Which one was Powell?"

Greed, money, *and* lust. A trifecta of sin, but to give Jane even that much was to open the door to more questions.

"Did you care for him?" he finally demanded, frustrated by the same challenging persistence that he admired.

"He amused me."

Jealousy shot through him, startling him with its force.

"As did his wife," she said. "But I was not one of his many lovers." He raised an eyebrow at that. Powell had not been the most discreet but neither had he been terribly indiscreet, other than in bed. "Oh, don't look so shocked that I know of that. He confided in me that he meant to seduce me before we even boarded the carriage."

The jealousy turned into a rage. If he had not killed the man, he likely would have then. To try and seduce a young woman with his wife in the same carriage took enormous gall.

"You look so fierce. He only half meant it," she said with a thin laugh. Her face was pale and drawn. She looked tired and he wanted nothing more at that moment than to hold her and protect her, to give her some of his strength. "You know how these men are, they flirt and seduce but it is all to while away the time. I take none of it seriously."

"The man was a bounder," he said, his voice tight and low. He stood up and retrieved a blanket from the cupboard where they were stored. He paid a woman to come by monthly to dust, wash, and launder, make certain the woodpile was full and the larder had enough provisions to last him at least a night or two. He usually took his meals at the inn down the street, but he liked to be prepared for every eventuality. He spread the blanket over Jane. "I am going to light the fire in the bedroom, too, and then you can sleep."

She rested her head back on the arm of the sofa. The image of her sleepily waiting for him stayed with him as he readied the bedroom. But when he returned her eyes were fully closed in slumber. He wavered for a moment. He needed to go into town, conduct business while he was here, buy food and other supplies. After hesitating, he lifted her up, blanket and all. She snuggled against him, her eyelashes fluttering.

"I'm moving you to the bed, Jane," he said softly. "I shall undress you so that you are more comfortable."

He wasn't certain why he felt he needed to tell her of his intended actions. He had undressed and tended to her body dozens of times, and yet, as she grew stronger, everything was changing. She nodded her head against him and that consent satisfied him. He pulled down the coverlet on the bed and laid her down on the cool sheets. The fire in the hearth would soon chase the chill from the room.

He undressed her as dispassionately as possible, focusing on her still healing injuries to distract him from the woman he desired. Finally, he tucked the coverlet around her, and then laid the blanket above that.

She reached for him, and he bent over, pressed a kiss to that hand before tucking it back under the covers. How many times had he lain beside her to lend her his warmth? That was all she wanted. Yet, as he left her, slipped quietly out of the bedroom and locked the door, his chest was full with tenderness, with the dream that she reached for him for something more.

The bed was empty, the sheets tangled up, but he found her in an instant, stretched out before the fireplace, wrapped in a blanket. One bare leg stretched out, one knee bent and tucked toward her chest. All that careful awareness, all that sharp intellect, softened in sleep, melted into a simple beauty.

He felt dizzy, oddly buoyant. How quickly his world had turned over, sideways, inside out and unrecognizable. How swiftly this one woman had become the center of his new existence. When he thought of returning home, he had thought of returning to her.

She awakened the fullness of both his desire and his more tender emotions—emotions he had long ago discarded as weakness. But he did not feel weaker for them now. Instead he was invigorated. He was...

In love.

As quickly as he thought the words, he heard Badeau's voice in his head.

Do not be fooled by love, my son. It has been the undoing of too many good men.

Gerard had never thought to ask his mentor if love had been *his* undoing. Certainly he could see the dangers here. Already he had broken his code, strayed from his path. Already he was entertaining a life vastly divergent from the one he had known, one in which he and Jane could be together, away from the darkness. He had not known the depths of the dark in which he lived until she had come into it, illuminating everything.

He shrugged out of his coat, undid the simple cloth at his neck and then lowered himself to his knees by her side. How difficult would it be to start a new life? To walk away from his clients, from even his grandfather's requests, to be a husband. To be, perhaps, a father.

A dark tendril of unease threaded through him, but he pushed it away. He didn't need to think so far ahead.

Although painstakingly planning and designing multiple iterations of the future were elements of his success and the reason he had not only survived thus far but also amassed a respectable fortune, he did not want to look beyond the next day.

Tomorrow and tomorrow and tomorrow…

He had never been a coward and yet now he refused to consider any iteration but the one he wanted most: Jane to be his. She shifted, her head lolling to the side. The creamy expanse of her neck called to him but he satisfied himself by imagining his tongue licking down its length, his lips coaxing sighs of pleasure from her lips.

His gaze trailed down to where the skin of her shoulder revealed by the blanket was still bruised. The reason he would not yet make her his own the way he wished to, body to body, inside of her. That uneasy, foreign sensation of guilt slithered through him again. A casualty, but Jane should never have been one, and yet she wouldn't be in his life if she had not. Could he regret that injury?

Did she?

She must know what they had been doing these past few days as they recounted stories and shared their truths. Even as they struggled to hide some part of themselves, they were seducing each other's minds. Each touch built on the foundation created with words. Not the way love was described by troubadours but the very unusualness of its nature made him doubt it less, made him doubt Badeau's warning more.

She shifted again, lifting her chin, her eyelashes fluttering, her back arching slightly, and then those pale blue eyes were gazing at him.

"How long have you been back?"

"Long enough to imagine every way I wish to make love to you." But that was not true. He had only barely scratched the surface of his desire.

She flushed, and the pink glow pleased him. He reached for her outstretched leg, took her foot in his hand, studied it. Not a dainty foot but well formed, strong. He kneaded the muscles with his fingers as he explored this small part of her body that he dared to touch.

She let out a sigh and he looked up to catch an expression of absolute pleasure on her face. The sight fascinated him, enticed him, made him want to give her every sort of pleasure, to see her undulate with climax, melt with post-coital languor.

"I did not know a foot could feel so…" She rested her head back against the stone of the mantle again.

He laughed. He did not know how it felt. No one had ever touched him so. But he knew well that pleasure came in unexpected forms. He moved his exploration to the soft skin of her ankle, fingers gliding firmly over the flesh and bone.

"Where were you?" she asked.

"Business," he said simply. But he wanted to tell her more, share the details of his movements. That he had visited his banker here in Frankfurt, that he had sent correspondence to his man in Paris, to his client in Vienna. Tied up threads that needed to be tied.

"I suppose I must accept that very unsatisfying answer. I was terribly bored in your absence. I could not find a single book other than the Bible in this room."

Which, of course, meant she had looked. The flat was carefully devoid of anything that would reveal his identity.

He had been given his mother's name at birth: Moran. But even that name had not always been hers. She had changed it when she'd left her family for life as a courtesan. He kept Moran for the first twenty-three years of his life until Badeau's death when he wished to honor his memory as a son.

A son.

He had yearned for a father in his early years. He had told Jane that Badeau was more of a father than his own of blood, and the man had left Gerard everything he owned, but there were times he had hated his tutor, times his tutor had betrayed his trust in ways Gerard could never quite forgive, even if he understood.

"Locking the door would not have been sufficient if I had truly wished to leave." The words chilled him. He knew this to be true but there was significance to her statement. That she had checked the door, and that she had not yet wished to leave. Yet. At some point she would.

"I won't let you go," he said, the words meant as a warning, although when the time came, he was not certain how or if he would force her to stay.

He felt the loss of her as keenly as if it had already happened, as if some part of himself had been cut away. And try as he might to harden himself, gird against the impending loss, he could not.

The expression on Gerard's face was inscrutable, as if he had thrust a mask upon it to keep her from seeing him. A reminder that after all they had shared, all the stories they had told, there were still secrets to be kept. Not that her identity would be a secret long if he made any effort to inquire about who the third occupant had been in Powell's carriage. Surely in Vienna the Brumbles would have enlightened everyone that she had not in fact been traveling with them as she ought. Vienna. Where her father awaited her. Where by now he knew of her loss. Vienna, where Lady Jane Langley would have been engaged in helping her father with any matters of business he needed to conduct as he supported the congress's efforts. She had been so excited to be a part of that world, to use her mind.

The reminder of Vienna, of a life so distant from this little world of Gerard and Jane, where other people were enjoying the vibrancy of intellectual pursuits without her, stiffened her spine. She was Jane Langley after all.

"You have to," Jane said at length, with a simple shrug. "I will not stay."

"I love you."

Her heart clenched at the three simple words. In some other place and some other time, she would rejoice to hear them from him, and yet, she would never know him this way had circumstances been different.

"Hah," she scoffed coldly, "you Frenchmen and your love. A cliché, I think. What you are is a murderer. An assassin. A tool for someone." Tension radiated from him. The words were no less than the truth, but they were hurtful.

"What makes you think I didn't plan everything on my own?"

She sat up, drew the blanket back around her, shutting down the softer side of her, latching on to the fight.

"Oh, I'm certain you planned the event. But how did you

pick your target? Lord Powell, for as we have determined your target wasn't me. Why him? Had you ever met him before?"

"You are obfuscating." He shook his head. "You are mine. This is not simply for now." He said it with such surety that she thought perhaps he was right.

She made the mistake of looking into his eyes. His dark gaze caught her, dared her to speak the truth. He dipped one finger into the ashes, pressed it to her neck, the dark remnants of fire still warm on her skin.

He drew his finger down the flat plane of her chest to where it came to meet the rise of her breasts. He was marking her. She saw the words take shape, in French, in Italian, in Portuguese. Some words she understood: Mine, Love. She understood why too, when he switched to German, then to Hungarian, down her arms, her bare breasts, the words streaked, smeared away as his hand held her, thumb slid over nipple. She recognized the Russian letters and the Greek, on the soft expanse of her belly.

She let him, because this moment might be the closest she ever came to experiencing love for herself. That this strange man even wanted to claim her in such a way astounded her. That her heart desperately wanted to answer shocked her even more.

He moved lower, brushed across the curls between her thighs. She shivered again, but shifted ever so slightly, gave him room to—his finger stroking her, then inside her. She opened her eyes, found him watching her. He was marking her in every which way possible, making her his. With every moment more, she wanted to let him, she wanted to give herself over to his keeping, stay here in this room, nowhere, under his hands, in this silence, but she couldn't.

She reached down, lay her fingertips on his wrist. He withdrew, slid his fingers down her leg so that she felt him mark her with her own moisture. There was no Lady Jane here, no Jane even. Just woman and man, with the thin walls of civilization holding them back from the rest of night's creatures.

"When I leave—"

"Jane, you know I cannot let you."

"You say you love me. Then let me go and trust that I will not reveal you."

He leaned over her, cradling her head, brought her mouth to his. The rough fabric of his shirt rubbed against her. She parted her legs to cradle him between them, against her, knew that she was tempting her own control, her own ability to make either of them stop.

Lady Jane Langley. She said her name in her head, repeated it again till the words began to hold some modicum of meaning. *Langley. Jane.* But his mouth was everything, a world of swirling colors and rich warmth, where she would never be cold, never be hurt, always be in the cradle of his hands.

She broke away, burying her face against his neck. "If you really love me, then would you not want my love in return?" She lifted her head again, challenged him to meet her gaze. "As your prisoner, any love I professed would be… false."

Distorted.

She admired him and desired him.

"I *cannot* let go of you." But this time he was not referring to her ability to identify him. She looked away from the tortured need of his gaze and stared at the now dark pile of ash. She understood that agony and confusion. Her world had upended and apparently his had as well. And though she had said she could not give him her love, her heart ached. Somehow, as different as they were, they had found something akin in each other, experienced some sort of communion of the souls. It was very like love. Perhaps it even was the seeds of such an emotion, but it didn't matter. She pushed herself from him, reached down, buried her hand in soot. With her other hand, she pulled at his shirt, not caring when she heard the tear of fabric.

"Gentle, love." His hand stilled hers but she slid her fingers around, took his wrist between her fingers, and brought it to her mouth. Lips pressed to that thin, sensitive skin where she could feel the pulse of his blood, she lifted her other hand.

"Here," she whispered, palm flat against his chest. Then she lowered his hand from her mouth to her own breast, above where her heart beat. She met his eyes, still blinking away the wetness from her own. "In some way, you are right. I am yours. My heart, that ephemeral space the poets call a soul. Everything. But still, I will leave you."

Gerard pushed her words out of his mind, pulled her against him and embraced her in his arms. "We'll go south, live by the water. The days will be slow and warm, the beds soft and we'll both start anew where no one knows us."

She said nothing, but shifted so that she curled up against

his chest and he felt the heat of her breath on his skin, giving him everything and nothing. He tightened his arm around her. She gasped and he quickly released her, scooped her up and carried her to the bed.

"You should be resting."

She held her eyes closed. Her eyelashes were damp, a fat drop of water clinging to the dark fringe before it fell, ran across her cheek.

"I've slept most of the day," she said. "And we're supposed to join Mrs. Koch for dinner."

He shook his head. "I think perhaps it is best if we don't." The idea of having to pretend for even so much as an hour, was too much. "I shall give our regrets."

He lay down next to her, stroked her arm, her cheek, until she fell asleep.

Even now, this love he felt for Jane was strange to him yet completely sensible. She was not some feeble-minded being; she understood the world and the strings that pulled at it, the tensions created. She viewed life as if she stood on a mountaintop. Perhaps it wasn't the sea to which he should secret her. Perhaps Switzerland, the Alps, some chateau in that stark beauty. By a lake. The fantasy was building in his mind.

Her body softened fully against him, her breath deep and even. He eased himself off of the bed and made himself presentable.

He would go down and make their excuses, then he would venture out into the town once more.

She had asked him to trust her, but she did not know about torture, and keeping her with him was protecting her as much as himself. He was tempting fate, he knew. If she woke, if she decided to leave, then she would. If not today then someday.

He needed to convince her to stay before that day came, because he had no way to hold her other than the force he was no longer willing to use.

Chapter Eight

When she woke and Gerard was gone, Jane didn't hesitate. Her movements were economical, protecting the arm that still needed to heal, silent in case he heard noise and came to look. He could very well be in the sitting room or somewhere else, but it didn't matter. She was alone in a town big enough to find shelter.

Unless he stopped her.

She went through all the motions of her escape, gathering what food she could, the letter opener from the desk as the meanest sort of weapon, and then, in the darkness of the alley behind the building, her chest ached hollowly, her stomach hurt, and her eyes burned. The freedom to leave weighed down each step. He had let down his guard and now she would leave. She would never see him again.

Nausea sickened her as she stumbled through the shadowy cobblestone streets toward the edge of town and the posting inn that would surely be there. The farther she went, the more she understood he would not be stopping her. She had never felt more alone.

Yes, there was the physical aloneness, the awareness that she had traded the safety of his company for the dangers of a woman traveling alone. But there was also the emotional, the void that was so much greater and terrifying now that she understood what she was missing.

Resting against the cold stone of the nearest wall, she shook with silent tears. Until she wiped at her eyes with the back of her hand, took a deep breath, and forced him out of her thoughts, focused on logistics. She would not cry over him again. Nor would she let him find her the way his tutor had found him all those years ago, which is what would happen if she showed up at any inn in the middle of the night alone and penniless. But the moon was only a sliver, and without light, the darkness near complete. She did not dare to ask directions, to leave a trail so easily followed, or to speak to the sort of strangers like to be out at this hour of the night. Perhaps the best course of action would be to hide near his apartment. He would not expect her to be so close. But the idea of going backward, of being near him yet apart, was impossible to bear.

Instead, wrapped tightly in the warm coat Gerard had purchased for her, Jane snuck through the town, avoiding lights and people, toward the cathedral whose spires she had noted when they first entered the city. In the shadows of the graveyard, she found a place to hide for the night, but she didn't sleep. It was possible Gerard would find her and she was wracked by her own duality of emotion. In some way, she wanted him to, wanted to cede her will to his, give in to his warmth, his love, the impossible life he suggested. After all, the road between her hiding place and Vienna was long and surely fraught with danger. There was no guarantee she would make it. Or that, still healing as she was, she had the strength to endure whatever obstacles she might face.

But she would not have made her escape if she did not have a plan, and here in Frankfurt she had the best chance of survival. When the first light of dawn broke the sky, she righted her appearance and ventured into a shop, knowing even as she did so that if Gerard searched for her, with each contact she was leading him to her.

Tired and wary of the stares that accompanied her foray into the Jewish quarter, she finally located the Rothschilds' banking offices and as she had met one of the Rothschild sons in London, and they recognized her father's name, she was able to obtain credit. She would have sold her necklace, been fiercely happy to be rid of its reverence of reason, and managed some other way if she had had to, but the bankers were sympathetic to her plight. They had heard of the accident and Lord Powell's death and seemed inordinately interested. Unease sent gooseflesh down her skin and Jane carefully did not mention Gerard.

The rest of the journey passed relatively peacefully. She hired a coach and a woman to act as her maid, and arrived a week and a half later in Vienna. Most of this she imparted to her father, who listened over a stack of papers, as if the fact that his only child had turned up alive was of little importance. Yet she knew it was. This was simply her father's way — to focus on matters at hand.

"Did anyone search for me?" she asked abruptly, stopping her own narrative.

For an instant, there was only the sound of paper crushed

in his grip and to her ears it signaled a pause, an indication that her father was deliberating his answer. What was there to deliberate about that question?

"I was told that there was. Naturally, by the time the news reached me, I had grave doubts about the success of any further search. Still, I sent Patrick."

Patrick. One of his grooms. The man could barely speak English, let alone German or French.

"We are sorely understaffed, Jane. And the chances of you being alive…" He was making excuses. Her father never made excuses.

"What did you think happened to me?"

"The carriage was ransacked, goods stolen…"

Not by Gerard. Her heart hitched at the sound of his name in her head, and her eyes stung with unshed tears. She, who had rarely cried before that fateful day nearly a month earlier. So opportunists had come upon the carriage and taken what they could. She could hardly blame them after seeing the wreckage of the countryside even months after the last battle had ended.

"Everyone accounted for except for me."

She tried to imagine being in her father's place, eminently practical—assume the most likely thing to have happened. After all, who would imagine that Jane wandered off looking for help? Her father knew that she was as practical as he. She would have stayed near the road, if possible, and waited for the other coach. Of course, her story was far from the truth. And the truth was just as fantastical.

Her heart constricted. Her chest ached. The room felt painfully small. Her eyes stung again, and she quickly looked down to hide from her father the upwelling of emotion. Not that distress would be remiss after an ordeal such as she had gone through—even the watered down version she had presented to him.

"I was…distraught." Her father's voice caught on the word and she glanced at him quickly, catching the tortured expression on his face, the first indication that he had truly cared if she lived or died. That expression undid her. The tears burned her eyes and dampened her skin.

"It was too much to expect that there would be more than one survivor," he said.

Jane froze and she blinked away the tears rapidly. "More than one? Who else?"

Images of that day flew through her head like a shuttle on a loom and she struggled to remember exactly what had happened and who had been where. Lord Powell for certain had died. Lady Powell had certainly looked dead, and Gerard had confirmed the coachman's death.

"Lady Powell." Her father's gaze was sharp upon Jane again, watching her reaction. "Her injuries were great and I am told she has no memory of the accident. She is recuperating in Darmstadt until she can be moved to Paris."

Did Gerard know? Had he let two people live? And if so, why? Jane's stomach felt as if it had been caught in a vise and it was difficult to breathe deeply.

"That is wonderful," she managed to say, and yet, dread seeped through her. If Gerard did not know, if Lady Powell had witnessed her husband's murder as well, then Gerard was in danger. Which was a ridiculous thought. It was a danger of his own making. No matter how she still hoped his actions had been honorable in some way, a secret mission for France or England, he had denied that idea.

She wanted to see him, demand answers, know if he had intentionally let Lady Powell live. He was not infallible, but she could not imagine he would miss such a detail.

"Tell me again what happened." Her father's expression was stoic once more, determined.

She shook her head, struggling to bring her thoughts back to the present moment, to her father's demand. She should tell him the truth. She could do so without revealing what she knew of Gerard's identity. The fact that Powell had been assassinated might be significant politically for England. Her act of silence might be one of treason. Yet *instinct* held her back.

Her father doubted some element of her story, but what reason would he have for that? Unless he thought her compromised by brigands and ashamed of it. Or he doubted the accident was an accident, in which case he must know more about Powell than she. Know that he'd had enemies who wished him dead. Or one enemy.

Perhaps Lady Powell remembered more than her father admitted to. But if so, why lie? Unless there was more to this intrigue, something far more complicated than she could even imagine.

"I do not wish to recount it again."

"You will have to," he said. "If not now, when you reenter society."

He was right. People would be curious and the death of the Powells and Jane's disappearance and subsequent reappearance would not have gone unnoticed. But their motivation would likely not be the same as whatever her father's unspoken one was.

"I need to rest," she said, letting her very real exhaustion show. "I am not yet myself."

It was the truest statement she had said to him that hour, but she wasn't certain if she would ever again be herself. Now she had secrets, ones she kept from her father. Now she had known something very like love, and had chosen to leave it behind, and that knowledge settled as a constant ache in her chest, in her stomach, and in her throat. Any ideal she had thought she might have had, she had discarded in lieu of something else that she could not yet fully understand.

"Jane." Her father stopped her as she was halfway out the door. "I should never have let you travel without me."

His pain hurt her and yet it was such a relief to have seen his agony, to know that her father loved her no matter how frugal he was with affectionate words. Again, she considered sitting by him, revealing all that had occurred, but the words stayed swollen in her chest. Instead, she offered her father a smile and shook her head. "Hindsight."

Chapter Nine

Jane's new gown was relatively simple, gold silk with small puffed sleeves and a strand of tiny pearls along the bodice. With the gilded frames, chandeliers and sconces, and the mirrors that reflected that golden candlelight, the dress allowed her to blend in to the soiree and not stand out more than the nine days' wonder she already was.

Her ordeal—the version she told in which a farm wife had taken her in, followed by days of unconsciousness and even more days of immobility—had whet the imagination of all the hangers on, the Viennese socialites, the petty princes and lords attached to delegation, those relatively unimportant in the proceedings, and just below the affairs of Tsar Alexander and Metternich were the salacious thoughts people imposed upon her experience.

Not that they were entirely wrong. Even though nothing permanent of that month remained other than a slight pain where she still healed and the bruises on her chest, she remembered Gerard's hands on her body as if his touch had marked her indelibly. But *they* did not need to know that. Still, people questioned her constantly. Jane bore it because there was some questioning of her own she wished to do.

After a few days of indulging in absolute inactivity, the like of which she had not known her entire life, she attempted to throw herself into assisting her father, as she had since the age of seventeen when, during the week that her father's trusted secretary was ill with the ague, she took over the matter of his correspondence. It had seemed as though every experience Jane had to that point had prepared her to be her father's factotum. It was said that Queen Elizabeth had spoken six languages, corresponded with her cousins (Jane, Edward, and Mary) about matters of religion and philosophy. It was her example Jane sought to emulate when she diligently did all that her governess and tutors asked of her, and then sat up late in the library teaching herself German by flickering candlelight, which was why her father's sudden unwillingness to entrust much work to her or to include her in several meetings hurt. As a result, passing her days among the men of the British delegation was more tiresome than invigorating, and her mind returned again and again to Gerard.

He might not be forthcoming about why he killed Lord Powell, but others would know who might wish the man dead. She would be discreet, of course. She didn't wish anyone to suspect she knew the crash was anything other than an accident. Those who didn't know such a thing did not need to know, and those who did might not be as generous about her life as Gerard. But she had to know. Was there perhaps an honorable excuse for his actions? Did any of that matter?

Yet she was compelled.

Thus she was dancing with Alistair Whitley. She had never paid the man any particular attention before. He was of an age with her, which was why she was making something of a sweep through the junior clerks. It was easy enough to ask small questions about the Powells when talking about her perilous adventure.

However, Alistair Whitley seemed completely unaware that he had been the focus of Lady Powell's amorous attentions, and from the first moment Jane showed any interest, Mr. John Penman, younger son of Baron Munset, hovered around her like a bee.

"Yes, it was a rather harrowing experience," she said, when the end of the dance brought her to the edge of the floor with both the young men by her side. "By the time I was conscious and able to make any decent decisions, the Brumbles had long given up on me." The dig was ungenerous of her, but the couple and Sir Joseph Grimsby had called upon her shortly after her arrival in Vienna and the thrust of their conversation had been the distress they had experienced and how wrong she had been to switch carriages. She did wonder that the search for her had not been lengthy and comprehensive. After consulting a map upon her arrival in Vienna, she had ascertained that the abandoned farmhouse where she had stayed with Gerard had not been very far away from the main road at all.

"I am amazed by your fortitude," Penman said, admiringly.

"Fortitude," she repeated with a laugh. "I traveled with grief heavy in my heart for my lost companions. I was very relieved to learn that Lady Powell is alive and recovering, but I imagine Lord Powell will be much missed by the delegation. Although I was never quite certain what was his area of expertise…"

"Women," Penman said.

"Spices," said Whitley at exactly the same time.

"It was a poor jest," Penman said quickly. "Lord Powell was a great ambassador for England. He spent many years here in Vienna during his youth."

Penman's faux pas tightened his lips and she didn't get much more from him. In fact, the majority of her interviews progressed no further than that. People recalled Powell as a dry wit, jovial after his first glass and frequently cuttingly cruel when deep into his cups. In London, she would have resources to investigate more deeply—into his finances, his connections. Here in Vienna she was limited. A visit to Powell's former mistress, Lady Heathland, revealed that the man had dabbled in investments. Shipping, specifically. That he had taken his wife's dowry and used it to invest in the spice trade, apparently successful enough to be generous with his gifts.

"But why speak with me if you wish to know more about him. Why not talk to his last mistress?" Lady Heathland pointed across the room. Then she glanced at Jane with a sly look. "Or were you his last?"

Jane choked on her laughter in surprise.

"No?" Lady Heathland said. "A pity for you. He was a bit of a fool at times but a rather satisfying lover."

Jane wished to ask more about the diminutive blonde across the room, basic things even, such as the woman's name, but Lady Heathland was far more interested in discussing all the affairs among those presently gathered in

Vienna. With that many dignitaries packed into the relatively provincial city of Vienna—it was no cosmopolis like Paris or London—intrigues abounded. Simply beginning her careful questioning uncovered a myriad of ones in which she had no interest. Yet, gossip was currency. A currency that was useful for delicately ascertaining the name of Albertina Abbing in as circuitous a way as to disguise her true interest in the woman. Useful, as well, as an entrée into that interview a day later when a studiously offhand comment about a French comte had her and Mrs. Abbings laughing like old school chums. With no one else about to introduce them, they did so informally.

"The famous Lady Jane Langley," Mrs. Abbings said. "Your story of survival and intrepidity has certainly made the rounds."

Jane blushed at that, the pleasure of successfully making the connection she wished overshadowed by the guilt of knowing she had survived where this woman's lover had not. But she could hardly offer her condolences to a near stranger.

"I assure you, it is not what I would wish to be known for."

Mrs. Abbings nodded. "Your father must be beside himself with joy to have you returned safe and sound. I know I would be to be rejoined with a loved one thought dead."

Jane smiled vaguely, trying to hide her confusion at the oblique way the woman seemed to reference Lord Powell. Did Mrs. Abbings think Jane did or did not know about their affair? She wanted to test the waters but the question was how to do so politely?

"I believe his assistants are more relieved," she said.

"Ah yes. It must be very exciting to be in the thick of all the negotiations. I do enjoy having so much society here in Vienna. One cannot take a step without stumbling upon an interesting person."

That much was true, and if Jane had not had her odd excursion with Gerard, and then on her own, she would have enjoyed the scene much more. Those days on the road she had missed the work that had once given her life so much meaning, but now, at her father's side, even the small amount of work he did send her way no longer interested her in the same way. She did it all perfunctorily.

"It's quite stimulating here, but from what I understand there's a decided lack of negotiations."

Mrs. Abbings laughed. "Men, they always take such a circuitous way to get to the point. Take Lord Powell. I was well acquainted with him, did you know? He was a man who liked to tie three or four stories together before coming back to make his final, always brilliant, point."

This was true. It had been part of the man's wit and sense of humor. But more importantly, the woman had just offered the perfect opening, as if she had desired to establish more of a bond with Jane and understood using Powell was one way to do so.

"Did you meet here in Vienna?"

"No. In London. I promised to show him around my home." She blinked rapidly as if she were about to cry, but then smiled through the incipient tears to describe a night at Vauxhall. She did an admirable job of hinting at an affair without ever actually mentioning such a thing. It was clear that despite Lady Powell's presence, she had expected the affair to continue here in Vienna.

"Ah, I thought perhaps it might have been here, that perhaps business concerns had taken him abroad. Shipping, I believe?"

Mrs. Abbings shrugged. "I did not concern myself with such things."

A few more minutes of conversation suggested this line of questioning was a dead end, but Jane could not dismiss the woman. Mrs. Abbings kept bringing up new topics of conversation.

Returned to her room in the early hours of the morning, Jane set her thoughts on Powell to pen and paper. She said nothing of Gerard, phrased her interest as stemming from a fictitious offhand comment the Powells had made as they traveled across France, and then sealed the letter. Lord Landsdowne would have been her natural confidant—he already held one of her secrets—but it was entirely possible that he had ordered the Powells' deaths. Yet if that were the case, then the reason would be political, and honorable, for Landsdowne put England and family above all else. And Gerard refused to admit that his reasons were in any way honorable, which was why she was sending this letter to Lord Landsdowne after all. Because, not knowing Jane's connection to Gerard, Landsdowne might reveal his own. Or, if Gerard had confided in his grandfather, then…in that case Jane did not know what. It was hard to think through this particular iteration. Everything Gerard had said pointed to the client being someone else, but Jane wanted it to be Landsdowne.

When she laid her head down on the pillow, she closed her eyes, and despite understanding that she was torturing herself, unnecessarily revisited each moment she had spent with Gerard, from the carriage to his apartment. Her chest ached at the memories that were painful, sweet, and tinged with the darkness of guilt.

After a few days more, life in Vienna began to fill Jane with a certain malaise. She remembered with some chagrin a conversation she had had only months before with the new Lady Templeton—Gerard's sister-in-law—in which she had defended the right of the great powers to decide the fate of Poland. But here in this city, the injustice of the jostling for position and power was impossible to deny. Although representatives of nearly all the countries on the continent had gathered, the fate and legitimacy of kingdoms, principalities and duchies fell to a very few, and were variable depending on their treaties and alliances, their personal goals, or romantic liaisons.

It was not so much that Jane's opinions had changed, but that the extremity of her practical nature had been broken. Or perhaps not even that. She had shared so many stories of her life with Gerard, ones on which she had rarely thought, had pushed to the side, and in the telling a pattern had emerged. Again and again, she had taken the side of the less powerful.

The image she had had of herself did not fit with this newer understanding, and the two were hard to reconcile, as it was hard to reconcile her feelings for Gerard. She no longer knew herself, and thus her time in Vienna was unfulfilling. But she went through the motions, assisted her father, attended soirees, balls, and the theater. Packed a month's worth of a London Season's outings into a week.

At the theater one night, in the company of her cousin, Princess von Wolfstein, she stared at the stage where the actors so earnestly, yet ridiculously, engaged in their work and was at once overwhelmed by it all. She excused herself, slipped beyond the velvet curtains of the box, through the well-oiled door, and into the empty corridor. She stared blindly at the wooden floor with its bright red carpet.

The air shifted. There was barely a sound, nothing more than the slightest scuff of soft leather against wood to alert her that she wasn't alone. Fear chilled her skin and she started walking, away, away from what she did not dare to face. Footsteps louder, faster and then with a rush that had her gasping for breath, she was swept back against a hard form, a hand clasped over her mouth, an arm around her waist.

She knew that hand, she knew the scent of the man behind her. Fear buoyed into a giddy joy. That dreamlike episode after the accident had been real. And he had found her.

Finally.

For the first time since the day she left Frankfurt, she realized how much she had wanted him to follow her, to come for her, to prove that his words of love were as lasting as he proclaimed. Unless he came because he saw her as a threat. Yet if so, she had been apart long enough to do damage if she chose to.

"Don't scream," he whispered, and she wanted to laugh.

"Gerard," she said, his name barely more than a breath against his skin. She nipped playfully at his fingers, a kiss that made her want to press more upon his skin. He groaned, the sound delicious against her ear. "Don't you know you should wear gloves at the theater?"

She turned in his arms. He was handsome, dressed like a gentleman, as he hadn't been during their time together. If he escorted her out into the open space no one would ever question that he belonged.

He laughed, and then the look in his eyes darkened. Her pulse quickened. Energy coursed through her, surging up to meet that look.

"This way," he said, leading her down the hall. For the briefest moment she wondered if anyone would see them and recognize her. But then there was a door in the fabric-covered paneling of the wall, an easy one to overlook, for storage or some other such thing. He led her inside. It was dark, but a window high up illuminated the small room in shadows. A storage room, indeed, with chairs, and rolled up carpets stacked against the wall. But then she was in his arms again, pulled tight against his body. His head dipped down. The touch of his lips was nothing like the ones shared in the candlelit shadows of the burned-out cottage. There was nothing gentle about him now. He was taking from her, demanding, and she gave him what he wanted, eagerly.

She lost herself in the taste of him. And then his mouth on her cheek, her jaw, the lobe of her ear.

"I should abscond with you right now."

"I wouldn't go."

"I could force you." He punctuated his words by pushing her gently against the wall, pinning her there with his body.

"But you wouldn't." She gasped the words out over the overwhelming pleasure of his mouth on her neck, his tongue on her skin. "And you know why I couldn't stay."

"Because you wouldn't give up your life as the daughter of an earl for love."

"Certainly not. At the very least, it would require that I love you." The words felt dishonest, but they were only the truth. If she did love him, if she did admit to such a thing, she was certain he would never let her go. He caressed her nearly bare shoulder, revealed by the dress she had dared to wear because the signs of her injuries had finally faded. His lips followed and she shivered deliciously under the touch.

Then his mouth was ravenous and his hands were searching, grabbing at fabric, and caressing her leg through the voluminous cloth of her drawers. She knew what would come next; she remembered the touch of his hand at the center of her, inside her. She remembered it and wanted it. Even here, even at a theater in Vienna, she was his. She didn't think to stop him, didn't worry about being found.

She needed this. Him. If they were found, it would be scandalous, and there would be nothing left for her to protect, no reputation to speak of. Everything would be out of her control.

From his seat in the pit, Gerard had watched Jane leave her box. An unexpected opening, but he had taken it with alacrity, made his way swiftly up the stairs. He had planned only to speak to her for a few moments, but when he found her standing in the middle of the hallway, looking utterly exhausted and low in spirits, he had wanted nothing more than to sweep her up in his arms, take care of her, take her somewhere safe.

This dark room, her body against his, his fingers exploring her center, this was not safe. But from the moment she had turned in his arms, plans, intent and reason all fell by the wayside. What he needed was Jane. To make Jane his. She sighed at the touch of his fingers on her, stroking where hair met damp folds. And he parted those too. She squirmed when his finger touched some place more sensitive than the rest, which seemed to grow harder and heavier, fuller at that touch. Heat pulsed through his body.

She would not admit to love but if this was not love, perhaps he didn't need that word. He could be satisfied for eternity with the expression on her face, the joy with which she greeted him.

"Come with me, in any event," he urged. "We'll go to Switzerland."

"And rusticate?" She said the word with such derision that he understood immediately. Neither of them would want a safe life, away from society, hiding simply so they could be together. Yet, he wanted her more than anything he had ever wanted in his life.

"There will be a way."

He hooked her leg over his arm, then unfastened the falls of his breeches with his other hand and pulled aside the voluminous material of his shirt to free himself. He rocked against her, naked flesh to naked flesh.

She felt so good. And it was Jane in his arms. Jane, who knew him like no other, who listened to his stories, connected disparate strands and challenged his understanding of the world. Jane, who made him want to be the honorable man that a young Gerard had once thought he would become before he'd ruthlessly stifled every softer emotion he had ever had under the very need to survive.

"I didn't tell anyone about you."

He shook his head. His world was focused on her damp heat parting around him as he placed himself where he wished to be most.

"I didn't think you would," he managed to say, and lowered his mouth to her neck, breathed in her scent. He wanted to be enveloped in Jane, in her touch, her scent, her mind, in this woman who had become a symbol of everything good to him.

"This will ruin me."

He paused. She was wet and hot against him. Temptingly soft.

"Do you care?" He waited for her answer, holding back despite the deepest urge to push forward, drive himself up into her. He had never wished to force her to be his. That was where the comparison with Badeau's actions broke down. Badeau had wanted Gerard to learn the futility of running, to recognize the power and greater cunning of the tutor. While Gerard did not intend to let Jane go, he would not force her to leave with him, to do anything that made a return to her old life impossible. Despite the manner of their meeting, he wanted her with him willingly.

"No." Her hips rocked against him, the invitation he wanted more than anything, and triumphant he surged forward. He sucked in his breath at the feel of her parting for him, surrounding him, muscles gripping him. He grasped her hips tighter and pulled her down to meet him. Her own sharp inhale sounded in his ears. He'd hurt her. Of course he had.

He'd been first.

Blood thundered in his head, surged through his body, with the primal satisfaction of claiming her with his body. He didn't stop. There was no need to with her clasping him between her thighs, pulling at him with her hands. He heard nothing except the rushing of blood in his ears, the pounding of his heart, her breathy little cries against his ear and the slick suction of his flesh and hers coming together and parting again and again.

"Jane," he said, his voice a guttural exclamation against her neck. She cried out again, and he found her lips, took the sound into his mouth even as his body trembled with his release. The world, sight, everything was lost except the scent of her. The scent of them.

He moved against her more slowly, savoring the feel of her around him. He didn't want to move, to step away and admit reality. "I'll find a way."

She didn't speak, but he felt the touch of her lips against him, and he shivered with renewed sensation. *Too much.* Yet he still didn't move, even when the exploration of her tongue brought all of his sensitized skin to something more overwhelming than climax. Her touch pierced through his armor.

"You won't want for anything," he said. She was the daughter of an earl, one who was not in impecunious circumstances. He had not the wealth of kings but certainly he could provide her with the comforts to which she was accustomed.

"Other than my position in society and the respect of my friends. You are nobody, Gerard."

Cold slithered down his chest, coiled around his heart. He resisted the truth of her words for a moment, focusing on her heat, on the pleasure that still thrummed through him.

Then, slowly, he slid from her body. Her words were matter-of-fact and in her world they were true, but not in his. He held the lives of men in his hands. Whether as courier, spy, negotiator or assassin, he'd changed events countless times, as much as any one of these diplomats did with the ink of their pens.

He refastened the falls of his trousers, aware that he was sticky not only with their pleasure, but also with her blood. Blood. His memory flashed with the image of her nearly crushed under the carriage, despite the obvious pain, staring at him with that same matter-of-fact expression. This was the Jane he wanted. Strong and assured. If she ran away with him so easily, he would doubt her.

Her gown dropped between them, the curtain closing on this act. He knew well what he must do next. He would win her for his own, and in doing so…in doing so he would prove to her that he could exist in her society as much as she did.

"You care so much for the approbation of society."

"Perhaps I do," she said, lifting her chin slightly. The movement made him smile.

"Then I shall simply have to find a way for you to have society and for me to have you." Easier said than done, but not impossible.

"You think Lord Landsdowne will help you?"

Gerard stilled, the cold spreading. He ran through the stories he had shared, hundreds of thousands of words chattering in his head as he tried to sort them, to find where he had failed in his attempt to share his life without revealing his identity.

"My father and he are great friends," Jane said. "The story of his scapegrace son and his seven bastards is not unknown to me."

He had been careless. Of course, he had been careless to let her live, and to let her escape. *This* was what she had meant that night in Frankfurt. The stories had all come together for her more than he had realized. He had not imagined that she would have enough prior information to decode the disparate knowledge. His carelessness was yet another way in which she had changed him, made continuing in his life of shadows impossible. Carelessness led to death. But Jane would not be the death of him, despite what she had said. She was light and life. The life he wanted for himself.

He considered her words. His grandfather was the reason Gerard's work was what it was. There was a cool respect between them. Gerard had valued it more before he had met his half brother, the heir. Still, it was not impossible that the Earl of Landsdowne would officially take him under his wing and introduce his wealthy bastard grandson to society. The purchase of an estate, perhaps the procurement of a baronetcy or something more…

"My grandfather owes me," he said, leaving the details for later thought. His words were an understatement. The scales were tilted far in Gerard's favor.

"He owes no one. If you think he would acknowledge any debt then you don't know him as well as I. Of course, I've been sharing a table with him every other week for the last three years."

This he had not known, as even once he had determined her identity, he still had known nothing about her other than that she was the daughter of Lord Langley, friend to his grandfather. He did know that Lord Langley was well versed in the history of the German states and principalities and related to at least one dynastic family.

"The only thing I do *not* know…" Her voice was a pained whisper. "Is he the one? Is he responsible for Lord Powell?"

"No," Gerard said. It was more than he should admit but he could give her this much. She was silent, her expression inscrutable.

Then she reached around him, opened the door slowly. Light seeped in around the edges. She peeked through the opening, but he did not look, did not care. Tumultuous thoughts and emotions ravaged him. He had never known less who he was.

"There is no one there," she said. "I think it best if we part now." She tried to move around him but he wrapped his hand around her waist, blocking her way, clinging to her and ashamed of his weakness.

"This is not over, Jane," he said roughly.

Not over. Of course, it wasn't over. He was written indelibly on her skin, on her mind. He was a part of her soul now, had awakened that part of her that she had long ruthlessly ignored. It was not over but she could *not* be with him.

"Why did you kill Lord Powell?" she asked, clearly startling him with the question. But she needed to know.

"I cannot tell you." Frustration stiffened her at his words. "To do so would place you in danger. As it is, I am loath to leave you. If anyone suspects…and they will suspect, out of an abundance of caution."

She had thought of this but it seemed ridiculous that

anyone might consider her a threat. She was a British subject in the middle of delicate negotiations. Assassinations conducted here would be closely scrutinized, might cause war anew.

"No one would dare assault me. Not here with my father, with half the courts of Europe in attendance."

"This is exactly where they would. When the death of an unimportant woman would barely take notice."

"You flatter me."

"You are important to *me*." Liquid warmth coursed through her body and she wanted to push away from him, push away the desire to hold him close and be with him forever, go wherever he wanted. If by some miraculous method he managed to make it possible for them to be together— She stopped the useless, heartbreaking thought. Instead, she forced words out that had nothing to do with emotion, that were exactly the sort of statement the logical and reasonable Lady Jane Langley would utter. "It would be an incident of international importance."

"These people do not care about borders."

A frisson of fear added to her confusion. Who *were* these people for whom he worked?

"Tell me at least that he deserved his death."

His low laugh mocked her. "I am certain Powell would think not, but those who wished him gone thought he did. I am no hero, Jane. You cannot make me one."

"But I cannot believe—"

He cut her off. "You asked how I felt when I first killed a man. Then I did it believing I was doing something good. But death is merely a tool to an end. When we kill, we kill ourselves."

A deep pain constricted her heart. She did not need to know the specifics of the story of his first kill to understand the significance of its effect. Damn Landsdowne! Gerard had never had a chance. Given to an assassin to raise and tricked into committing an unjust murder in the name of honor, bit by bit Gerard had lost any sense of his own.

He wanted her to run away with him because he wanted a way out of the life he led. But she had said no, because she had been thinking only of herself, of her comfort, of *reality*.

She choked back a sob, pressing her fist to her mouth, blinking rapidly to stop the wetness from falling to her cheeks.

He reached out, brushed his thumb across her cheek, wiping at the tears.

"I want your love, Jane, and I want you. But I cannot change the man I have been, only the man I will be." His lips pressed against hers briefly, his breath warming her face. "Consider it. Us. It is not impossible."

Then his hand was gone from her cheek, and he was gone from the room, and she was alone. Far more alone than she had ever been in her life, because she'd had a glimpse of what it would be like to be with him. She wanted to run after him, draw him back, and tell him she would love him. She would run away with him. She would—

No. As he had said, he could not change the man he had been. It would be one thing if she knew fully who that man was, so she could make a decision based on facts, on knowledge. Instead, he was asking her to go against everything rational and to make a decision steeped in emotion.

The way she was still steeped in his scent.

Chapter Ten

The year was 1799. Gerard was sixteen and Venice had lived through two tumultuous years, first losing its independence to Bonaparte's France and then enduring the ignominy of being transferred as a possession to Austria. Gerard, though French by birth, had begun to identify firmly with the elegant City of Water.

It was more a part of him than any other. Its narrow winding passageways that opened up into bustling squares, the terra firma and the islands connected by bridges and canals, shadowy corners and life that paralleled the respectable life of day, all echoed inside of him.

The only admirable benefit of the brief French rule had been the end to the gates of the Ghetto, the corner of Venice that he had sometimes secretly visited, seeking an understanding of that part of his ancestry that had rejected him in Paris. He never admitted to any of the Jews within that his mother had been a Jew, but he learned of their ways, studied their language and scripture, held a certain sympathy for their concerns.

In 1799, the French were gone and the Austrians who replaced them were laughable, and from the first Badeau was involved in the resistance. Secretly, of course.

And Gerard, full of youthful passion and idealism, latched on to the cause as well. Despite centuries of intrigue, not very much came of the secret meetings. Until the day Badeau took Gerard into a windowless interior room and explained his dilemma. An Austrian was arriving the following day. The man knew Badeau or he would never impose on Gerard in such a way.

A simple matter of slipping powder into his drink at the inn. Anyone could do it, but he trusted Gerard most, and once the man was unconscious, Gerard could retrieve the important papers the man carried with him that were perhaps on his person, or in his room. Badeau depended on Gerard to discern.

A seemingly harmless exercise and one that would help the resistance, as the papers were supposed to reveal Austria's plans for the city. It was easy to do as Badeau wished. But when Gerard was upstairs in the man's room, the leather satchel with the papers in his hand, there was a commotion downstairs. A thundering of footsteps. The Austrian slammed open the door to his room and fell at Gerard's feet in a pool of vomit.

Dead. Because of him.

He stumbled out of the room, down the backstairs, past the maid scrubbing sheets who stared at him, and out into the night. He knew even as he went that he was being careless, that his haste would tie him to the death more surely than proximity. But he needed to escape the bulging eyes that had stared at him out of a terrified mask of death.

That had been Gerard's first kill and he had been horrified. Something had gone wrong. The Austrian was not meant to die, only to be inconvenienced long enough to obtain the papers. For hours, Gerard could not return to the house he shared with his tutor, could not reveal what had happened. Could not come to terms with the death he had perpetrated, with the images that snapped through his mind.

But he slunk into the house in the wee hours of morning, and in the darkness through which he had tried to tread silently, a hand shot out, grabbed him by the shirt and pinned him against the wall.

"Where have you been, boy?"

Gerard still remembered the harsh staccato of Badeau's demand, the angriest he had ever been. *Had he found out somehow? Of course, he must have. Badeau knew everything that happened in Venice.*

"I…I didn't mean to kill him." His voice had shaken with the words and tears on his cheeks had unmanned him. It was dark but Badeau would miss nothing.

Badeau slid his hand down and pulled the satchel from Gerard's shoulder.

"Did you get the papers?"

Gerard nodded, and then, unsure if his tutor could see the gesture in the darkness, sputtered, "Yes."

"Good. Next time you will not tarry. You will report immediately to me. And next time, you will intend to kill."

Badeau stepped away, his breath the only indication that he was still in the room. But leaving.

The meaning of his last command hit Gerard all at once

with the force of a punch to the stomach, knocked the wind out of him. Gasping for breath, he reached back to the stone of the wall to support himself. Surely he had misunderstood.

"Sir!"

The impatient swivel of Badeau's leather-clad heel on the floor sounded loudly in the room.

"Don't be tiresome, son. This is not a game. He had to die." Badeau confirmed the worst with those three short sentences.

"And the papers?" Gerard asked, desperately, needing some proof that what he had done had been for a just cause.

"We shall see. Go to bed."

Red tinged his sight, and he charged across the room blindly, trusting his senses and instincts, the ones he had trained, to find his tutor in the dark, at the foot of the stairs. He pulled his fist back to strike and then the impact of Badeau's knee, his arm, his hand brought the ground rushing up to meet Gerard's face. He slammed into the floor painfully, his teeth pressed hard against his lips. His arm wrenched hard behind his back, his left leg pressed up toward his back.

"Learn," Badeau hissed, "to fight only when you can win."

"You tricked me!" Gerard pushed the words out despite the pain, wanting some explanation if he would not have the satisfaction of bruising Badeau's face. "Was it even for the cause? Did his death accomplish anything honorable?"

"It is time to lose your missish ways. There are things in this world a man must do. After tonight, you are no longer a boy. Be a man."

Badeau bent down, pressed a paternal kiss to Gerard's temple. He could smell the scent of the older man's exertion, the leather of the satchel, and taste blood in his mouth. Then

the pressure of Badeau's hold was gone, and Gerard was left
alone, collapsed on the floor.

That was Badeau's second betrayal. But everyone
Gerard had ever loved had betrayed him. It was a reminder
to be wary, to trust no one. After that night, it did not matter
if Badeau was forthcoming or not because Gerard never
performed a task he had not researched. He refused to be
a puppet, to be manipulated so completely. If this was to be
his life, then he must be the master of it.

Powell had been killed because the man who had hired
Gerard could no longer trust him. He had fallen prey to that
all too common trap of whispering secrets while in bed with
his lovers. And his loose lips had cost them deeply.

It was a side matter that his newest mistress was an
Austrian spy who had seduced him purely to have access to
the English side of the negotiations at Vienna. His employer
had not known about that, nor would have cared if he had
known. Gerard did not particularly care either. After all, he
was not English. He had no loyalty to that nation despite
his paternity. But it was the sort of detail Jane would cling
to as proof that Gerard was an honorable man. As if he
needed to be in order for her to love him. Yet to give her
that would be wrong twofold. First, it would be deceiving
her, manipulating her to secure her affections. And second,
he was a man of honor in his own way. He was discreet. Did
not reveal the secrets of those who employed him. Did not
take on jobs he did not feel he could keep secret. And he
gave each employer that respect, regardless of country of
origin. Not that Szabo deserved respect, but he had paid his
debt to the man. He owed no one else on this earth.

It was late and the winter sun had set long ago, but there

was still business to conduct, some secretive and some less so. He slipped from persona to persona as he traversed the city with ease, using the most minimal of disguises necessary to protect his identity. But throughout the passing hours, his thoughts returned to Jane, to her cries of passion, her challenge, her— He needed to see her again.

The theater had long been over. By now she was surely asleep in her bed, and that was where he most wanted to see her. To make love to her again, this time slowly, to re-explore every inch of her as a lover. To learn what pleased her best.

It was easy enough to steal into her room. He had made his way into far more challenging strongholds in his life. He could make out her form on the bed, and as he moved closer, breathe in the fragrance she had worn earlier that evening, heating his blood anew. He reached out, gently rested his hand over her mouth, prepared to increase the pressure if she started too loudly. Her head shifted, and she let out a soft moan. Still asleep.

"Jane," he whispered, his head bent close to hers. "Don't make any noise."

"Gerard? What…" But then her protests stopped and her arms were around him, her hair brushing against his cheek, the fragrance of her in his nose and his heart. "I was dreaming of you."

He thought she might even then still be half asleep. Her voice was thick as she trailed kisses across his face, his neck. Each kiss burned his skin like a brand, marked him indelibly with the need to possess her in every way possible. The way she possessed him.

"I thought I was alive before but now I know I was just an infant."

He had been her first lover and yet he could have echoed every word she had said and it would have been true. In her arms he was more, better, hopeful for a future. He cupped her head with his hand, stopped her exploration, met her lips with his. The softness of her mouth eased the tension that coiled in his body. He studied the shape of it, the fullness of the lower lip, sucked it into his mouth, between his teeth, licked it with his tongue until she sparred in return, vying for power over his mouth with hers and he let her have it.

Jane pushed at him until he tumbled backward with her atop him, straddling him, her voluminous night rail pillowing over him. The last time he had seen her in a snowy white shirt it had been his, gaping low on her chest and high on her legs, revealing the peaks and valleys that tantalized him. This time, the gown was the respectable garment of an unwed young woman. He reached for her legs, found the bare skin of her ankles.

She gasped at that first contact of his hands, and then he stroked upward, under the cloth. She sucked in the skin of his neck, ravaging him with her tongue, and it was his turn to breathe in sharply. The skin of his fingertips tingled as he caressed her legs, circling upward, finding the hollows behind her knees. His body was awash in sensation from his neck to his fingers and even his toes, to places she wasn't touching at all.

She tugged at his shirt, and he was grateful that, in his need for stealth, he forwent so many of the layers required for society, the stifling cravat, the waistcoat, the coats that were more about style than substance. Instead, his clothes were basic and without ornamentation, intended for agility, for the ability to blend into the night, to merely pass a moment's observation rather than extended scrutiny.

His back arched off the bed as her tongue found his collarbone, licked a hot trail across his skin. Ah! She had a wicked, beautiful tongue. She used it in all the right places, all the right ways, as if she had an instinct for Gerard's body, and for what would please him most. But the pleasure was torture and made him impatient, made him want to roll her onto her back once more and take control. He slid his hands up to her thighs, gripped the firm, silken flesh. She paused in her ministrations and he rocked his hips up experimentally. Despite the layers between them, his swollen flesh rejoiced at the hint of her core nestled at the apex of her legs.

"I want to see," she whispered.

See what? And then he understood and laughed. See his cock, physical proof of his desire.

"And I wish to see you, but that will have to wait, unless you believe a lamp at this hour will not cause alarm."

"No more than the squeaking of this bed."

He stifled the bark of laughter that had almost spilled out far too loud. "I would venture to guess that no one will come to investigate that."

"I suppose they might think I was enjoying self-pleasure." Her voice was muffled against his skin and yet he heard it clearly.

That image froze him, and then burned him hot, the way her tongue continued to do.

"Have you?"

She pushed herself up on her arms and he could make out the shape of her face, the outline of her nose, her chin.

"I've explored my body. I think it a rather natural thing to do."

"Though the church does not believe so. Any of them, as far as I can tell. One never thinks of a young woman engaging in any sort of illicit behavior at all."

"Yet we expect men to engage in such. I would be more surprised to hear that I had been your first."

He was amused and troubled at the same time. And he was bereft of her mouth, forced to think about things he did not wish to consider.

"I am not my father."

"Perhaps not. However, I'm not ignorant. I know I was not your first."

"No. Not my first." His first had been the girl in Florence when he was fifteen, and after that there had been a very small handful of lovers. His work and the shadow of his father's dissolution and irresponsibility had not left much room for Gerard to indulge in physical pleasures. But there were times when he had given in to desire, and times when desire coincided with his work, when seduction had been the most direct means to an end.

She bent her head down, blocking his vision into complete darkness, and pressed her lips to his cheek. As she followed that with her tongue licking a hot line to his ear, he relaxed back into sensation.

"You were mine."

"I know," he murmured.

She laughed, the breathiness of that exhalation feathering against his skin deliciously. "I had never thought on it before, but now I find it very unfair that women are born with proof of their virginity and men without. If it had been the opposite, perhaps the laws would favor us."

The idea twisted everything on its end. He looked up

at Jane, her body a shadowy silhouette against the room's darkness, and imagined how her face would look, those light blue eyes, as she so effortlessly challenged everything society took for granted.

Lust surged within him, overpowering thought. This was *his* woman. In this world or any upside-down one, and he could no longer wait to be inside her, to feel her flesh cling to his in the most intimate way possible.

"Perhaps." He shifted his hands, pulling at the cloth of her gown until it bunched about her waist. He grasped her hips with his palms and urged her upward. "But no more talk. Take me in your hand. Guide me into you."

He cursed the darkness that did not let him watch her face, watch her movements, and yet, that inkiness added to the anticipation. Her hand wrapping around his cock was sweet relief and yet pure torture. Then the pressure of that hand eased as her fingers swept over him, studying him. And that touch, filled with curiosity, made him impossibly full, his muscles, blood, everything physical and earthly about him straining against his own skin.

"Jane…" He uttered her name as a helpless plea.

"Mmm." She shifted, and the warm center of her hovered over him. His hips bucked upward instinctually, and she gasped. He gasped, too, at the contact, at the tantalizing sensation of her welcoming flesh. Her hand fumbled between them, trying to move his length into place.

"Let me." He rolled her onto her back and covered her body with his own, nestling again between her legs, his cock against her core. And slid between the wet folds.

She was tight around him, but she lifted her hips, wrapped her arms around his back and he thrust in deep, till he was enveloped fully in Jane, nothing separating her skin from him. He buried his face in her neck, breathed her in deep, and paused there. *Home.* A place where for once he belonged.

"You fill me up so completely," she whispered. "I hadn't known how empty I was before."

Physically he was inside of her, but again, he could have spoken those words and they would have been true. Emotion welled up inside him, inside his chest, stealing air.

"Jane," he said again, everything bound up in her name, in that one word. She rocked her hips against him, urging him into motion and he answered the call. He needed her for everything, for this visceral pleasure, for the cerebral connection, for the understanding in her eyes, and for the challenge that he rise up to be a better man, and in doing so that he find a way to claim her.

She wanted to believe in him and he wanted her to be able to. He wanted to be able to believe in himself. He licked her skin the way she had explored his, lifted his hips slightly so that he could slide his hand down her stomach to the curls beneath that were slick with their exertion, found the rise of flesh hidden there.

Even as his hips continued to thrust and retreat, as her pulse at her neck beat against his searching tongue, he stroked her, listening to the cadence of her breath, the hitches and releases, the clues to her pleasure.

Her body tensed and she gripped him tightly everywhere until at once she arched back, hips rising, a moan escaping her lips. Her release triggered something deep in him, something primal, and he grabbed her hip again in one hand, and the back of her head with the other. Claimed her mouth again with his own as he pumped into her. She was his. His. His.

He came deep, teeth bared in a soundless cry. But even in the triumph of his pleasure, of making her his one more time, he was undone.

"It's almost dawn." Jane's whisper in his ear woke Gerard from the slumber he had not intended to enjoy. Certainly not here and certainly not so deeply that, if she had not awoken him, he would have stayed asleep in her arms.

Her arms, where he was surely crushing her. He started to roll to the side, but ended up hovering, staring down at her. Her outline was more distinct now and the nearly imperceptible shift in the midnight blue of the sky beyond the window made it clear that Gerard had stayed past any advisable hour. Not that any of his actions were advisable. At least to a man who wished to keep his wits about him, save his sanity and perhaps his life.

He was in bed with the daughter of an earl. Had claimed her as his own with his body, had vowed to find a way to make her his own forever.

"Lady Jane Langley," he mused, studying her.

"Does it change your opinion of me?"

"I should have guessed. My grandpere, he had spoken of you. And of your father. But I confess, your powers of deduction in this matter were far superior."

"There is a family resemblance. Once the stories matched in places, I discerned the features you share with Lord

Templeton and Lord Landsdowne. You do realize, I have likely spent more consecutive days with Lord Landsdowne than you."

That of all the women in the world this one was so intricately twisted into his life before he ever knew her astounded him.

"As you've suggested. But I assure you, if I go to him, I will prevail."

Her fingers stroked his face, buried in his hair, the sensation painfully, pleasurably, sweet. But she said nothing. She did not believe him. And nothing he said could convince her. Action was what was needed now.

"It is a matter that must be handled in person," he said.

"You'll leave Vienna?"

"As soon as possible." He took her hand in his and bent it backward gently, pressed his lips to the tender skin of her wrist. Closed his eyes. Gerard had never been religious, and it had been years since he had even thought of something such as a higher power, but the touch of his lips to her skin felt strange, felt almost like…a prayer.

Gerard had gone utterly still, his lips pressed to her wrist, and Jane listened to his ragged breath, her own held. She watched him, as she had watched him for hours while he slept, holding him inside her, enjoying the pressure of his body on hers even when it grew uncomfortable, and marveling at the strangeness of them being together in this strange bed, in a strange city, with servants and her father only down the hall.

"I..." *I want you to succeed.* But she couldn't say it because she wasn't entirely certain if she did, if she knew what his success would mean. Certainly, if he went to Landsdowne then that man, one whose opinion she had respected for so long, would know of the folly of her emotions. "I don't want this night to end." That much she could say, because here, in Vienna, this night, this bed, was a world apart.

He let go of her hand and rolled to the side, sitting up, looking out to the window. She followed his gaze. The curtains were parted and she could see that the sky had lightened to the gray haze of dawn.

She understood what he saw. It didn't matter if she wanted the night to never end. It already had. Still, she struggled to express the thought that slithered through her mind. "If you go, it changes everything."

"Everything changes and nothing stands still."

She laughed softly. How like this man to remind her how well suited he was to her in so many other ways. "If Heraclitus and Plato believe it, then it must be so," she said, taking a deep breath. Letting him go did not mean she was bound to some silent promise. Letting him go...it meant she could wait and see. "I suppose this is good-bye then."

He shook his head. "Only good day."

Gerard would go to Landsdowne, and if that didn't work, he would find some other way. And she knew Landsdowne wouldn't work, and there likely was no other way. Yet... she'd set the challenge and quixotically, Gerard would meet it, would do anything to meet it. She knew that the way she had understood some aspect of him from the first moment her gaze locked with his.

She fought to temper the unfurling bittersweet pleasure

in her chest but it remained stubbornly. After all, not once in all of her twenty-three years had she had something to look forward to. Someone.

He kissed her and she lifted her lips to meet his, wrapped her arms around him, soaked in everything of him that she could, memorized the shape of his lips and the sensations the kiss engendered in her. Then she watched him leave via the still open window. She didn't move from the bed to watch his progress until he was gone from sight. She didn't want to hold her breath at each foothold and each noise, wondering if he'd fall or be found. Instead, after Gerard was gone, Jane gave in to the grief that tore into her until she sobbed into her pillow, breathing in the scent of Gerard on her body, all too aware that the stickiness between her legs was the only proof left that he had been there at all. Reality did not end with the daughter of an earl and the illegitimate assassin grandson of an earl living happily ever after. Unless happiness could be had away from all of one's usual society, friends and family, looked down on by the rest of the world. Knowing that one's husband had lived a dozen or more identities and never knowing if she could trust the one he presented her to be the truth.

The tears dried on her cheeks as she examined that thought. Did she trust Gerard? She had no way of confirming the stories he told, but she had taken his word as truth. Had used the fact that he openly kept secrets as proof that what he did share was not based in lies. Had felt more comfortable because she knew his grandfather and half brother so well. But he was likely a man used to lying. Perhaps he did so without thought.

She had given him everything of herself. No…she had

not. She had kept part of herself whole, knowing that this was impossible.

Jane was used to keeping things to herself. There was no bosom friend with whom she shared the emotional fluctuations of her days. But then again, until recently, there had been no emotional fluctuations of this magnitude. She had not bonded with her cousins or the young ladies of the *ton* over the meaning of a glance or the slightest touch from a handsome gentleman. Her closest friend was likely Lord Carslyle, and that because he offered her a brotherly masculine escort, with no expectation of anything more than that friendship.

But now, now she wanted a confidante, someone with whom she could puzzle out everything that confused her, the emotions that made her want to go against her intellect. It was strange to think that Gerard was in truth the closest thing she had ever had to a friend. It had been one thing to leave him in Frankfurt, to have the goal of returning to her father and reaching Vienna. Now, he had left her and the loneliness she felt at that loss grieved her most of all.

Chapter Eleven

Gerard did not leave Vienna, not immediately. After all, he needed to make certain he did not leave Jane in danger.

After bathing, breakfasting, and changing into clothes befitting that of a courier, Gerard went to a bookshop on the edge of Leopoldstadt. The neighborhood had once been the heart of the Jewish community but was no longer such. Instead, Vienna's Jewry was spread in pockets across the city, attempting to stay below notice, breath held that this congress would positively affect their fate as Napoleon had changed that of the French Jews. Not that Gerard particularly cared, but several of his clients did.

In any event, for years now he had collected correspondence at Buchhandlung Dornacher. Correspondence and information. The narrow store smelled of dust and leather, of old wood. The ceiling was low and books were crammed every which way. To one side there was a wooden counter piled high with books and behind that counter sat a woman Gerard knew well enough. She and her brother, Peter, had inherited the store from their father some years ago. Though he knew her brother as well, he preferred to deal with Eva.

"Herr Amsel." One of his many aliases. This one the servant of an unnamed man, the intermediary between the men of Berlin and of Vienna. It was easier to act as his own servant, to appear unimportant. It did not make his life less endangered, but it protected his identity in other cities. In Vienna, too, when he wore other disguises. "There have been several letters awaiting you."

He had shared a drink more than once with this woman. Shared a bed for an hour or two. He did not visit her without a token of acknowledgment, but today it was harder to carry on the flirtation. He simply wanted information and Eva was a nexus of information in Vienna.

"Fräulein, there has been talk."

She laughed, the dark curls by her temple bobbing with the movement. "With this many strangers in town I should be surprised if there were not."

He acknowledged that with a smile and shrug.

"Lord Powell," he prodded.

"The Englishman."

"I hear a carriage accident."

"That is what they say."

"What do they not say? And who is careful not to say it."

Her black eyes glittered with amusement. He offered another smile. They were two people who did not matter sharing the humor of the situation. Intrigue about things that hardly mattered either, at least to them. Someone, somewhere, would benefit financially. It would be neither of them.

"There were survivors."

Gerard nodded. "Then they should know."

"Exactly. The young woman is asking questions about Lord Powell." A chill ran down his spine even as the bookseller continued to talk. "Why would she if it was simply an accident?"

"Interesting. That is the conclusion one must come to in such a case." He shrugged as if it were inconsequential. Inside, his uneasiness was growing. It was still morning, but if Jane courted danger, being in the safety of her room would not save her. He had proven how easily the security of the apartment could be imperiled.

"If your employer is involved, he is now compromised." The bluntness of Eva's speech was even more chilling, a deliberate warning, foregoing all the vague words. "If your employer was involved...*you* are compromised." She held out his correspondence, a thick stack of different-sized missives.

"Me?" Gerard laughed, taking the letters. "Yes, they always kill the messenger."

He laughed, but even before he noted that one of the letters was from his client, Imre Szabo, his uneasiness had grown to full alarm, and he was already making plans, plans for how to keep Jane safe, for dealing with the Hungarian Wolf. No wonder Eva had warned him. She knew that he had some dealings with Szabo. It was likely she knew Szabo was the one to have ordered Powell's death.

He stepped away and turned for some semblance of privacy. Tore that letter open. Bit back the curse that filled his mouth.

I have paid you in full for services rendered. I need proof that services were indeed rendered.

Proof. Damn it. What could he say that would convince Szabo Jane was not a threat? Gerard asked for paper and ink, wrote a letter that he folded and sealed. Then thanked Eva and promised to visit her soon. The letter to Szabo, as well as the rest of his correspondence, he took with him as he traversed the narrow streets of the city yet again.

Gerard could no longer visit the bookstore, no longer go about on the disguise of his own servant, for if Szabo wanted to question Gerard, a servant would be a target. He was not unduly alarmed by Szabo's desire for answers. The man had paid his bill and expected no complications. That Lady Powell and Jane survived were not in itself problems for Szabo, but likely the nature of Jane's appearance had alerted him that something was different. But that did not mean Jane was in any imminent danger. If she was, she would already be dead. No, Szabo wanted to ascertain the damage and the reasons for Gerard's softness. Had it been a mistake or calculated action?

On his way, Gerard hired a boy on the street to take a letter to his client. Long beard, reddish hair, elegant clothes, the boy would likely report when he was quizzed as to who had given him the letter. A return letter would be sent to a certain inn frequented primarily by Greeks and Eastern merchants in the commercial part of the city where one of the grooms had directions to forward all of his correspondence on to the bookshop. It was not an infallible method of protecting both his communication and his privacy, but thus far, with all his other safeguards, there had been no issue. However, these were not ordinary times. He had never before given an employer reason to doubt him. And doubt him Imre Szabo did.

In an alley, the red beard and wig disappeared beneath his coat. His waistcoat was quickly turned inside out, the fanciful design of animals and vines on silk exchanged for a simple checked pattern on a coarser fabric. The dual-sided garment was a particularly useful design, and transitioned him from gentleman to merchant for any who gave him simply a cursory glance. If he focused attention where he wished it to be focused, they rarely noticed the rest. The disguise would not hold up to extended scrutiny, but today he did not need it to.

His next stop was a tavern known to cater to pugilists and Valentin Bohm was exactly where Gerard expected him to be at this hour, holding court among younger men who wished to gain knowledge of the sport.

He was somewhere in his fourth decade of life, but Gerard had first met him some twenty years ago when Badeau took him to watch one of his informal matches, held at an estate in the Austrian countryside. Several years later, Gerard learned that on the side, or perhaps his pugilism was on the side, Bohm was in a similar line of work to Badeau. At times rivals and at times allies, they were always friends.

Gerard knew the instant Bohm recognized him, although not a fraction of the man's demeanor changed. Gerard stepped back outside and waited for Bohm around the corner. Together, they ambled along the narrow street, beneath the looming city that had been built vertically from lack of space.

"What brings you to Vienna?" the man asked.

Though Bohm knew Gerard's name, he did not know his

aliases, and in an odd reversal, it was what protected Gerard from Bohm knowing too much. He did not know Gerard's clients or his work, but all of that was about to change.

"Do you still hate the Wolf?"

"Szabo?" Bohm spit on the ground, his face florid instantly. "Do not tell me you are the one he hired to kill the Englishman."

"Does everyone know of this?"

"I am certain by now even Metternich. The spies he has put into place for this congress are far superior to the usual."

"Ah," Gerard said, rubbing his chin. He had been in Vienna not two months ago. He knew that the foreign minister had commissioned the minister of police Sedlnitzky with gathering intelligence on all the visiting diplomats, but he had not known the extent of the web. "Well, the answer, my friend, is yes."

"My friend? You expect me to keep this secret? Though you know how and why I hate Szabo."

Gerard did know. Bohm had once been married.

"Money is money." But that callous answer was not why he had taken the job. "And yes, I need to hire you."

"I am not in the business any longer. I make my money off the young nobles. I teach them to fight. They invite me to their estates, give me gifts."

"I need you to protect a woman from Szabo."

"The Langley girl."

Cold dread settled in the pit of Gerard's stomach. The unease he had felt for the last several hours crystallized into something bordering on fear. It was one thing for Eva to know. She traded information and it was her business to know everything in Vienna. She then wrote it into novels that she sent to a publisher in London that Gerard had sold for her. It was another for Metternich to know. But that Bohm knew added another layer of danger. It meant that Szabo actively had people watching Jane's every move, that it would not be enough for Jane to stop whatever questioning she had been doing. Some campaign of erroneous information would need to be spread to make Szabo drop the scent.

"Yes."

"You intend to retire as well, then."

The expression in Bohm's knowing eyes was pity. He, more than anyone, perhaps, was able to make that leap of logic, to understand the iterations of decisions that would lead to a man wanting to protect a woman with his life. Gerard's sigh welled up from the deepest places of his soul. Bohm was correct. He had made his choice when he had let Jane live.

"Marry, a passel of kids, a farm, perhaps." The last was a joke, and Bohm smiled wryly in acknowledgment.

"I can protect her, but if Szabo truly believes hers is a necessary death, I will not be enough. London will not be far enough away."

Gerard nodded. He needed to deal with Szabo before he left Vienna.

He stopped back by Leopoldstadt and the grassy expanse of the Prater, the park that bordered the Danube, because hours had passed since he'd last seen Jane and he could not stay away. He hoped only for a glimpse of her in the midst of the extravagant picnic she was scheduled to attend that day.

He had changed his clothes yet again, dressed finely but plainly as befit Gerard Badeau, the Frenchman of independent means visiting Vienna merely for the spectacle of dozens of regal heads gathered together in one place. Although he was ostensibly the most himself, the man who interweaved with society freely in Paris, he felt strangely as if he were wearing a mask.

It was a cool day, but every attempt had been made to keep the guests warm even with the wind off the river. Aside from fire pits, there were furs and lap blankets, warm bricks and other devices. He nodded to people he passed in the crowd as if he knew them. Many he did know...but not as Badeau, and thus could not acknowledge. When he saw one or two that he did indeed recognize, had met here or there as Badeau, he made a point to stop and converse, to present as innocuous a front as possible.

His gaze stopped on every colorful group of revelers, on the bright skirts spread out above large embroidered blankets, on the sea of hats perched above artfully dressed curls, searching for just one head of light brown hair, one decisive nose and set of full, pink lips. One set of light blue eyes that saw everything, saw right into him. That cut him to the quick, stripping away any disguise he had ever worn. As she did now, their gazes meeting across the expanse. He was hollowed out by a gaping sense of nakedness, of being overexposed and vulnerable, and yet, at the same time, the radiant light of Jane's face filled him with infinite strength. He had never more wanted to live, free and as master of his own destiny.

She was dressed like a spring flower, bright yellow silk pooling about her legs where she sat in a small group of men and women. In one hand she held a glass of what he imagined must be champagne. She tilted her head slightly to the side, the movement a question. And well she'd question him; she always did. She had likely believed he had left Vienna already. He had thought to catch a glimpse of Jane, satisfy his soul—his *soul*. He repeated the word with disgust, yet even the disgust felt hollow. Yes, damn it. He had thought to satisfy the soul he had not believed in, had not considered in years.

The soul that craved more than observation or a speaking glance across a crowded park. Studying the field, he glanced at her companions and recognized one. A young woman who was uncomfortably familiar. Under a frothy pink confection of a hat sat the blond-haired Mrs. Abbings, the widow Lord Powell had met in London last summer with whom he had exchanged passionate letters for months. But Abbings, for all her secrets, was not connected to Imre Szabo and the shipping concerns that the Wolf shared with the late Lord Powell. Though to some she might be equally dangerous, she should not pose a danger to Gerard. Except for the fact that she was conversing with Jane.

Gerard did not believe in coincidences. Although he was beginning to believe in fate—a fate that was forcing him out of the role of observer, out of the sidelines. With a sense that the earth was shifting beneath him, Gerard stepped forward into the bright Viennese sun.

Jane's heart beat wildly in her chest. He was still in Vienna! Excitement warred with panic as she watched Gerard progress across the park toward her. She admired the stark beauty of his face, the caged strength of his body visible in every step. He had come for her yet again, but this time they were not in the dark solitude of her bedroom or the empty corridor of the theater. This time they were in broad daylight, in public. She was sitting with the Prince of Ligne, amongst others. And Gerard was the illegitimate grandson of the Earl of Landsdowne. If that was even the persona he meant to go by here. In any event, no matter his identity, she could not acknowledge that she knew him. It was too odd an acquaintance, surely.

She blinked. Somehow he had disappeared from her view. Where had he gone?

"You are very serious, Lady Jane," Mrs. Abbings said, and Jane looked to the other woman in alarm and stomach-tossing guilt. She had first met the Austrian widow in her quest for more information about Lord Powell, and thus some sort of window into understanding Gerard's motivation. Would he realize that? Though she believed she had learned as much as she could from the woman already, Mrs. Abbings had apparently decided that Jane was *très amusante,* and had sought her out at several events.

In London, where Mrs. Abbings had been living for the last several years since her husband's death, they did not run in the same circles. But here in Vienna, the social circles overlapped, collided, and distorted. It was quite odd on any given night to be an arm's length from three monarchs.

"I thought I saw an acquaintance," she said, and returned her attention to her companions.

Mrs. Abbings laughed, the sound throaty and full. "I look right and left and my gaze falls upon too many of my acquaintances." She was a voluptuous woman, in tone and in body. She had a way of speaking that made Jane feel as if she were the most important person in that woman's world. That sort of ability to make one feel special was an interesting talent. Jane had seen it before, amongst some of the members of the House of Commons, among some actors and the best hostesses of London. She, herself, had never mastered it and was particularly conscious this afternoon that in comparison she was quite aloof.

It was an observation she had never had before but somehow since her arrival in Vienna she had become an outsider to society. It did not matter that they welcomed her, or that she knew dozens of the attendees. It was some sort of lack of attachment in herself. Strange and disorienting.

Where was Gerard? She *had* seen him. He had been walking toward her. Where had he gone?

She spotted him again several minutes later, chatting with a man she didn't recognize, laughing and acting as if he had not a care in the world other than to be festive on this startlingly sunny November afternoon. Consumed by thoughts of him, she lost the threads of the conversations around her. She extricated herself from her companions. She wanted to go to Gerard but he likely had a reason for not approaching her immediately. Instead, she glanced at him as she walked toward the Danube. He made no sign that he had seen her but she knew, she just *knew*, that he would be as intensely aware of each of her movements as she was of his.

A cloth pavilion had been set up not far from the bank of the Danube and the canvas flapped in the light breeze. Inside, there were refreshments and chaise longues. It was quieter here, away from the orchestra and the crowds. She accepted another glass of champagne from a servant and stood at the edge of the structure, looking out at the sparkling water.

"The breeze seems to have the same idea as me."

Happiness and satisfaction surged within her chest, making her as buoyant as the boats that bobbed on the Danube. He had followed her.

"And what is that?" she asked lightly, turning to face him. Up close he was more handsome than he had been across the park. And he was tantalizingly within reach. But still, they were not alone.

"To do away with the pins confining your hair."

The way his hands had run through her hair the night before. She could feel them even now, his fingers sparking sensation along her scalp. The space between them grew hot and she turned back to the breeze blowing off the river.

"Will you still be here tonight?" she asked. It was late in the day for him to begin any sort of travel and if he was still in Vienna…if he was still in Vienna, she wanted him in her arms.

"Yes," he said, his voice low and tight. "I cannot leave just yet. Not until… Jane." The very serious tone in which he uttered her name made her look at him again. There was a warning in his eyes. "You need to stop asking questions."

She flushed, embarrassed that he knew how she had struggled to uncover his motivation. Did he know her failure as well?

"How did you know?" But this, too, was a stupid question. The fact that Gerard knew meant that her questioning had not been subtle enough, meant that people were paying attention to her actions. "Forget that. *You* tell me. Why did you kill Powell?"

"Let it go." He urged her forward, behind the pavilion, onto the wooden stairs that led down to a boat dock. "Listen to me carefully. We are stealing time as it is. I cannot tell you about Powell and you cannot try to investigate the matter. At the moment, I believe you are still safe, but the wrong question, the wrong person... I cannot leave for London if there is a chance you are in danger."

Frustration made her furious. "*Why* can't you tell me? You trust me enough to love me, to say you want to be with me forever. *Marry* me." She had never said the word before, neither of them had, but now it was boldly out there.

"Yes," he hissed. "Yes, I am asking that much of you, though I do not deserve you. The why does not matter. I am a mercenary, Jane. On occasion, an assassin, as you have named me. Can you love me despite that?"

She didn't answer. Her emotions went against every moral and rational thought she had.

He brushed the hair back from her cheek with his knuckles. "Protect yourself. Keep my woman safe for me."

His touch was gone as quickly as it had come and he rocked back on his heel in the insouciant slouch of the gentleman of means about town. Yet his possessive words stayed with her. *Keep my woman safe*. She wasn't his woman. Never would be. But she didn't need to repeat the protest again. No matter how much he tried to claim her with words, no matter how many times their bodies joined, even as her heart yearned to meet his, she would never be his woman.

Even if his actions were noble, it would be difficult to look past the misfortune of his birth. She didn't need to marry a nobleman but she did need a man well respected by society, whose position in it would not stifle her own interests. The world was not kind to people with neither power nor wealth. Her position in society had offered her enough power to force a man into exile.

"And stay away from Albertina Abbings. Don't look like that. You well know she was Powell's mistress. Your continued proximity could lead to unfortunate conclusions." Jane didn't like the command at all, wanted to tell Gerard she could very well do what she liked, but she recognized that impulse for a childish contrariness. Perhaps she was angry and frustrated to be kept ignorant on a matter that seemed so very integral to her life and her future happiness, but Gerard did love her. This *was* Gerard's area of expertise. If she was ever to trust him, in this matter she knew she should.

"She might be hard to stay away from," Jane said with a smile, aware at the edge of her mind that withholding agreement was a petty way of maintaining power. "I think Mrs. Abbings has decided we should be friends."

"Why is that? Is she grieving? Has she asked for last remembrances of her lover?"

The suggested behavior was so different from Mrs. Abbings' actual behavior that Jane stared at Gerard in shock. He was right. It was odd that Powell's lover exhibited few expressions of grief.

"Perhaps I have finally made you listen to me. This is no jest."

She nodded. "I do understand, but…can you not see how it is for me? To love you on blind faith?"

His lips set grimly. "Not on blind faith. You know exactly what I am."

"But I don't!" She didn't believe him. He could not be as

mercenary as he said. As callous and cold. In rational men such as politicians, intellect, wisdom, and the ability to put emotional responses aside to make decisions for the greater good might be revered, called reasonable. But Gerard did not claim to believe in a greater good.

How could love blossom in such a barren place?

Gerard left the Prater furious and helpless, knowing his fury was an impossible thing. He wanted her to love him for who he was, but how could he ask that of anyone? How could she truly love him? Perhaps, she did not. She had certainly not said as much.

Did it matter? He wanted her and was determined to have her. Perhaps his love for her was an excuse to leave his life behind and to begin a new one. If that were so, he didn't need her at all to do that. He could be the man he wished to be on his own. But that thought didn't excite him and a future without her was not nearly as bright.

It would be so much easier to not feel this twisting knife of shame and yearning in his gut. To not desperately wish that he could magically be the man who inspired trust and admiration in her.

Exhaustion swept like a wave over him. He stopped in surprise, rested a hand on the cold stone of building to his left. Yes, he had had little sleep but that was not unusual for him when he was in the midst of a job, and for now, that was still what this was.

He blinked, cleared his vision and continued on. He had faith in Jane's intelligence now that she knew the danger. He could have entrusted her with another task, with redirecting her interest in Powell publically so people would think it had been for another reason. Jealousy, perhaps. Her proximity to Mrs. Abbings might be fuel to that fire but he did not want her near the woman and the other new dangers she entailed. The last thing Gerard needed was for Metternich to think Powell's deal was more complicated than a falling out with a partner in trade.

For a brief moment a more complex plan titillated his mind, a Machiavellian one in which he used Metternich and the congress's concerns to ruin Szabo completely. Bohm would be willing to assist, no doubt, but such a complex plot was not worth the risks when all Gerard wished was to keep Jane safe. The simplest plan was the best, which meant redirection, and if not that Jane was Powell's lover (the mere thought sent a burning fury through the pit of Gerard's stomach), then by some other obfuscation.

Another stop at his rooms, where he changed his clothes, added new details to his disguise, this time dressing for stealth, for mixing into the Viennese populace, the surroundings, completely. This afternoon he would see Szabo.

The word spy was an inglorious one. It meant a man doing work for his country without their protection. Or for some other employer, which was even less glorious. It was always understood that if caught Gerard had acted on his own, was not connected to the client in any way. Not that Gerard had ever been caught by anyone other than Badeau during the early days of training.

Regardless, spying compounded by the act of assassination made Gerard's past actions unforgiveable. One Voltaire quote summed it up quite nicely. "It is forbidden to kill. Therefore all murderers are punished unless they kill in large numbers and to the sound of trumpets."

He was not a soldier. His actions would not be excused. This had never bothered him before. Or rather, not since that first death, since he had come to terms with the life into which he had been thrust. And it did not bother him now. For the first time he was acting fully on his own behalf to ensure that he could safely leave Jane in Vienna while he traveled to London to see his grandfather. A request of this magnitude could not be made in a letter written in code. Written in blood, even.

Though Szabo often dealt in the shadows, he was in fact a wealthy man of business, supposedly respected by his peers, and as such, his schedule was strikingly regular. Moreover, he was a man of habits, from his morning pastries to the time he arrived at the squat building on the banks of the Danube where he had his main offices. His partner, Ambroos de Groot, dealt with shipping across the oceans but Szabo managed continental affairs, transportation via rivers and across mountains, all the details and logistics necessary to sell the goods they imported from across the world.

He was an enterprising man, and Gerard might have respected him if it were not for Bohm's story. But he did know Bohm's tale, and half a dozen others, and thus he resented the debt he had felt obligated to repay, the debt that had put him under Szabo's thumb.

At the same time that it galled him that his last job would be one he had not wished to complete in the first place, his distaste for the work would make it easier to walk away, to be satisfied with a life out of the shadows. Jane had mocked the idea of them rusticating and Gerard had laughed with her, understanding. But he craved peace.

And he would have it.

The bustling activity around the riverfront warehouse masked the six men guarding the front office. A casual observer would only notice the one man standing attention by the door. However, the others Gerard spotted easily. There would be an equal number at every entrance and exit to the building, if Szabo had kept to his usual specifications.

He observed the warehouse, through the shift change and as darkness fell over the city. Szabo liked to come and go from the river, and if Gerard's goal were an ambush, that would be the weakness he would utilize. For a moment he allowed himself to enjoy the fantasy of killing the man, the way the grand plan of ruining him had been a pleasurable digression in thought. However, assassination came with its own consequences, few of which were directly related to the Powell matter, and would likely mean more loose ends to tie up. Therefore, Gerard's plan to keep Jane safe would have to be more complicated than mere assassination.

He did not wait for Szabo to leave the warehouse before crossing town to observe the man's lodgings. The townhouse was in a respectable part of the city, housing Szabo's mistress and three daughters. A family man. Two families, as his wife lived in Budapest with his other children.

The building was as much a fortress as the warehouse but with its own weaknesses. Gerard did not intend to exploit any of them unless absolutely necessary. Instead, he ascertained the mistress's plans for the evening, a ball which most of Vienna society would attend. It was not the normal order of things but as much as the congress complicated matters, it was making this one simpler. At the ball, he would sow the seeds of his campaign.

The ballroom was well lighted, and filled with people in masks or dominoes. Despite the pretense of disguise, it was easy to see that nearly all of Austria and its visiting potentates were there. The Emperor of Russia, King of Denmark, and the Archdukes of Austria were in attendance, dancing, ordering supper or partaking in refreshments in the rooms adjoining the gallery.

Through the crowd, Gerard passed like a wraith, noticed only when he wished to be. It was relatively easy for a dark-haired man in a domino to blend in with all the rest of the dark-haired men of Europe.

He spotted Jane from the line of her back, the space between her jaw and her shoulder at just the right angle. Lust surged through him, heat gathering in his loins, hard and urgent, as if he were an untried youth…and yet, with a man's knowledge that made the desire that much more fierce.

As he moved toward her, he took in the details of her appearance, the costume that was intended to amuse but not obscure. Rather the opposite of obscure. The thin white cloth, in imitation of a toga, gathered high on her shoulders revealed the long lines of her slender arms. She wore long gloves that drew attention to each elegant movement or gesticulation. Gold rope tied beneath her bosom… He stopped there, enjoyed the two smooth rises of flesh above the fabric.

He was lost.

He shook his head mentally, continued to survey the crowd, and spotted Bohm. Relief thrummed through him. He made no attempt to acknowledge the man. After all, if Bohm did not already see him, he would soon enough. Gerard continued on, until he was close enough he could hear fragments of the conversation Jane shared with her father and another man. Something about Saxony and whether England would in the end support the legitimacy of the king Napoleon had brought to power or deny it.

He was now close enough to catch her gaze, to watch the corner of her mouth quirk just the tiniest bit, her head cock ever so slightly. As a conversational tidbit erupted into a punctuating laughter, Gerard stepped forward.

"Lady Jane," he said with a bow, insinuating himself into the conversation. He felt the inquisitive stares of her father and the other man.

"Forgive me, Mr…"

"Badeau, yes, of course, introductions were rather hasty yesterday." He surreptitiously watched Langley for his reaction. It was unlikely that his grandfather had mentioned his name ever to his friend, but not impossible.

She laughed. "Mr. Badeau, I did not forget *you*, simply your name. Papa, Mr. Tuttle, allow me to introduce you to Gerard Badeau. Mr. Badeau, Lord Langley and Gavin Tuttle."

He had never met Langley before, though he had heard of the man through his grandfather. It was fascinating to see him side by side with his daughter. Some of Langley's graying hair was the same light brown shade as Jane's, and his heavily lidded eyes were the same clear pale blue. They shared some mannerisms as well, but there the similarities ended.

"Badeau... French?"

"By birth," Gerard said. "I have lived abroad since the terror." It was not the strictest truth, but it was an answer that usually put Englishmen at ease, one that suggested Gerard's family was well born enough to fear the wrath of France's citizens.

And, under normal circumstances, this was the man whose permission he would request to marry Jane. But this was not a normal circumstance. Jane was of age to consent on her own and if Gerard did choose to abide by that social nicety, he would do so only as a formality.

"What brings you to Vienna?" This from Mr. Tuttle. Gerard was not particularly interested in the man. Still, he had assessed him out of reflex, first from a distance and now at closer quarters. Somewhere in his thirties, the man had the look of one attached to the diplomatic corps, used to copious paperwork and drudgery.

"The menagerie," Gerard quipped. The expected laughter eased the tension of new acquaintances and into the more congenial space, he added, "And a matter of business to which to attend." It was a fine line to walk to try and portray the epitome of gentlemanly insouciance at the same time as reassure Lord Langley that he possessed a certain amount of gravity.

Understanding slammed into Gerard's chest like a sack of stones. He was attempting to impress the damned man after all, but all of it was merely shades of truth. A sham really. He exchanged banalities for a handful of moments, aware that Jane was watching him intently. Too intently.

"Forgive me, gentlemen. My true purpose is to ask Lady

Jane for this next dance. With your permission?"

Jane obligingly smiled and took his arm, but when they were a few steps away from her father, she questioned him. "What are you doing here?"

"Dancing with you," he said, even though they were still on the fringes of the ballroom as he surveyed where best to join the dancing figures. "Will you dance with me?"

He sent her a teasing grin, but her more serious expression was not what he expected in return.

"Isn't it dangerous? In public?"

He tensed, re-examining everything at the mere suggestion. It was habit to constantly think about dangers, so much a habit that he had not questioned his actions.

"Gerard Badeau is not connected to anyone from whom I anticipate danger."

"But I am, as you have said, and thus everyone to whom I speak is suspect, no?"

She was right. Those disguises that were only meant to deflect attention could allow someone to see the shape of his ear, or the slope of his shoulder, and take a second look. And wearing a domino as he was, perhaps he was even more recognizable. It was the sort of mistake Gerard had never made before. The sort of mistake that would get him killed. Get Jane killed.

He scanned the crowd, spotted Bohm again, but no one else that raised alarm. Certainly there were other men and women of intrigue here, but none yet focused on him.

"This way." He ushered her into the long gallery that paralleled the ballroom. Here it was less brightly illuminated, darkened alcoves perfect for trysts.

"My father will wonder that we are not among the dancers."

"With this crush your father will not notice," he said, finding one of those alcoves empty and drawing her into it, into the deepest shadows of the accommodating draperies.

He pulled her against him, bent his head to the soft lobe of her ear. "Here, then," he whispered. "Dance with me here."

She lifted her arms, fit her body to his, far closer than they would if they were to waltz in public where anyone could see. He took a step forward and she followed his lead. There was no room for a proper waltz but he turned her in place, small steps that rotated them around and around, that made her skirt billow out against his legs and her breath turn to laughter.

He had always enjoyed dancing, had understood its appeal even when not being used to advance his agenda, but as with everything else, with Jane it transformed into something else entirely.

"What a boy you are!" Jane said, looking up at him, her lips pursed in amusement. "The fierce assassin, spy, whatever you are…"

"Hush. Even here the walls might have ears."

She wilted against him.

"I don't think I am made for this sort of intrigue and secrecy. I prefer the game of chess, strategy but actions taken visibly. A game board everyone can see."

"What I do…everyone who is looking can see that too."

She nodded, but rested her head against his shoulder, swayed to the distant strains of the orchestra. He moved with her until they were dancing once more, hip to hip, chest to chest, thigh to thigh.

"I can regret nothing about the way you came into my

life," he murmured. "But I do not wish you to be endangered. And you are. My warnings of this afternoon...I have thought through the puzzle again and again but the easiest solution to throwing others off the scent presents other problems."

"No riddles," she said, pushing away from him, irritation clear in her voice. "Speak plainly if you are to at all."

He hesitated. "There are some who believe you would only make inquiries into Powell's matters if you know too much and thus need to be eliminated. We must give them another story that they can believe."

"Ah, that Powell and I were lovers? I would never have been his lover and could not bear to be thought to have been so, no matter the danger to my life," she said with a laugh. But she was trembling.

"I won't let anyone hurt you."

"When the danger was you..."

He pressed his lips together against the anger and impotence. She was right. As Bohm had said, if Szabo truly wished Jane dead, Bohm alone might not be enough defense.

"Come with me to London. I can protect you there."

"And say what to my father? That man you just met? *He* is my lover and I intend to elope with him?"

"No, but that sounds rather good now that you've suggested it." The boldness of it did appeal to him, as did the suggestion that Jane would indeed be willing to elope.

"You are impossible."

He lifted his hand, cradled her head, and ran his thumb over the soft skin of her cheek. He wasn't certain yet how he would forge their path forward, but forge it he would. "*We* are impossible, but inevitable."

"Gerard." Jane said his name on a sigh, exhausted, confused, and made dizzy by his nearness. The idea that someone would target her for death specifically was anathema to her very sense of the order of the world, an order that Gerard had upended and continued to spin, as if she were a planet set off its usual axis.

The reasonable thing to do was to demand Gerard never bother her again, to pretend the sad matter of Powell was of no interest to her. To act as if she were still the same simple Lady Jane Langley who wished to assist her father in his diplomatic dabblings.

Simple. Dabblings. These alone were words she would not have previously used to describe either herself or her father. They seemed accurate to her now when nothing was simple.

Why was she drawn to a man who professed to be a villain, to kill for money with no greater, more honorable goal? Would she have formed such a tendre for any other man with whom she shared an intense experience? Or was it that when he listened, he focused entirely on her and he thought about what she had said? He didn't underestimate her or assume that her sex made her inferior in any way at all. And he saw beneath the facade she had presented to the rest of the world, found the woman who needed desperately to be cared for and loved.

Were those reasons to love a man? Were they reasons to throw everything else that she valued away? He was strong, intelligent and handsome, but he used his skills for his own gain. Did not respect human life, though he had let Lady Powell live. Had let Jane live.

Gerard's breath was warm on her cheek. His lips touched her ear again, and liquid warmth slid through her body, gathered low between her thighs as his lips moved to her neck. Her own lips parted in a desirous question, full of the need he had awakened.

There was this as well, the heat of his touch, the way her body wanted his.

"What I intend is that we convince him your interest in Powell stems from your work for your father. But I need your assistance to do so."

"Which is why you are revealing so much." She quickly discerned what was said and not said. "Now I know that Powell's death was due to something other than his work for the crown. I must assume his shipping interests." Gerard's sigh sent a little thrill of triumph through her. "I'm certain Lady Heathland would know who his partners are, if any live here in Vienna. I'm getting close, aren't I?"

"This isn't a game."

"No," she agreed. It wasn't a game. She had first wanted to know more to better understand Gerard. Then, she wanted to know because he would not tell her. Now…the threat was directly against her life. It was her right to know. "Well, then. How may I help you?"

"There is someone here tonight, a woman, who we must convince. Hearing Powell's name from your lips, she will relay the information to others concerned."

"So, I shall say…to someone—"

"To me."

"Is that not a risk?"

"She does not know me."

Jane raised an eyebrow. "I think you are overconfident."

"Jane—"

"As you wish," she said dismissively, ignoring the look of outraged male pride. She did not wish him to lie to her and she would not do so to him. "I shall say to you that I suspect Lord Powell had other loyalties. His family will be outraged by the suggestion of treason. But if I only say that he is missed, then why was I asking questions? And who are you that you would be interested in this discussion? Perhaps I'd better drag one of the junior clerks into this. Confuse them with a story about how I've ascertained that…" She wracked her brain for something and thought of the conversations she had been having with her father just before Gerard arrived. "…Lord Powell did not in fact have any ties to Saxony and that we may rest easy."

"Saxony," Gerard mused. "That is a good choice."

A small pleased pride snaked through Jane.

"And you are right. One of the junior clerks might be safer."

That pleased tendril grew inside her. As if she needed his approval.

"If all goes well, I shall leave tomorrow."

The conversational switch was abrupt, and that tendril withered, replaced by a nervous sort of fear and anticipation.

If he left…if he spoke with his grandfather, asked for help in forging a life accepted by English society, he would understand at last that a union between them was impossible, that— She couldn't think beyond that, would not let herself. If he left Vienna, he was setting in motion more than simply an illicit affair, more than this ominous intrigue in which they were currently engaged.

These few days in Vienna, these few nights, each morning he had said he would go and then there he was again, brightening her life. Here, where royalty and the people of Vienna intermingled freely, there was less to separate Jane from Gerard, less to make the idea of them together impossible.

"You'll come to me tonight?"

He stilled, as if she had somehow offended him.

"What is it?"

He did not answer.

"It is one thing to not tell me about Powell, but it is another entirely to hide your thoughts from me now about this. When you claim you are leaving for London tomorrow *because* of your love for me." She felt a bit like a shrew using his love to manipulate him into answering, but she was frustrated, too, tired of being kept in the dark except for when *he* chose to eke out some small bit of knowledge. Tired of him thinking he controlled everything, their fate, their lives.

"It is just…this is the first time you are asking me to come to you."

Her breath fled as she took in his words, his pensive expression, the gaze that was half embarrassed at his confession. She had not expected vulnerability. But he was right. It had always been Gerard pushing her, invading her space, taking over her life. In return, she had pushed him away. She had never before invited him in. He thought it meant more than it did. It was no great sign of love. Instead, it was one of lust. She wanted one more night. One more night before it was over.

"Then you will come to me? I will make it easy for you and leave my window open."

He laughed and then shook his head. "I cannot. I will need to ensure our work tonight took root. But there is an inn on the edge of the woods. Das Holzbeisl. Meet me there tomorrow."

She frowned. "You will not leave for London?"

"For one day for us to be Jane and Gerard, away from intrigue and Vienna, away from the world, knowing everything? For that I will wait one more day. Soon enough you will be mine in every other way."

"Knowing everything…" She laughed. "To know you is to know a man of secrets he will not reveal."

"I have not lied to you."

"I must take you at your word on that…and I do," she said with a sigh. At the very least, he would still be in Vienna one more day, one more chance to convince him not to go to Landsdowne, not to seek absolution from society if doing so was in pursuit of her.

He escorted her back into the ballroom much later than the end of the dance she had promised him. She looked for her father but, if possible, the ballroom was even more crowded than before.

"She's here." She followed Gerard's gaze to a woman not all that far away, bedecked in jewels and frills, with a riot of curls and a hoarse laugh. A merchant's wife or a mistress perhaps. Jane looked at the woman's companions, tried to ascertain more. "Jane," Gerard said, a note of warning in his voice. "No questions, simply the conversation conducted near her."

"I understand."

They didn't speak again until he delivered her to her father's side, until all the small and necessary pleasantries were said. Then Gerard was gone, absorbed back into the crowd.

A sea of faces out of which she would need to find one of those junior clerks, and that woman once again. Her stomach clenched, but she took a deep breath and focused on the task at hand, idly fingering the silk rope that edged her dress. It was a trifle, a small matter of erroneous gossip to be imparted. Really, the sort of thing woman of the ton did on a daily basis for far less dire reasons. And she was not alone. Gerard had not said, but she knew—he would be watching until the deed was done.

Gerard wanted to speak with Bohm, but he didn't dare. The ex-pugilist still had his devotees, was not unknown in Vienna. It was part of what made him the perfect guard for Jane, especially at these peculiarly Viennese gatherings where all of society seemed to mix.

Instead, he circled the perimeter of the room, keeping an eye on Elda Schmitt, Szabo's mistress. She seemed to be having an enjoyable time. Though Szabo kept a tight rein on his household, he also liked to make his mistress happy, and encouraged her to attend as many social events as she wished. There were only a handful of these that Szabo ever attended as well.

He caught the glint of gold in Jane's brown hair as she walked arm in arm with a young, blushing man. A junior clerk, Gerard presumed, who had little idea that he was being maneuvered into exactly the position Jane wanted him. Jane laughed, and clung to the man's arm. Flirting.

Jealousy tugged sharply in Gerard's gut, even as he marveled at this view of her. From the first moment that he had held her cheek in his hand, their world had been the intensity between the two of them. Even though he knew the wide smile and knowing eyes were intended to obfuscate, it still startled him to see her use such a tool. Jane's natural flirtatiousness stemmed from her seriousness, her willingness to meet a man's eyes while discussing the most complex or the simplest matters. She did not shy away from life, and that was arousing and appealing in and of itself. But this…it was not in Jane's nature and yet she did it brilliantly. The poor clerk was clearly under her spell.

There. They were a mere hand's breadth from Szabo's mistress. He knew exactly when Powell's name was dropped, not from the shape of Jane's lips as she rounded her lips around the word, but from the way Szabo's mistress turned her head sharply, and then back again, studiously pretending she wasn't listening when everything in her posture clearly indicated to Gerard that she was. Excellent. He had little doubt that this information would come back to Szabo this night. Szabo would still keep an eye on Jane, no doubt, but if she stopped asking questions altogether, he would assume this matter of Saxony had been the reason, some other political intrigue that did not concern him directly.

Gerard stayed a little longer, watched Jane disentangle herself from the hapless young clerk. Observed her enter a dance with a minor German prince. He wanted to rip the prince's hand from hers. He wanted to hold her in his arms, dance with her here before the orchestra, amidst all the other dancers. But she had not invited anyone else to come to her room this night. Only Gerard, despite everything. Despite the way he had threatened her life and then continued to do so merely by having let her live.

She loved him. She had said she did, and the words were a balm to Gerard's scorched soul. *Soul.* That word again, as foreign and as natural as its twin, *love.*

He knew well enough that she claimed love was not enough for her, that she needed security and a life in which she was accorded the same respect as a wife as she had as Langley's daughter. She deserved that and he would give it to her. He would find a way.

But first he had to keep her alive.

As he left the ball and stepped out into the dark of night, exhilaration quickened his pulse, made him breathe deep of the cold air that ached in his lungs. If all went well, this night would be his last night of intrigue, the final piece in a job that had been both unwanted and profoundly affecting. After this he was truly his own man and would never work for anyone other than himself. He could nearly taste the freedom that idea invoked.

Freedom. Soul. Love.

What had become of Gerard Badeau?

Chapter Twelve

The room at the inn on the northern outskirts of the city was in his name, or at least the name he went by here in Vienna, and she did not give hers. She met him in the bold light of day, no spies, no servants, and no need for extraordinary secrecy. Anticipation soared through her as she climbed well-worn wooden stairs to his room. This time she was coming to him of her own free will.

The third door on the left, the proprietor had said. The door was a dark wood, the center polished smooth by the touches and raps over the years. She knocked. The door opened. Her stomach gripped and tumbled at the sight of his dark eyes, his dark gaze, the intensity of his desire.

Gerard.

Space, light, extinguished between them. The thump of the door closing, the turn of the lock, sounded distantly in her head as that desire devoured her, lips on lips, bodies overlapping. They pulled at each other's clothing, undressing at first in a frenzy and then more languidly, taking their time as he unlaced her stays, his thumbs caressing circles onto her back.

Finally naked they stood, their skin golden in the afternoon light. She had never had a chance to admire him before. Now, her heart as full as her desire, she could. She traced the hard planes of his chest, trailed her finger down to his hip. He reached out and she stopped him, trapped his hand in hers, lifted it to her mouth. She pressed a kiss to his knuckles and then to the bones of his wrist. The length of his arms intrigued her. She had admired his lean strength before, but now it was hers to explore. The suntanned skin, dusted with hair, the corded muscles. She wanted to lick it all and she wanted to cry.

"Gerard," she whispered, her voice breaking.

"Ma chere." He pulled her against him, whispered to her in French, soothing her. "My love, my beautiful, brave, intelligent Jane." She understood the words but it was his voice and the language that washed over her with the comfort of home. His home. His language. He had said he had no country that was his, but now in his voice it was clear that the language of his childhood was his first, the one he dreamt in. The one he loved in.

He *loved* her.

Loved.

His love had overwhelmed her at first, felt impossible. But now…

Such an amazing, incredible thing to have grown out of death, out of the strangest of circumstances. To have met a man who could see her for who she was, not as someone's daughter or a flush dowry or any other superficiality. *Not that money is a superficial—* She thrust the pragmatic thought from her head. It did not belong here in this room, where all that mattered was this moment together. Here, emotion reigned. Here, she could love him.

She lifted her hand between them and touched the warm skin of his chest, reveled in the beating of his heart beneath. He had marked her with his love that last night in Frankfurt, but she could not and did not wish to mark him. She could make no promises. No promises but this afternoon.

She trailed her fingers over his sculpted chest, over the small nipples so like and so unlike her own, explored the nubs that hardened at her touch. Desire surged like a wave within her, powerful and all consuming, drawing her under. She gave into it, drowned in it willingly. She kissed his chest, the delineation of muscle, with her tongue. Every sense was centered there as she breathed him in, tasted him, listened to the rhythmic beating of his heart. Primal music.

"How…"

She paused infinitesimally, but his question trailed off, continued the trail of her tongue down his beautiful body as she waited for him to continue. She knelt as she reached his hips, the male part of him, which was erect and intriguing. She took him in her hands and marveled at the contrast of hard and soft, rough and smooth, beautiful and strange. This she had taken inside her, was how they had joined hip to hip, until nothing separated them, until they were nearly one being.

"How do you manage to unravel me?" His voice was hoarse, nearly guttural. "This isn't simply pleasure."

She had no measure for comparison but the wonder in his tone filled her with a deep, very female sort of satisfaction, made her feel for the first time the wonderful power of being a female. Here, in the privacy between two people, a man and a woman, they were utterly equal.

"No?" She was unsure what to do next, other than what she wanted to do, and yet, that seemed so... "May I kiss you?"

There was a moment of silence, a hesitation, and she wondered if he had understood what she meant. Then he choked, "Yes."

Yes. Then this was something that was done. Not some strange creation on her part. She breathed in deep, then feathered her lips over the hard length of him. Out of the corner of her eye, she caught the movement of his hand, closing into a fist, his wrist and forearm radiating with suppressed tension. But he made no other motion or sound. If she were hurting him, he'd surely say something.

She touched him experimentally with her tongue, and his hips rocked toward her. She licked the length of him, slowly at first, and then, encouraged by his soft moan, at her will. His hands gripped her upper arms firmly and she loved the pressure of his fingers on her flesh. She slid her tongue under the slight ridge that encircled the tip.

"Jane, come here."

Dizzily, she let him pull her up against him, let his mouth plunder hers once more. She could feel him hard, hot, throbbing against her and the simple knowledge of it sent a damp heat settling between her thighs.

"My turn." The gravelly rawness of his voice as he matched it with forceful action thrilled her. He swept her off her feet and, breathless, she looked up at him from where he placed her on the bed, looming over her, never more than a few inches away.

She reached for him and he grabbed her wrists, pulled her arms over her head and held them there with one arm. "Let me pleasure you."

Let me pleasure you. The pleasure she knew was his kisses, his touch, his body joined intimately with hers. Her body tingled in anticipation. He let go of her wrists and bent his head. She gasped as his mouth lowered to her neck and she arched her head back to give him more access. But he had moved on, down her body the way she had explored his. It felt as if he was everywhere, his hands, his mouth, his tongue. Even the simple contact of his thigh against hers sent fire running across her skin. It was as if each lick, each caress, were a strand, a thread, a piece of some grander tapestry of pleasure that he was weaving across her body. She followed each thread until he moved on and that one was left trembling, a maw of desire. He managed to find places she had never imagined would be sensitive, she had never thought of beyond the bath, and turn them into greedy centers of need.

Unravel me, he had said. As his mouth trailed down her body, she finally understood. His mouth closed over her, soothing her for the briefest moment before his tongue moved, kept moving, shooting tendrils of pleasure through her body with each lick. She had never imagined such a thing, imagined these ministrations as part of what occurred in sexual relations, and yet it was perfect.

Pleasure gathered, grew, until she started to shift her hips to escape the mounting pressure, the need for something. As if she were gunpowder about to explode and yet she didn't know how, didn't know by what mechanism she could find such a release. She moved frantically beneath him, hands finally weaving through the curls of his hair as she gave in to the sensation, to him, to her desire.

She scattered everywhere, into little pieces of thread fluttering through air, caught like sparkling dust in the afternoon light, floating down. He moved, loomed over her, settled his hips between her thighs, and the thrust of his hardness into her languid body was the most delicious thing in the world. She wrapped her legs around his, her arms around his back, and grinned over his shoulder at nothing.

At everything.

He'd unraveled her but now he was threading the loom again, putting her back together.

Until he unraveled her again.

The afternoon passed leisurely. Jane studied his body the way she had studied French, German, and Italian. Paid attention to what actions elicited involuntary moans, or made him lose control. In that plain, nearly bare little room, they made a home for themselves, a world that was just for them. But the sun shifted through the day, until it sent long shadows across the floorboards. She would have to return soon. Her father expected her to attend a dinner with him that evening, but with Gerard beside her, the long lines of his body beautiful as he rested, eyes half open, she wanted to stay. She wasn't done touching him, tasting him, or simply looking at him.

"I'm leaving tomorrow," he said. "Everything has been taken care of. You will be…safe."

The words cut through the relaxing warmth of satiation. These last weeks had been an odd idyll. As much not a part of reality as their time alone after the carriage wreck. But if he left, now, on the quest to win her, everything would change. Most of all, he would go to England and she would still be here, in Vienna, indefinitely.

She should urge him not to go, but the words were too harsh for this place, for the intimacy between them. She wanted to linger here in their own little world of the bed.

"Tell me a story," she begged, as if they were still on the road, learning everything they could about each other. Only now he knew her identity and she his. The secrets they still had were simply a matter of excavation over time.

"I have six half siblings, four of whom still live. Templeton, who you know, is one."

She nodded.

"After my birth, my father returned to England, begat his heir, then returned to France. My understanding is he wished to be out from under his father's eye." Jane laughed. Vincent Templeton must not have known his father very well if he thought Lord Landsdowne's reach ended at England's borders. "My eldest sister, Marie—when I found her she was married and with child. Happily, it seemed, in a simple life, and ignorant of all the rest of us. There was no reason to disturb her and so I did not."

"I assume then that she is still happy."

It was Gerard's turn to nod.

"Then there was Florian. He was born the year of the revolution, the year my father fled France for Spain. I found his grave, tiny, for that of a newborn. His mother was still alive but...not well."

"Why did you look for them? All you have in common is an absent father."

"Does your father have any bastards?"

The question shocked her. It shouldn't have, but it did.

"My mother died so long ago. I know he has a mistress, but she is not...she is not paraded about. And there are no children, I know that much. If he has sired any with any other woman, supports any other households, I do not know of it. And I believe I would."

"You were curious enough about siblings to be able to answer my question," he said pointedly.

"I concede the point. I suppose I would want to know, though I do not believe I would go so far as to acknowledge them."

"As I myself am a bastard, I have nothing to lose."

She nodded.

"And...Jane—" There was a note in his voice, something she had never heard from him before, something ragged and painfully honest and it pulled at her heart. "I am a man without a country, without people I call my own. My mother left her family for life as a courtesan. I was taken from her side at a young age, trained for...for death." It was chilling to hear him finally admit it. This was not his matter-of-fact description of his life; it was something else, a pleading for her to understand. "You say I walk in the shadows, but I also walk alone."

"You want a family." His sharp inhale was her confirmation. She reached out, pressed her hand to his chest. He grabbed her hand and drew it to his mouth, kissed it. Maintaining control. Of course. *That* need, she understood fully.

"Clara was born in Spain with the pox and died early of

it. Then Giana."

"The one you found in a brothel."

"The salacious detail is always the easiest remembered."

"It is also one of the few details you offered. Salacious makes the best stories."

"True."

"And is she family?"

"I did not realize…I have been a man of action. Ruminating on the whys and wherefores were not part of my training. Unless, of course, it is to assess an opponent's weaknesses."

"So you put her in that convent without much care for her desires and without any established relationship."

"I considered myself her guardian."

She nodded. Women were subject to the wills of their guardians across the world, submitted to their decisions because there was often no other recourse. But Gerard had not been this girl's guardian in truth, thus, if she was so against a convent, why did she go?

"Does she write to you?"

He looked surprised. "Frequently. Long missives about embroidery and the making of mulled wine, for which apparently the convent is famed."

She laughed.

"Does that mean something to you?"

"I cannot be certain, naturally," Jane said, "but I suspect that she very much would prefer a brother than a house full of sisters."

"I had no life to offer her." Yet he wanted to draw Jane into his. "Only the money I had earned. But enough of this. You wanted a story and I have given you a list."

"You've laid out the tale of a man searching for his

family."

"And learning that a man makes his way, makes his life and his family." He rolled over, looming over her so quickly, caging her between the sinewy lengths of his arms, between the weight of his hips and the softness of the mattress beneath. "And you, Jane. I choose you."

The enormity of his statement clenched around her heart, gutted her with the weight of his expectation and his need. She wanted to do it, to be everything for him, everything he needed, and yet…she was not his savior, not a haven into which he could hide.

She didn't wish for either of them to cling to each other as some sort of escape from their lives. Not that she had anything in her life to escape. She had, at least she had had until Gerard had upended it, a perfectly enjoyable and respectable life.

She met his voracious mouth with her own, wrapped her arms around him, around the smooth, muscular planes of his back, and though her heart leaped toward him, wished nothing else but to be a soft home for his, she could not tell him, *Gerard, I choose you.*

When they were breathless and languid once more, Jane rested her head on his chest. For the first time that he could remember, Gerard was completely content. This woman against him, the late afternoon light filtering in through the window, illuminating dust motes as if they were fairy sparkles. Such a fanciful thought, and yet that was how he felt inside, as if this moment were happening to someone else, some man who deserved this woman and a normal life.

"Don't go."

The air shifted around him.

"To London, you mean," he said.

He tensed, but she stayed where she was, as if nothing had changed. Yet, the silence was full of the knowledge that it had.

"Yes. Stay here. Let us enjoy this time we have together."

He wanted to, wanted to desperately, but the minute they left the inn the world would flood back in. If he wanted to make her his for more than stolen afternoons, the sooner he acted the better. The only reason to linger was if this was all they would ever have.

"You doubt I will succeed."

She rolled off him and stared down at him, unflinching. "Yes...and no. You think you have power, but when have you ever asked or demanded something of the people for whom you work? You are a servant to them."

She was here with him. She had come to him, and the look in her eyes...he had recognized it because that was how he felt inside. Yet the words were cold, an echo of what she had said to him that night on the road. And she meant them.

Jane would not be happy with a man who lived his life at the beck and call of others, or living on the outskirts of society. He had seen her among her peers in Vienna. As much as she was his, she belonged to that life. If he wanted her, he would have to belong as well. An impossible feat, but he had done the impossible before.

She shivered, sat up, slid off the bed, and then looked around the room for her clothes. She needed an answer, but what could he say that would appease her, that would convince her of their future together?

"No…and *yes*," he said finally, throwing her own words back at her. "In some ways you are right. Powell, all of this, is a result of a debt that needed to be paid. No matter how powerful one is, at some point, you must pay the price."

As his grandfather would. Jane doubted it but as well as she knew Landsdowne, she had never known the parts that Gerard knew.

"You think you are powerful? What great kindness did someone do you that a man's life is the price?"

His jaw tightened. She was determined to push him away. He watched as she slid her chemise over her head and then started on the more difficult task of her stays. Her body was covered to him, another wall between them. It was understandable. Their love went against common sense. What woman would put herself under the protection of a man who kept secrets, a man she didn't trust?

Secrets. There were so many he could not share, but perhaps there was another story he could tell that would give her the information she craved.

He put a hand on her shoulder, and she dropped her arms, released her breath in a shudder. He lifted the ends of the lace in each hand and they stood there in silence as he worked.

"Before Badeau's death—"

She froze. "Badeau?"

"My tutor, but I loved and hated him as a father. In his last years, he was more and more ill. He asked me to come with him to Turkey." He laughed. "That mission was in fact for Landsdowne."

His hands rested on her back for a moment before he

lifted them and took a step back. She picked up her dress and then turned to face him.

"When was this?"

"1810." The hostilities between Russia and the Ottomans had renewed. Landsdowne had wanted information, and to help the nephew of a friend. It had been intended to be a quick trip into and out of occupied territory.

Jane shook her head.

"In any event, while there, Badeau visited a doctor, discovered his ailment was a canker of the stomach. There is more I am not at liberty to say, but we…we had to leave the area under the worst of circumstances. I could have managed on my own, but with Badeau, nearly crippled from the ineffectual treatments, it was more complicated. Szabo orchestrated our escape."

"Szabo?"

Gerard let out a shuddering sigh. "Powell's business partner and the man who orchestrated his demise."

She pinned him with her gaze, direct, curious. "Why are you telling me this? Is this not information dangerous for me to know?"

"Yes, but it is also dangerous for you not to know from whom you may be under threat."

She swallowed hard. He wanted to take her into his arms, to protect her from everything, even himself, but her arms were wrapped around herself now and there was no room for him.

"So," she continued, "he knew Badeau and thus your identity as well, so when he called on the debt, you could not refuse?"

"No. He knew us under different names, but yes, I could

not refuse."

"From everything you've said about this man, there is no love lost between you. Why not just disappear?"

He slid an impatient hand through his hair. "Because if I did I would have to leave this life entirely behind. And Szabo is not one to forgive and forget. If he ever did choose to find me, it is possible he could. Anyone under my care would be in danger as well."

"Giana."

Gerard sucked in a breath. "Yes, and my younger brother as well. And now...you."

She shivered.

"So there you have it."

A story that told both of his power and powerlessness. Not all his decisions were for monetary gain.

"I would make you my confessor, tell you every moment of my life, as dark and cold as they have been, and lay it out for your judgment if I could. But this knowledge, it is the type that endangers people. Powell was killed for such tales."

Her face was drawn and tight, the opposite of how she had looked in bed only half an hour earlier.

"Imagine Landsdowne publically recognizes you, his illegitimate grandson, encourages his close society to accept you. Imagine you buy yourself an estate, show off your wealth...is that the life you want?"

The life he wanted. He closed his eyes and for a moment a vision of verdant grass, laughing children, and Jane filled his mind. He wanted a family and peace. Landsdowne was not necessary, and it chafed at his pride to have to go to the man and ask for help, but to have Jane he would do what was needed.

"Do you love me?" His own heart ached as he waited for her answer.

"Yes," she choked. "I do. But tragedies are written about fools who think love is enough."

His lips were tight, his jaw tight, but inside his heart was unfurling.

"Say it again."

"That we are fools?" she said.

He shook his head at her attempt to make it seem like the admission was less than it was. "That you love me."

She laughed derisively and stepped into her shoes. Then stumbled as he whirled her around and pulled her close. He grabbed her chin in his hand and stared down at her.

She looked back, eyes wide and searching. There was nothing but the taut air between them, the pulse of her skin against his hand.

"You have to let me go," she whispered.

"Don't be a coward."

She pushed at his hand and then at his chest until he took a step backward and she was free.

"I'm going to return now."

"To what? To your father? To the congress? Will satisfying your intellect alone be enough of a life for you now that you know how much more there is to be had?"

His answer to that question for his own life was no. From the traces of thought and emotion that flickered across her face, he was certain his point had been taken. He took a deep breath.

"Then go, Jane. But this is not over."

Chapter Thirteen

She didn't see him the next day, or the next, although she scanned the crowds hoping for a glimpse of him. She kept turning corners and attending events with the faint hope that his face would be the next one she saw, his voice whispering in her ear, his hand reaching to draw her into a waltz. But that wishful expectation jarred with the knowledge that he had left for England on his impossible quest. And with Gerard gone, Vienna felt empty.

He had warned her to stop asking questions, to stop inquiring into Powell's death, had suggested she was drawing the wrong type of attention, but Gerard's absence was proof that the only danger was to her aching heart.

Even so, Jane heeded him and avoided Albertina Abbings and Lady Heathland, and anyone else she had sought out purely for the sake of investigating Lord Powell's affairs. However, Mrs. Abbings was not so easy to shake and Jane not rude enough to dismiss her in any overt way. It was Mrs. Abbings who Jane happened to be standing next to when the sound of indulgent hoarse laughter made them turn to catch sight of riotous curls gathered up with a sash, to see the mysterious woman Gerard had instructed Jane to gossip in front of but not attempt to identify.

"I cannot imagine why *she* is here," Mrs. Abbings said, disdain dripping from her voice.

Jane hesitated, struggling to keep her curiosity at bay. She had promised Gerard she would not inquire and yet in this situation it was only natural to do so.

"Elda Schmitt," Mrs. Abbings said. "Of course you don't know her. Why would you? But she is the mistress of a merchant. Lord Powell's business partner, in fact."

Tension thrummed through her body as her mind engaged, but Jane struggled to look disinterested. "Oh?"

"A very crude woman. Thinks that because her lover, who by the way has a wife and family in Buda, is a wealthy and powerful man, she is an arbiter of fashion. She is nothing but a common whore."

Jane coughed, looking about quickly, hoping no one had overheard that exchange.

"I see I've shocked you. There is much you don't know."

Jane had wanted to know more, but now she felt the danger here. She needed to find a way to extricate herself from Mrs. Abbings.

"I imagine it isn't for my ears. If you do excuse me, my father is waving at me." Jane didn't wait for a response, but as she went to join her father, she spared a glance at Miss Schmitt and found the woman staring back at her. That brief contact sent a frisson of fear through Jane. It was surely nothing, merely the sense of having been glanced at. But nonetheless Jane vowed to avoid Mrs. Abbings and Lady Heathland and anyone else remotely connected to Lord Powell.

The following days she stayed good to her word. She stuck close to her father, did her best to be the dutiful daughter, the one who could assist him with anything that occurred. He gave her only the most menial of work, and she caught him staring at her in odd moments.

Life grew uncomfortable, and when Silviana, the Princess von Wolfstein, returned to Vienna from a brief trip to the countryside and invited her for a day of shopping, Jane agreed with alacrity.

"It is so good to be able to spend time with you," Silvie said as they walked down the street, Silvie's footman in tow. She was Jane's second cousin, and the last time she had seen her was several years ago in London. They exchanged regular, if infrequent, correspondence, one of the ways in which Jane practiced her German and maintained knowledge of the details of life abroad, as Silvie was frequently traveling, unperturbed in the recent years by Napoleon's army cutting its swath across the continent. She was intrepid, to the point that Jane had often thought her wandering a sign of foolishness more than intelligence. But now, strolling together through the busy Baroque streets of fashionable Vienna, she was inclined to adjust her opinion. Or adjust her opinion of herself, for she would not be a hypocrite and judge her cousin with one standard and herself with another.

Silvie was neither flighty nor stupid. She merely had a lust for life that was not satisfied by the narrow boundaries of her small country.

"The patisserie is very good, I assure you," she said,

pointing at the cake shop to their right. "I am thankful these high-waisted styles allow me to indulge. But if you don't mind, I would love to stop in this store first. I have begun collecting antique porcelain. Collections are always such odd things, but after I read Father d'Entrecolles' book on Chinese porcelain, how I came upon that book is an entirely different story, I had an absolute fascination."

Jane laughed. She knew little more than the basics of porcelain production, and was not particularly interested in the wares other than their usefulness when hosting dinner. But she followed her cousin into the store. Soon Silvie was engrossed in the little porcelain boxes, engaging the proprietor in a discussion about their provenance and craftsmanship. Jane wandered away, perusing the aisles filled with goods, some of which seemed more broken than desirable.

The store was narrow and winding, a series of small connected rooms that took up the ground floor of a four-story building that might once have been a townhouse but now seemed to be cut up into individual apartments. Each little room was devoted to something different, from oil lamps to armoires—that last room had been very difficult to navigate. As she reached a room that fit her idea of what might once have been kitchens or a scullery, another customer entered. From her peripheral vision, she had the sense that he was a larger man, and really, he took up so much space in the tiny room. He was moving closer as if he wished to pass her. She looked to the side. Past her was one more shelf and then a door, possibly a door to the back alley, although she was disoriented in this winding space.

Jane stepped closer to the shelf, the edge of the wood

uncomfortable against her, but the man did not pass. Instead, he crowded her. She whirled around to give him a proper dressing down for practically accosting a woman. A fist hit her rib cage. "That's a knife I've got," a harsh voice said, and she recognized that the fist was wrapped around a blade that came to a sharp point. "Leave with me or you won't be leaving alive."

She jabbed her elbow back instinctually, and then a sweaty hand clasped over her mouth even as the knife dug into her side, stinging as it penetrated cloth and broke skin.

"Don't say a word," the man said with a grunt of effort as he yanked her toward him. "Unless you want it to be your last."

She looked around the room, so far from where she had left Silvie and the proprietor at the front of the store. She had thought nothing of venturing back to this corner to examine the wares. If she screamed, how fast would someone respond? Would it be before she'd been stabbed to death?

As she thought through the iterations of possible events, the man shuttled her to the rear door of the store, which led out into the mews. He pushed open the door and a gust of cold wind blew in.

Why was he trying to kidnap her? Did he perhaps want Silvie? There were any number of political reasons the princess might be threatened, but there was only one reason for Jane to be. Unless this was not a premeditated attack but some insane man intent upon… She did not wish to finish the thought.

She walked slowly, trying to give herself time to find some way to escape. Was there a carriage waiting down the lane? Or how else did he intend to transport her? Would she be able to signal help?

A loose stone beneath her foot gave her an idea and she forced herself to stumble. He tried to hoist her back up, the knife just grazing her flesh and causing a new stinging, but there was space, space to slam her heel back against his leg and then twist away.

Free of his grip, she ran for the open door, aware that he thundered behind her, gaining ground. He slammed her down. The ground was hard and cold beneath her, his weight heavy. Then the pressure of his body was gone and instead of the gravel of the man's voice, she could hear grunts and the sound of a struggle, of bodies engaged in a fight. She rolled to her side. There was a thundering of footsteps away from her. She looked down the alley where another man, in a dark green coat, raced after her attacker. At the end of the alley, the green-coated man hesitated, looked over his shoulder at her, and then came to a full stop, a full turn, and headed back her way.

She scrambled up from the ground in case this man was no more of a friend than the other. She had thought at first he must be an employee or patron of the store, but he cut a fierce figure with a nose that looked to have been broken multiple times and a large, muscular frame.

"Are you all right?" he asked in heavily accented English.

"Yes, thank you. Fortuitous that you stumbled upon us when you did."

The man's expression was rather grim as he shook his head. "If he had entered from the rear, I would not have been able to save you." He said the dire words as if he were criticizing himself for not being *more* heroic.

"Mr…"

"Bohm."

"Mr. Bohm, I do thank you very much. I have no idea who that man was—"

Bohm laughed humorlessly. "But you do. That was Szabo's man. You were supposed to stop asking questions."

She stared at him. "I don't understand."

"Badeau instructed me to protect you in his absence, but it is difficult to protect a woman who does not heed advice."

"How do I know this is true?" Despite her question, she believed him. The pieces fit into place in her mind.

"I have known him for a very long time, since he was a boy. But I can give you no proof other than my identity and my reputation. Ask any sporting man who Valentin Bohm is and you shall know of me."

A pugilist, then. Perhaps this was a complex plot to gain her trust, but she went with her instinct. "Would you accompany me home?"

He nodded.

As they made their way back through the store, Jane attempted a defense against his previous accusation. "I did, in fact, heed his advice," she said and then sighed. The conversation with Mrs. Abbings had seemed so innocuous and yet she had been drawn into a mistake. "He did not tell me he had hired me a bodyguard."

"I believe he did not wish to alarm you unnecessarily, or draw undue attention to my presence."

"I certainly am alarmed. And apparently need one very much. One *not* in the shadows." They had reached the front of the store and Silvie was still there chattering with the owner of the store as if there had been no commotion, nothing amiss anywhere else. When Jane stepped up to her and excused herself from the rest of the outing, Silvie looked at her with a frown, her gaze likely taking in every tear and speck of dirt on Jane's dress. Jane shook her head slightly and thankfully Silvie took the hint, turning her attention to Bohm.

"I know you, do I not?"

He smiled. "As I was telling Lady Jane, I am famous here in Vienna."

"Herr Bohm, yes." The proprietor was nodding now, too. Jane knew the recognition was a false sort of validation for her instinct. A famous man could as easily be a villain, but she had chosen to believe Bohm. He had, after all, just saved her life.

"I am not feeling quite the thing, cousin," Jane said.

Silvie sent her footman for the carriage, and used the few minutes of waiting to complete her purchase. She was a bit nonplussed to discover Bohm would be accompanying them, but in the carriage Jane explained a small portion of the events, that she had been set upon by a man determined to abduct her person. Silvie was suitably horrified and Jane wished for a moment she could confide everything to her cousin, discover if here there was really a kindred soul, someone who might understand or help Jane to better understand the recent events, the changes within herself.

Instead, Jane begged Silvie not to mention the incident to anyone, and the drive back to Jane's Vienna residence was filled with a falseness that discomfited her. She had never had reason to not be forthright. She understood and practiced discretion but fabricating events was a different matter entirely. Yet, she would simply have to live with the dissonance of her actions going against her values.

Once the door of the apartment had closed behind her, Jane started shaking. She wrapped her arms around herself, eyes stinging. Then the shaking grew worse and her teeth chattered as tears streamed down her face.

"Lady Jane, you had better sit." Bohm stopped, and she was aware that he spoke with a maid before he guided her into the sitting room. She let him direct her, his hand on her arm. Her face was hot, even as she shook uncontrollably.

"I can't stop shaking." He arranged a lap blanket around her on the sofa as if he were her maid. She murmured a thank you and wiped at her eyes.

"It is a normal reaction to a shocking event," Bohm said. "You've held up admirably."

Admirably. She had survived the carriage accident, traveled across many German countries and Austria, and had an affair with a man who was both spy and assassin. Comparatively, the incident in the antique shop was not any more traumatic, and yet— A sob escaped her. She covered her face with her hands, all too aware that a stranger was witnessing this collapse.

"Jane, what happened?"

Fear whipped through her. A strange reaction and yet at that same instant she knew it was because she had so much to hide. She took a deep breath, wiped the tears away, and looked up at her father who was striding into the room, a maid with a tea tray nearly on his heels.

"This man." She gestured to Valentin Bohm, aware that her hand trembled wildly. "He saved my life. Someone tried to abduct me."

"Where was your maid or your footman?"

"I was with Silvie. I thought perhaps the attempt was intended for her." That was an obfuscation, as that thought had been brief and easily disposed. "However, I am concerned... Herr Bohm, would you mind if I return momentarily?"

She rose, folding the blanket and placing it on the sofa. The action calmed her, steadied the residual trembling.

"Of course."

She walked with her father down the hall to the room that currently served as his study. It was pink and filled with delicate things and certainly had not originally been intended to be a man's sanctum.

"Father, I am concerned that this event had to do with Lord Powell's death. It isn't as if I didn't understand the meaning beneath your questions. So I want to know, why do you not think his death was an accident?"

She was not quite lying and that was the only thing that kept Jane from blurting out everything that had happened. But she could not reveal Gerard. If she must be a liar to protect him, then she would until she was given a reason to reveal him. Furthermore, Gerard was merely a tool, a dagger, so to speak. The one who needed to be brought to justice in the event Powell's death was unjust was the one who hired him.

She was making excuses for Gerard and it made her feel despicable and hopeless. How could she love a man who was dishonorable?

To support that irrational love, she was fishing for information. It was beneath her, and yet...

"Jane, this is very serious. What happened?"

"We were in an antiques shop near Michaelerplatz and a man put a knife to my side and instructed me to calmly leave with him or he'd hurt me. I struggled against him, but when he dug the knife into my side, making it clear he intended his words, I worried that I would not escape his knife fast enough if I did scream for assistance. I was on the ground, he was running away, and Herr Bohm was in fast pursuit. I hoped Herr Bohm, though I did not yet know his name, would return with the criminal for questioning. Herr Bohm did return, though not with the man."

"Jane…"

She gestured to her side. "My dress was ripped and I was bleeding and did not feel I could continue shopping in such an instance. I asked Silvie to keep the matter secret. I wanted to speak with you."

She could see the thoughts swiftly moving behind her father's eyes. She could only imagine their content.

"You did the right thing, my dear. We do not wish to create panic in Vienna. It is best to investigate quietly and not draw undue attention to the English delegation."

Although they were only on the fringes of the delegation, as English, their behavior would reflect on the rest, though it would be hard to surpass the more widely discussed, scandalous affairs of Talleyrand, Metternich and the Emperor Alexander, or to be more circumspect than Lord Castlereagh and his wife.

"What is happening, Father? Why have I been targeted?"

"I am not certain, but perhaps it was truly for Princess von Wolfstein."

"You don't believe that."

He sighed. "Why do you doubt me?"

She could have asked him the same. Except, she was, in fact, concealing truth from him. She suspected her father of the same. Perhaps it was her guilt that made her shade him with her motivations. *That* thought made her retreat.

"I would like to hire Herr Bohm for my personal protection while we remain in Vienna," she said simply.

"Who is this man?"

"As I understand it, he is a pugilist by trade. I am not certain what quirk of fate brought him to my assistance, but I am grateful."

A quirk of fate named Gerard. A quirk of fate that had changed everything six weeks earlier—the decision to travel with the Powells, Gerard's decision to let her live, the unimaginable ability of love to flower between two unlikely people.

"I am certain that a footman would be sufficient, but you have had a difficult month, and I wish to set your mind at ease. I shall speak to the fellow and if his reputation is honorable, will do my best to fulfill your request."

Anger seethed at the demeaning way in which her father addressed her, yet Jane smiled her gratitude. He had always appeared to show her intellect the greatest respect, had not judged her by her sex, but now, ever since she had arrived in Vienna, despite availing himself of her skills, he treated her as if she were nervous and prone to hysteria. As if she needed to be placated and coddled.

Of course, her father *had* just walked in on her sobbing like the worst sort of weakling. But though she could not reveal it to her father and risk exposing Gerard, Jane's fear for her own life was very real and grounded in fact.

And that fear deepened when her father came to her

the next day.

"Jane, my dear, I'm sending you back to London. With Mr. Bohm as your guard."

A chill ran down her spine at the words. Her father would not reveal so much, would not do anything so drastic, if he did not believe the threat to be serious. If other people he respected had not concurred. She wondered what interviews he had had that morning to form his opinions. Who had he spoken to? Who knew what? She was beyond frustrated that despite her questioning she had unearthed very little and accomplished nothing other than to put her life in danger. It was not the sort of actions she prided herself on, and she could not excuse herself by saying that it was out of her realm of experience. Wisdom and intellect were talents to be used when faced with new challenges. If she were only ever faced with tasks with which she was familiar, then she might as well be an automaton.

"Apparently your questioning has attracted unwanted attention."

"Apparently," she agreed, her tone uncharacteristically sarcastic.

"The reason *I* questioned *you* so closely is that we do have reason to believe that the accident was not in fact an accident. I imagine you were spared simply because you were unconscious. Perhaps these villains thought you dead."

"What does this have to do with England's aims?"

"I'm not certain," her father said, surprising her with that confession. "What this has brought to light is that Powell's last mistress was an Austrian spy." Jane blinked, more pieces of the puzzle coming together. The way Mrs. Abbings had attached herself to Jane, seemed inordinately interested in

Jane's work for her father. "Powell's death may have been related to that or to his role as an advisor on German affairs, as his wife was born in Saxony." Jane had known the last, it was why she had chosen Saxony for misdirection. But was it her questioning that had made that reach her father's ears or was the connection in truth one that was suspect?

But more interesting and frightening than that question was her father choosing to make this revelation at all. He was rarely so forthcoming about subjects he considered secret. Of course, for so long she had been his confidante and privy to many of those secrets, but still.

"Or it may be due to his partnership with Imre Szabo. The man is known as ruthless. I do not know."

Her father was worried enough to confide in her, to send her back to England, although perhaps that last was simply that she had become more trouble than help. In any event, if her life was in danger, then so was Gerard's.

No man was infallible and in his attempt to attain his goal, he was essentially stepping out of the shadows, out of his known world where he could protect himself, and into the public eye.

His goal: to make it possible for them to be together as more than secret lovers. And more than secret lovers meant marriage. Marriage to Gerard. A shared bed in some country home, where the air was sweet with hay and sunshine. The idea flashed through her mind so overwhelmingly that for a moment she forgot where she was.

Then she thrust it out of her mind. Suddenly a life with Gerard was appealing because she was no longer satisfied with the life she had. In a certain way, returning to England now was a failure of her intellectual life.

Perhaps Lady Jane Langley had not truly been reborn that day that Gerard happened into her life, but nothing was the same. Perhaps in London it would be different. She would settle easily into a routine, one in which she explored interests that did not revolve around her father's affairs. She had tried to please him, to mold herself into his son for so long, but she was not his son and never would be afforded the respect he would give one. The weight on her chest lightened. As much as she grieved at the truth of her father's respect, or lack thereof, this was a moment full of possibility, in which she could explore her own interests in whatever direction they might be.

London. Home. She was ready to return. Moreover, Gerard was in England. In a matter of days so would she be once more. Her heart bounced a bit in her chest, felt impossibly full. Perhaps, just as she had perceived her relationship to her father differently than the truth, she was viewing that with Gerard as a false dilemma. If he were truly able to gain his goal, an estate, the approbation of society, perhaps even a title, then why not marry him? Why not grasp happiness where she could?

Chapter Fourteen

Gerard stopped only briefly in Paris, settled certain accounts, read and returned correspondence. He sat in his apartment and stared at the wall that had been repaired since the day, nearly six months earlier, that his half brother, having learned of his wife's infidelity, had punched a hole through it.

Gerard felt oddly kindred with that wall. Like a hole had been punched through him, though not yet patched up. Perhaps never patched up. And perhaps the wall needed a hole in it. He was half inclined to reinstate it.

After all, those weeks with his brother had been the beginning of a schism within himself, one that had made him susceptible to Jane's appearance in his life. What if the order of the events had been reversed? Would his first meeting with Jane have been fatal for her?

Sitting there, in the closest thing to a home he had made since Badeau died, it was easier to see the events of the past weeks with some perspective, to understand that he no longer wished intrigue and death to be his life. Life—he was realizing that the one he had thought he enjoyed was merely a half life, as Jane said, a shadow life.

"Monsieur." Baptiste, his servant, entered the room with a letter. "The courier is awaiting your response."

The Fenningham School for Boys. Gerard opened it, shaking his head as he did so. In the last year, he had received a great many letters from the school's exasperated headmaster, all bemoaning the young man who refused to stay on the school's expansive estate.

This, too, had had an effect on Gerard, and perhaps in some way, Thomas had been a catalyst for change as well. Though Gerard had long supported the boy and his mother, her death had put Thomas entirely in Gerard's care. And the boy had shown his kinship by running away during the journey from London to Fenningham.

Apparently this would be the last time, from Fenningham's at least, as the headmaster suggested the boy not return. Of course, one would have to know where Thomas was to even consider making him return. Luckily, Gerard had a very good guess. Re-settling his brother was one more mission to accomplish while in London.

When Gerard arrived in London, as expected, he found his rooms at the Billingsley were already occupied. At half past eleven in the morning, the fourteen-year-old was enjoying a deep sleep in Gerard's own bed. He stared at Thomas, at the light brown hair so different from his own. In Thomas, the Templeton features were not so marked.

He let the boy sleep, unpacked his bags, and rang for a maid to draw a bath for him. The Billingsley had a fleet of maids who cleaned the apartments daily, although many residents had their own valets or additional servants. Gerard had never stayed in these rooms long enough to feel the assistance of additional servants was required. However, servants lent consequence, and it was time to establish his identity as more than an absentee tenant.

It was time to do a great many things. As he waited for the bath, he sat down at the table and started penning a series of missives. One to his brother, Marcus. Others, in code, to his servant in Paris, his man in Berlin, his banker in Frankfurt. He needed to disentangle himself from the residences and buildings he owned under other identities.

He needed to begin unraveling the web of obfuscation and cut any possible ties between them and Gerard Badeau.

Gerard had called upon his grandfather at his London home only some half dozen times. The first time, he had sauntered through the cavernous rooms of the house as if he were not affected by the opulence. He had seen more elegant and luxurious residences across Europe and was determined to exhibit that worldliness. It had been a young, poor man's attempt at evening the playing field, and his grandfather had no doubt seen right through it. In the few interactions Gerard had with Thomas, he had seen that same youthful bravado, although in Gerard a rigorous training had backed it up.

On this afternoon, Gerard noticed each carving and ornamentation. This house was built on the labor of men such as himself, and men who worked in the fields. On generations of labor. Yet, he, too, had benefitted from that labor, had gained a gentleman's education because of it. But Gerard had worked for his own wealth. Yet this ostentation was what he was angling for. A title. A house. Outward trappings that exhibited his wealth.

"Gerard Badeau," he said to the butler, handing him his card.

"His lordship is not at home."

"He will be at home to me. It has been an age since I have had the chance to reunite with my grandfather."

In all the years, aside from his conversations with Marcus and Jane, he had never claimed the relationship publically. However, as Gerard lived on the continent for the most part and under so many different aliases, he had never felt the loss of the connection. This was a new day.

"I shall see, sir."

He led Gerard to a sitting room. This was one he had waited in before, a large portrait of his father as a young boy hanging over the mantel. Each time Gerard had seen it, he had stared at that face, trying to understand the man the innocent child had become. Fathering bastards was nothing out of the ordinary for a man like him. For any man, really. But his father had done nothing to look after their care.

He heard the creaking of the Bath chair long before Lord Landsdowne entered the room, pushed by a footman. The contraption was huge and made his grandfather look small and frail, and of course that was likely what he intended.

"Gerard, this is unexpected," his grandfather said, holding out his ring-bedecked hand with a smile. Gerard stared at the jewels that winked in the light. Obeisance was what his grandfather expected.

Gerard laughed. "Then you are slipping."

Landsdowne nodded, pulling his hand back in. "I am an old man. It is to be expected." He turned to his servant. "Leave us. And close the door. I do not wish to be disturbed."

Shaking his head, Gerard took a seat, crossed his legs. "I've come to hang up my hat. No more spying, no more covert work. I've found a woman I wish to make my own and thus it is time for a respectable life."

"A woman. That is truly unexpected."

"You thought me a monk?"

"I thought you…untouchable by love."

Gerard didn't blink, but the statement saddened him. Perhaps he had been that way. But he did love. He loved Jane. He loved Marie and Giana and Thomas. He loved the siblings he had never known and never would. He loved Marcus, even as he found his half brother insufferable. He had loved his mother and Badeau, despite the betrayals. And he loved the old man before him who defied the confines of his body to be one of the wiliest minds in Europe. So many different types of love. They had been there all along but unacknowledged, compartmentalized to avoid any weakness.

"No longer."

"You want a gift then. For me to settle an annuity or some sort upon you. So you can afford this woman."

"Grandfather, I am worth some hundred and fifty thousand pounds at my latest reckoning. I am certain a wife would be *comfortable*. But…there are other barriers to the match."

"One hundred and fifty thousand pounds? That should certainly take care of most barriers," Landsdowne said with a laugh. "What is left? Her father does not wish to align himself with the illegitimate grandson of an earl?"

"You have never publicly acknowledged me," Gerard said. He paused for a moment, tempted to ask his grandfather why that was, but at the same time admitting he wished to know felt like a weakness. "But no, the woman herself objects."

"You announced yourself as my grandson tonight. Is that what you want?"

Gerard met his grandfather's intent stare. Everything within him cautioned him to keep his secrets, put up a false front, but he was tired of lies. "In part. More than that, I want a title."

Landsdowne barked a laugh. "You do not dream small."

"No."

"If this woman will only have you with a title, perhaps some other country... I am certain titles are being redistributed in France."

The gallows humor jest did not sit well with Gerard.

"She is English. Only an English title will do."

"And that is her price?"

Her price. Jane had never directly asked for such a thing but she did not want to lose her social position. There were few ways to overcome the stigma of illegitimacy. Landsdowne's public support, and that of his friends, would be a help. As would Gerard's wealth. However, a title would ensure it. And no, Gerard could not afford to dream small. But the details were not necessary for Landsdowne to know.

"Who is she?" his grandfather pressed.

In the normal course of things, Gerard himself, acting as his grandfather's informant, would be bringing this sort of gossip back to his grandfather for the man to use as he saw fit. Landsdowne did not like being surprised, but no doubt he would be.

"Lady Jane Langley."

Landsdowne's eyes widened and his mouth moved silently. "She is not for you."

"She is, in fact, mine."

His grandfather's fingers tapped on the edge of his chair, his lips thinned. He was thinking through the matter and working toward his conclusion. Gerard waited. He knew his grandfather's process. "Langley will kill me. Does he know?"

Gerard shook his head.

"Money, an estate. That is all I can offer you."

"Not enough."

"I cannot go to the Regent and request—"

"Why not?"

"If they know about you— You are one of the few men whose discretion I trust. You must understand that the intelligence you have gathered for me no one can know."

That stopped Gerard for a moment. "What did you do with that knowledge if not protect England?"

"It is not so blunt. Guidance to England must be done subtly, lest people act out of pure reaction. I have my enemies."

But his grandfather's reasoning was flawed. Gerard had taken pains for his identity as Badeau to remain untainted. Unless Landsdowne had said something to someone, and the idea was ludicrous, there was no reason that his support of an illegitimate son should reveal Gerard's work as a spy. "They need know nothing. Surely enough gold and your support could buy a minor title."

"I cannot take the risk, Gerard. There will be questions into your past."

"You made me what I am."

"I made you into a gentleman, despite the circumstances of your birth. I paid for your education."

"In death and machinations."

Landsdowne frowned. "Machinations but not death," he said sternly. "Not once did I instruct you to kill."

"It was the logical progression. You entrusted me to Badeau's care."

"And he taught you the art of diplomacy," Landsdowne said, grabbing his cane from the side of his chair and standing up. He looked agitated.

"Of secrecy and spies, of intrigue and assassination."

His grandfather's mouth twisted in something resembling disgust and the expression knifed through Gerard. "It was you then," Landsdowne said. "Lord and Lady Powell."

"An interesting leap." Gerard's eyes narrowed in concentration. But the puzzle was not long unsolved.

"How else would you have met Lady Jane?"

Gerard nodded at the deduction. It was not a very far jump at all to one who knew all the facts.

"Why?"

It always came back to this. Why Lord Powell? Of course Lord Landsdowne would wish to know. And Jane wished to know. It was such a simple story. Powell's bedside murmurings to his Austrian spy mistress had ruined Szabo's chances of a royal contract. As successful as Szabo was, he had regretted his low birth and envied Powell. Gerard's stomach roiled. How similar he had become to Szabo, reaching above himself, wanting something that a bastard born to a Jew should never hope to attain. Wanting Jane. "There are some secrets to which you will never be privy."

"What have you become?" His grandfather was shaking his head, judgment heavy in his eyes.

Gerard forced himself to smile and to keep his fists relaxed. He had never before hated his grandfather or the life that he had lived.

"If you will not assist me, we have no more business to discuss." Gerard started to take his leave and then stopped, one question still burning in his mind. "Why me? Why out of all the bastards did you choose me? Do you even know what became of the others?"

Landsdowne seemed to deflate at that. He shook his head. "Do you know?" His voice shook. "There were five others. Your father…after you, he demanded I stop interfering in his life."

Gerard laughed harshly. "And you did?"

"At that point there was only little Marie… Her mother, a widow, had remarried. There was no reason to intervene. I kept track of the others, but…"

"What of when he died?"

Landsdowne was silent. He looked to the portrait of his wife and two sons, all of whom had died before him. "They were not foremost in my mind."

G erard walked back to his rooms, eschewing a hack for a chance to sort out his thoughts in the brisk air. His gut churned.

His grandfather had never intended for Badeau to teach Gerard the darker arts, regretted that he had not taken care of the other illegitimate scions. But he would not help.

A slow anger built and seethed inside Gerard. At his

father by blood and at Badeau, the father who raised him. At his grandfather. At fate and the life to which he had been resigned. A half life of which he had thought himself master, but he had been little more than a pawn. Jane had been right about that. Jane who would only speak the truth to him, who loved him despite it all.

Loved him but refused him.

The anger grew. At himself, at the world. At Szabo and even at Jane. He didn't deserve her but he could not let her go.

Fury flowed like a red wave inside him by the time he reached the Billingsley. Bitterness fueled the fire. The rage pushed at his skin, at his face, threatening to turn into an emotion perilously like despair.

He barely nodded at the footman who opened the door for him. The pounding of his feet on the wooden stairs matched the pounding of his heart. For the first time that he could remember, there was nothing of reason in him. As he opened the door to his rooms, he wanted nothing more than to throw himself on his bed and sleep. Not that he would sleep. There was more to do this day. Landsdowne was not the only path, simply the one Gerard had preferred.

"I won't return there. I won't and you can't make me."

He skidded to a halt and stared at the boy who stood in the middle of the sitting room, hands fisted and trembling with righteous anger. Gerard closed the door behind him and held his tongue. He needed to be careful not to misdirect his fury.

He took a deep breath and all the emotion cascaded into exhaustion. Here was this half brother of his who had had more of a youth than Gerard, who had the luxury of rebelliousness. He barely knew the boy, but instead of running away completely, Thomas had simply turned up in Gerard's rooms, which meant something.

"Then I won't."

The boy frowned. "I don't believe you. You always drag me back. You or that clod you hire."

Gerard slipped out of his shoes and his coat and tore the cravat from his neck. Thinking, he walked to the window and stared down at the mews behind. Fenningham was out of the question at this point, but it was likely any other school would be equally loathed. He turned back to his brother and leaned against the window. "Before my work took me from London too frequently to care for you—"

"I don't need anyone to—"

Gerard laughed. "You certainly need someone to teach you manners. However, there is time for that. For now, you will reside with me. We shall find you a tutor and you may learn at home."

"Truly?" All at once the boy looked far younger than his years and Gerard recalled his last conversation with Jane. Family. More than any of the others, this one needed him.

"Truly. And now that we've taken care of that matter of business, pack a bag. We are off to visit Lord Templeton."

Thomas's eyes bugged. "That's…"

"Our half brother, yes. Apparently you do listen on occasion."

"But he's a lord."

"The honorific makes him no more special than you or I in the eyes of the law. And what of it, in any event? It does not make him more or less of a man." Just as Gerard would not be if he succeeded in his quest.

He ran a tired hand through his hair. He wanted to see Jane, to lie in her arms and feel her pulse against him. He wanted her to say she loved him again, but this time to say she was his, title or not, England or not. But those were foolish thoughts and there was work to be done.

Marcus, Lord Templeton, chose to spend the majority of his time at his country estate, where he had his soap factory and where he doted on his wife and daughter. Gerard had never visited his half brother at the man's home. The last time he had seen him had been in Firenze nearly half a year earlier. Theirs was an uneasy relationship that veered from friendship to…to something indefinable by anything other than the bond of blood.

Gerard did not believe Marcus had sway with anyone of import. His brother, despite his title and his role as heir to the vast Landsdowne fortune, was essentially a pawn in the schemes of others, as apparently was Gerard. But there were other ways in which Marcus might be useful. Such as Thomas, who needed a stable home, one that Gerard could not provide until this matter was completed.

They were expected, as Gerard had written to Marcus with the intention of bringing Thomas to stay with him for a brief while until other accommodations could be found. Now that need was more urgent. But the family reunion was awkward at best. Thomas stood stiffly at Gerard's side as he was introduced to Lord Templeton, then Lady Templeton, and their daughter Leona. The whole thing was made only less awkward when Leona asked if Thomas wanted to see her dog, Puffin. Thomas surprisingly accepted his role as playmate and agreed.

Lady Templeton lingered a moment more before excusing herself. Alone in the sitting room, Gerard ran a heavy hand through his hair and girded himself.

"I need your advice."

Marcus raised an eyebrow. "*My* advice? If I recall correctly, you were furious with me for saving the life of your quarry."

"You merely assured his death."

Marcus paled. "What do you do? What does our grandfather ask of you?"

"Let us walk in the garden." Gerard wanted to stand in the sunshine even though the day was cold. He wanted no shadows or hidden ears about as he told fragments of this story. *His* story. The one he had come to understand better as he shaped it for Jane.

The garden directly to the rear of the house was a neatly laid out series of hedges, sandy paths, and grass. The organized beauty made it easier to construct his thoughts.

"A man reaches a certain age, a certain place in life, and he reflects on what has passed thus far."

Marcus nodded.

"Thomas is young. I could not save everyone, but Thomas still has a chance."

Gerard felt the cool distance between them, the fine line between legitimacy and bastardy. If Marcus had ever been interested in knowing more about his half siblings, he had never pursued that inclination. He had had the stability of a known lineage, of the approbation of society. An easy life. Whereas Gerard had... In many ways Gerard had had a better life than any of his other illegitimate siblings. Yes, Marie had found contentment, but that was luck.

"Our grandfather's interest in me has been both a blessing and a curse." Gerard told an abridged version of his training and his work for Landsdowne. "Choosing to do such work for others? A man wishes to be the master of his own destiny, not his grandfather's puppet."

Marcus's lips thinned and he nodded in acknowledgment. Yes, Gerard's half brother would understand this. He had been so under Landsdowne's thumb that he had nearly lost his chance for happiness with the woman he loved.

Gerard ran a hand over his face. He had ridiculed Marcus privately, but now, now he was in a situation all too similar, struggling to find a way to be with the woman *he* loved, despite his grandfather's machinations. Landsdowne was not responsible for Gerard's illegitimacy, but he had certainly tried to shape Gerard's life to fit his own needs. Ruthlessly.

If their grandfather would not help him, then Gerard would use the training he had been given to help himself, the same way he had chosen to work for others.

"Over the years, I've amassed information that I have no doubt would be of use to England in her negotiations." All of it had been discovered in the course of his work, but did not compromise that work, was not directly related. He would not have to break his own code of secrecy and trust. "Men have been gifted nobility for less."

"You want a title," Marcus said flatly.

"I want a woman, and a title will get me the woman I want."

"Ah." Marcus laughed and the sound was slightly harsh.

"I see. Who is this woman that you would trade your life of independence for servitude to the crown?"

Servitude. That word again. No less than the truth. "Lady Jane Langley."

Silence met his proclamation, and then laughter.

"You do not aim low, do you? I would never in all my life have guessed, but I do see now why you are so desperate to gain yourself a title."

Desperate. Another word that unsettled Gerard. He detested feeling in any way inferior and for the great majority of his thirty-four years he had not once. Until faced with a desire that his mere birth had made impossible from the outset. But Gerard was not inferior and he had always made the impossible possible. It was why his services had been in such demand, why he had amassed a fortune, why he— He broke off his thoughts, disgusted with the weakness of his need to bolster himself in any way.

"Who should I see?"

Marcus shook his head. "All right, listen. Go to Horse Guards," he said. "There is a man there, Anche, who oversees the gathering of intelligence. If anyone can assist you in this endeavor, it will be him. I shall write you a letter of introduction. I know him well enough for that."

It was more than Gerard had expected. "You don't worry the family name will be dragged through the mud through association with me?"

"Yes and no," Marcus said. "I am angry enough with our grandfather to want him to suffer the consequences of his meddling in the affairs of others."

Gerard nodded. He had hoped for that. "Thank you. The other matter…Thomas."

"You wish me to take him in."

"Temporarily, until I have this matter settled and can provide something more for him."

Marcus shook his head again. "How strange this life is."

"He's just a boy. His life relatively easy despite his loss. I wish him be spared."

"Save him, save us all?"

Gerard laughed at the succinct mocking statement. But there was truth in there. "Something like that."

But Thomas would not be left and would not be reasoned with, and although Gerard knew it would be better for the boy, he relented.

"I am sorry, you know," Marcus said, pulling Gerard aside before he mounted his horse. "That our grandfather… that your life has been what it was. I did not know it was not your choice."

Gerard laughed again but this time it was without mirth. The horse snorted, too, as if it knew how ridiculous the sentiment was. Knew its rider was heartless to the core. "Don't fool yourself, brother. A better man than I would have made different choices, would not have followed where others led. I had a choice. We all do."

The following day Gerard called upon Mr. Anche, a slight, unprepossessing man with narrow eyes that Gerard understood instantly. This was a man well versed in intrigue.

It was strange to be standing there, dressed as any other well-to-do gentleman in London, using the name he most considered his own, revealing a considerable portion of his history, if not the specific details of the work he had done.

"I am fascinated, Mr. Badeau, by your background. I always wondered how that wily Landsdowne managed to know of events before my own men. If you were his secret weapon, then you are a useful man indeed." Gerard and a whole fleet of informants. "We'll find a place for you," Anche said.

Gerard frowned. "I'm not a spy."

"Reconnaissance, if you prefer."

As if the word used made any difference. "I don't work for any country. I am not looking for a position."

"Hmm." Anche picked up the letter of introduction from Marcus again, put it down. "Then what do you want?"

Everything inside Gerard buzzed with anticipation. This was his best, his only chance, perhaps, to gain what he desired.

"My knowledge for a title."

Anche laughed. "You are a bold man to walk in here and offer such a trade. French by birth, are you not? I am certain we can find crimes against England that you have committed."

"I very much doubt that," Gerard said with a smile. "And I assure you, I do have knowledge that Lord Castlereagh would find quite useful."

Anche waved his hand dismissively. "We are up to our eyeballs in information, Mr. Badeau. Most of it is irrelevant."

"There have been fifty-seven plots to rescue Napoleon from Elba. It is only a matter of time before one of these come to fruition."

"That is hardly news."

Gerard raised an eyebrow.

"Seventeen have been documented."

"My point, Mr. Anche."

"Why should I believe you?"

"Speak with Lord Landsdowne. I know he does not wish his machinations to be known by all, but I am certain he would be forthcoming if questioned. He and his 'Group of Eight.'"

"That pretentious coterie? A gentleman's club," Anche scoffed.

"This is my gift to you, free of charge, Mr. Anche," Gerard said. "Never take anything at face value."

"The king grants titles, Mr. Badeau."

"Yes, I understand. For services to the crown."

"Yes. I must consult with others but I need your word. I will have all the information you possess."

"That I am free to share, which is extensive."

"What is your direction? I will inform you at a later date."

Gerard gave the Billingsley. He was finished with a life of disguises. Giving up these secrets would be part of that.

He stepped out of the office, down the hallway, his boots echoing on the wooden floor, down the stairs and across the courtyard with its stench of hay, horse and exertion. He crossed St. James Park and then stopped in the center of it and looked around at a small park ringed with gray buildings, all shrouded by the damp mist.

He had one more stop, to see his solicitor. Regardless of the outcome of the meeting with Anche, he would need a home. The Billingsley was no place for a rebellious youth like Thomas.

Chapter Fifteen

The journey back to England was nothing like the one to Vienna. It passed uneventfully, her maid and Bohm by Jane's side at all times. Silvie, too, as her cousin decided to serve as companion and visit the country that years of war had made impossible to access. The only dramatic moments were those in Jane's head as she relived again and again the past six weeks as the couch jarred across the hard earth. She had the strong sense that she was traveling *from* her father *to* Gerard, not merely in the geographical sense.

"Jane," Silvie said one night as they dined in yet another inn's private dining room. Sometimes Bohm dined with them, but often, like tonight, he chose to give them privacy, and to dine in the main hall. "This melancholia is not simply due to the threat to your life. I know these symptoms. Love is a very painful affliction."

"Love itself is quite pleasant and uplifting," Jane said, hesitating. She wasn't certain how much she could tell her cousin, but she needed to work through her conflicted thoughts and perhaps Silvie would offer a perspective Jane lacked. "It is the fact that the man himself is not entirely suitable. I told him it is impossible, but I am no longer certain that decision is the wisest."

"How unsuitable is he?"

"Very. He is the illegitimate grandson of the Earl of Landsdowne." She saw no reason to hide that bit of information. After all, Gerard Badeau was the man who wooed her, who had been introduced to her father.

"I see. The illegitimate son of a royal duke, a prince or a king would be acceptable if he were in favor with his father and if he possessed some influence and wealth of his own. Your English society is so rigid. Unless there are extenuating circumstances you have not yet revealed, this situation *is* problematic."

Somehow Jane had hoped Silvie would say something more encouraging. Yet, her cousin gave exactly the response Jane most admired: the truth.

"When I was nineteen, the summer before I married, I fell in love."

"This does not sound like a story about falling in love with the prince."

Silvie laughed. "And so it is not. I fell in love with a rank and file soldier. Nothing to distinguish him from any other but that he was wild and had traveled the world, and I was impetuous and had not. I wanted his experience and I fell in love with him for it. But when he asked me to run away with him…I said no. Two months later, I was engaged to Von Wolfstein."

"You make it seem as if you were not truly in love with him."

"I ridicule myself to make the loss easier. My life with him would have been harder, grueling even. I would have been exiled from everyone I knew and cared for. But he made me feel alive and at the time I believed myself deeply in love. The only thing that makes me feel alive now is traveling."

"You do not love your husband." Something about that made Jane's chest twinge. Only a handful of months ago she would have thought nothing of a loveless marriage, especially one that had made Silvie a princess with the freedom and resources to enjoy life as she wished. Now, it all seemed so very sad, tragic almost.

Silvie sighed. "I do not know him. We have shared a bed, a dining table, the carriage en route to Vienna, and yet...he has his mistress and his duty to the country. I chose him but I resent him."

"So I could choose Gerard and a life... He is not impoverished but I very much doubt we would be invited or accepted to the society I currently frequent. Or, I can keep my friends and acquaintances, the respect of society and either live alone forever, or choose a man who is a stranger to marry, who will always be a stranger. And if I never marry, there are many who will pity me for that choice as well."

"Or you might meet another man with whom you fall in love who conveniently happens to be nobility."

"Or that," Jane said, but it didn't feel very likely, especially now that she had experienced everything she had. What other man would ever understand? Would ever embrace all the disparate facets of her character?

"Are you certain you love him? How did you meet?"

Jane's mind whirled. So many questions, so many things

to consider. She chose the easiest question first and opted for some part of the truth.

"On the road to Vienna," Jane said slowly. "He…helped me when I was injured."

"I thought an old woman took you in," Silvie said archly.

"Eventually." Jane met Silvie's gaze with a rueful smile. "What was I to say? I spent days in a man's company when I was bedridden and unable to move?"

Silvie laughed. "I suppose being injured put a bit of a damper on the affair."

"At least until Vienna."

"My mousey, studious little cousin. Always so proper and papa's little girl. I am shocked, my dear, to hear of your indecent liaison!"

"Ha." Jane laughed too. It was so good to be able to share even this small part of all the recent confusing events. To admit to caring for Gerard. To admit to his existence. And Silvie, of all people, understood.

Their friendship blossomed after that night and Jane was grateful for her cousin's company. It kept her mind off the intrigues and dangers of Vienna, the betrayal of her father, the fact that Gerard had likely discovered already that his grandfather would be of no assistance. But Silvie had asked if Jane was certain she loved Gerard, and that question she did consider, over and over again.

She had resisted admitting to love until that last night in Vienna, despite a heart that pulled toward Gerard like a lodestone seeking true north. She did love him. Did the fact that she thought love not enough make that love any less real? Any less true?

It had been so easy to place other desires above love

before she had understood the emotion, but it was no longer so. Perhaps, back in London, society would once again hold the same interest it previously had. The politics of Vienna should have held her interest. Instead, she had turned into a lovestruck and lovesick ninny, the likes of whom should only be found in gothic novels. Not that Jane had read any of those. Perhaps she ought to start and complete her transformation. And then run away with Gerard when he failed to rise above the stain of his illegitimate birth.

As the boat pulled up to dock in the early hours of the morning, the city that was so dear and known to her looked unchanged, made her feel almost unchanged, as if everything from the day she boarded a carriage for the channel and the day she stepped off a boat in the Thames had been a dream. But the man at her left, the guard Gerard had hired for her protection, was proof that it was not.

She glanced at Bohm out of the corner of her eyes. Their gazes caught for an instant and he nodded almost imperceptibly, letting her know she was protected. She wanted to see Gerard. She was furious with him. Furious and…eager. She'd admit that to herself.

After the carriage deposited them safely at the Langley townhouse, she took Bohm aside. She didn't want to wait for Gerard to come to her. "Will you find him?" she asked.

Bohm nodded and she had utter confidence in that short gesture. If only she had confidence in her own desires.

Gerard Badeau called on her that morning. Entering through the front door of the Langley townhouse, announced into the parlor by the footman. The knocker had only just been put back on the door. The servants, though they had received advance notice to expect them any day, were still adjusting to having Jane and Silvie there. But *he* was here. In London. In *her* house. Dressed fashionably and precisely, as if he were a man who cared about such things.

This was not the wilds of the continent, or even a foreign city apart from her usual life. This was London, her territory, and he was here. She waved her maid away. And then he was enveloping her, taking up all of the air in the room even as his breath mingled with hers, his hand cupping her cheek, hips, lips merely an inch from hers, even though the last time they had seen each other the tension had been thick and nothing had been resolved.

"If something had happened to you…"

She pushed him away, her conflicted emotions settling into pique. "Except you hired a bodyguard for me."

"And I am thankful I did."

"As am I, but you should have told me! I had to decide to trust him. I had no way of verifying that what he said was true."

Gerard was silent.

"Keep your secrets that you feel bound to keep, but do not treat me as if I am not capable, as if I cannot be trusted with the truth. You say you love me, but…the reason I am not married yet is that I do not wish a man who treats me as inferior." As her father did despite the years she had assisted him. Despite the knowledge she had amassed over the years, the fact that her judgment had never failed her yet. At least, not when she had enough knowledge to make an informed decision.

But loving Gerard had been one of those decisions.

At the same time, loving Gerard had not been a decision at all, which was why she had not resisted the emotion but had resisted the *unwise* decision to commit herself to him together.

"You are right. I endangered you even more." He looked incredibly remorseful. More than that, he looked... devastated. That excess of emotion angered her more.

"Oh, don't flagellate yourself over it. That isn't my point. If I wanted to be with a man who did not think me intelligent or strong enough to hear the truth, however painful or difficult it may be, then I might as well have married years ago."

"Jane." Gerard looked aghast. "I have never met a woman or man I have esteemed more."

She let out a deep breath, feeling her anger deflate. "Then promise me you will *trust* me."

"Come here." He pulled her into him and she let him surround her again. "I am done with secrets, Jane. I do not deserve you but you are still mine. I am still yours."

She buried her face against him. This man had been her caretaker as well as her lover. She could show him weakness because he did believe in her strength.

"I have not led an honorable life such as you would like me to have led."

"I understand that." She didn't like it but it was what it was. This was the man with whom she had fallen in love.

"Jane...I went to see my grandfather." His arms tightened around her.

"He would not help you."

"All these years I thought he knew what Badeau was

teaching me." There was pain in Gerard's voice, emotion breaking through the words. Her heart swooped up to catch his. "I thought he intended it. I understood that there was work Badeau wished me to do that was not likely to be what my grandfather had ordered, but I did not understand that there was a limit to Landsdowne's orders."

"The assassinations."

He buried his head in her neck, even as she still held her breath, as she struggled to come to terms with this man she held in her arms. He had told her so little of his life, and of the work he had done. But Powell, at least, she knew had been to repay a debt on behalf of his mentor. In a way it was an act of honor. Not traditional honor but... She closed her eyes against the stupid way she was trying to justify his actions. They were what they were. She had fallen in love with him despite them, and perhaps in part because of the rawness of his power. The angel of death.

"Jane." The note of pain in his voice made her chest ache. She stroked his back, breathed in his scent. "I loved Badeau. I wanted—needed—a father, and he was that. But what father..."

She swallowed hard, focused on his need. "I suspect he did not regret his life or his actions, and therefore did not feel he was doing you harm. There is always good with the bad." The need to prove herself to her own father that had inspired her to push herself beyond any perceived limits. She moved away so she could meet Gerard's eyes. "But it is not the life *you* choose. The past is the past."

Those dark eyes stared back, searching, intent upon her. "And my future?"

She sighed, but her chest remained tight. He wanted the

answer she could not yet give. Landsdowne had refused to help him, as she had suspected. What sort of life could she have with Gerard as he was? Perhaps this affair was no more lasting than Silvie's had been with her common soldier. Gerard's will had taken it this far. She could still stop it. Before this ruined her.

He was already in her sitting room, in her house. He had already been inside her body, joined to her in the most intimate way possible.

"You *want* to leave your life, Gerard. I do not wish to leave mine. But I do not see how you fit into this world."

"There might be another way. My brother directed me to a Mr. Anche."

Anche, the government official who not so secretly was in charge of informants and spies. She had met him before, had disliked him instantly for some reason she could not quite explain. He was a plain man and yet he was threatening, darkness beneath. But he dealt with secrecy as well. Perhaps darkness was a necessary trait to work with shadows.

"How do you know he won't arrest you? Not all your work has been on England's behalf. Surely you have done acts that would be considered treasonous for an Englishman." Gerard didn't deny it and a chill went down her spine. "You cannot trust Anche. Information for a title, I understand your goal, but it will not be a fair trade."

"What do you know of him?" Gerard asked. Implacable, determined to achieve his goal, so strong and yet so vulnerable because he loved her.

Loved her. Her eyes stung.

She looked away. "He came up out of nowhere, amassed power, ran his own department independent of the War

Office during the war. I have nothing to base my instinct on, but…"

"I am due to see him this afternoon." Gerard touched her cheek, wiped at the wetness she hadn't yet blinked away. "You needn't worry. I will be careful," he said. "I expect to pay more than my weight in gold."

She stepped into his arms and lifted her face to his. "I *am* afraid. Of what could happen to you, of what would happen to us if you do by some chance succeed and what would happen if you fail. But I love you. No matter what, know that. I do love you."

He crushed her in his embrace, his lips hard against hers, the kiss anything but gentle. The way his emotions were riotous inside of him. She would not yield, and he understood. If he did not understand, he would not now still be vying for her hand in every way he possibly could.

He wanted to hear her say it again, that she loved him. The words were still a marvel to him, both his own emotions and to know she returned them.

"Oh, I'm terribly sorry."

Jane broke away.

The sound of the door shutting filled the room. She brought her hand to her cheek, then let out a nervous laugh. Gerard looked behind him, confirming that whoever had disturbed them had chosen to leave just as quickly.

"My cousin, Silvie, accompanied me from Vienna and is acting as companion in my father's absence. She knows about you."

He raised a questioning eyebrow and enjoyed the way that Jane blushed.

"Well...she knows that you exist. Not how we met but that you are Lord Landsdowne's illegitimate grandson and that I love you."

It was strange to hear her describe him in such a way. Part of a lineage even if the wrong side of the blanket, and his grandfather had been unwilling to support him, although by approaching Anche and telling him about the part his grandfather had played, he had forced Landsdowne's hand. It was strange as well to know that Jane had discussed their affair with her cousin.

"She was there the day Szabo's man tried to abduct me." She rubbed her hands over her arms and Gerard drew her back into his embrace. His stomach clenched again the way it had the minute Bohm told him about the attempted abduction.

"I should never have left you."

"I feel like such a fool but my life was never truly in danger before."

The wreckage of the carriage, her warm neck under his hand. A year earlier and he would have killed her without a second thought. In that moment he hated himself.

"I think I knew from the first that you would not hurt me."

Each word she said was a dagger into him.

"Except I have," he said harshly. "And still I am asking everything of you, Jane. I don't care that I am what most people would consider a villain. It is entirely possible I will never be able to come to you and ask for your hand as a gentleman in society, but I want you. I need you. I will move heaven and earth to make you mine."

"So dramatic. Hopefully the celestial bodies may stay where they are." Her words were light and his lips twisted in acknowledgment. Except, dramatic as they were, he had meant every syllable of it. "Gerard, I...I want you to succeed. In the meantime, perhaps you would like to stay for lunch?"

Lunch, here in this townhouse, in broad daylight. He had already walked boldly up the front stairs as if he had every right to do so. He had left all the other iterations of identity behind. All that was left was Gerard Badeau. And she wanted him to succeed. The knowledge was a balm to his aching heart. He had told Marcus that all choices were his own, that was true, and now he was making a different choice. One that brought him to a strange moment of sitting at the long dining table in the Langley townhouse, with its polished silver and freshly cut flowers. To have Jane by his side and her cousin—Silvie—across.

The princess was of an age with him, with a face defined more by character and experience than by some ephemeral beauty, and over the noon meal they chatted about the weather, and the journey, about Vienna and the inconclusive congress that seemed to drag on far beyond its original intentions. Jane led the conversation from one relatively safe topic to another until, sitting in the parlor after the meal, enjoying the crackling fire and the pleasure of having had a good meal, Silvie turned to him and asked, "So, do tell me about yourself, Mr. Badeau—"

"Silvie," Jane said quickly, a warning note in her voice, even as she shot Gerard an apologetic look.

"It might be unsaid, but it is as obvious as if there were

a tiger in the room," Silvie said, persisting and directing her comment to Gerard. "I know so little but that this...affair between yourself and my cousin is something of a secret. Never fear I'll spill it, but I confess I am curious."

"My cousin is rude."

"Your cousin is curious," Silvie corrected her. "And I have never conformed to society's expectations. Why should I now?"

"There is very little to tell," Gerard said with a laugh. He rather liked Silvie, even though her questioning focused on him. "My grandfather, despite the circumstances of my birth, was kind enough to fund my education and ensure I could live the life of a gentleman. As I have. I have traveled much of my life but I call Paris home for lack of a more substantive place."

"And how did you stumble upon our Jane?"

"I am certain Jane regaled you with the best version of the story."

"The secret version," Jane said, her words rushed. "I did tell her that we met when I was injured, that you took care of me. That we couldn't tell anyone for the sake of my reputation."

He laughed. "So you left out the very romantic way I carried you in the rain for miles?"

She looked down. "There are certain moments when one is falling in love that one prefers to keep private."

That love surged inside Gerard, at how quickly Jane adapted the story, at how she picked carefully between truth and lies.

"So there you have it, Madam," he said. "Your cousin foolishly fell in love with me and now she cannot get rid of me. But I hope to convince her to make an honest man of me."

"There is more to this story," Silvie said. "But as curious as I am, as much that I feel in lieu of Jane's father being here, as her older, and very likely at this moment wiser, cousin, I need protect her interests, I shall leave it at that. My sense is that you are a chameleon, Mr. Badeau, that you would fit in anywhere, charm anyone if need be."

"Silvie," Jane said again, but Gerard held up a hand.

"It is quite all right, Jane. Your cousin is perceptive but it is no more than you yourself already know of me. You know my worst flaws and still you say you love me. A love I know I do not deserve."

Silvie laughed. "You are *good*, Mr. Badeau. I shall leave it. Jane, you are warned. Mr. Badeau—"

"I take no offense," Gerard said, even though inside his gut was wrenching. Though he was determined to make Jane his own, she had never committed to him fully. What if Silvie convinced her— He looked to Jane, whose hands were fisted, silently seething. "I must go. I am expected elsewhere."

"I shall walk you to the door," Jane said.

They walked silently down the stairs to the front hall. The footman stood at the door, ready to open it. There was little space for privacy here. At the bottom of the stairs, he took her arm, held her still for a moment as he lowered his head near to her ear.

"I am sorry about—"

"Never mind your cousin," he said quickly. "I will come to you after midnight. Which window is yours?"

She shook her head. "I will leave the garden door unlocked and meet you in the library. No need to scale walls."

"Warn Bohm, if you will. I have no desire to be attacked. Where is he, in any event?" He looked about, disconcerted that the man was not there. Bohm's presence was the only thing that allowed Gerard to feel at ease away from Jane.

"Gentleman Jackson's. He ran into an old pupil and the young man demanded he visit and tell tales to all his friends. As I did not intend to go out this morning, I saw no reason to keep him here."

Gerard pressed his lips together tightly. He could not fault the man. Or Jane. Though the townhouse was hardly a fortress, she was well protected. "Don't leave until he returns," he said.

"I won't."

"Then I will see you tonight." He lingered a second more, wanting to make the day progress faster to the hour of his meeting with Anche, but not wanting to leave Jane at all.

Finally he walked to the front door, which the footman opened. And in broad daylight, in full view of prying neighbors and anyone who cared at all, Gerard Badeau left the townhouse and descended back into the world.

The afternoon took him back to Anche, to that office that smelled of wood and sweat.

The man wasted no time in his conversation. "A barony. Alandale. It is a minor estate in Somerset that will be attached. Naturally, there will be a price as well."

Baron Alandale. Triumph soared through Gerard. Yes, Jane would still be relinquishing some level of position, he did understand the sensitivity of matters of hierarchy, but the schism would be much less. To gain such a position was an impossible feat for the son of a Jew, illegitimate by birth and barely acknowledged by both his mother and his father's family. Yet he would.

"Of course, the crown requires a test of loyalty."

Before Anche continued, Gerard knew. A darkness seeped into his bones even as he tried to shake it. This he should have expected. The information he shared was not enough. Of course not. He was a resource they could not let go to waste.

He wanted to say no, but how could he return to Jane and say that he had failed, that the most he could offer her was a home, material comforts, his love. She would lose her position in society. There were ramifications to their union of which he could only guess. More likely than not, Jane would refuse. He could not fault her for that. Her cousin Silvie would be satisfied.

He smiled tightly, pushing back the insidious terror that snaked through him, and presented to Anche only the calm, collected exterior, the assassin who would consider such a thing.

It was simply one more mission. The key to his freedom and his future.

Nothing he had not done before.

Chapter Sixteen

It was not unusual for Jane to stay up late in the library, nor even unheard of for her to fall asleep sitting sideways in one of the deep, high-backed chairs, legs dangling over the arms. But this night she did not sleep. She was too full of restless anticipation.

Her cousin's interference had surprised her. They were second cousins, their grandmothers sisters. They had only seen each other a handful of times throughout their life, and though their friendship had blossomed since Vienna, it was still relatively fledgling. That Silvie would think she had a right to say anything to Gerard still infuriated Jane.

Not that Silvie was wrong, which infuriated Jane more. She could not defend him. She loved him but as he said, she loved him despite the flaws she knew. She loved the way he was with *her*. The way he took care of her and made her feel beautiful, intelligent and, most of all, loved.

But who would he be once he left his life of shadows

behind? A man of leisure? She could not imagine Gerard enjoying an endless progression of dinners, routs, and balls. House parties and hunts. Though he claimed his actions had impacted international politics, though he was better educated than many of the gentlemen who made their way through Cambridge and Oxford, he did not seem particularly interested in the jostling of countries for strategic supremacy. As a landowner, would he find the local affairs interesting?

All of that assuming he was successful in his quest. What if he were not? How much was she prepared to give up?

He would not admit to it, but she knew he had been hurt, knew that in his attempt to be a better man, live a better life, the inability to escape the old was like poking a wound. She wanted desperately to be able to say yes to him, to take care of him the way he had taken care of her. To help him be reborn.

Though she had known Landsdowne would not be of assistance, she could not predict if his appointment with Anche would be fruitful. Apparently, the man had thought Gerard interesting enough to request a second interview. How much had Gerard already revealed? Powell? Surely not. If it were known that Gerard had killed a peer of the realm, there would be no secrets, no information, valuable enough to spare his life.

She pulled a book off the shelf. The first volume of *Cecilia*. She had skimmed it briefly years ago and dismissed it as overly sentimental despite the cutting depictions of characters in society, but now sentiment appealed to her. Now that reason had seemed to flee her thoughts. She was halfway through the third page when a noise at the back of the house made her tense, but Bohm was there, aware that Gerard would come. The man would not let anyone else enter.

Footsteps down the hall followed, then the door opened and the rectangular space framed a familiar silhouette. She stood quickly and went to him, even as he closed the door behind him. Tension thrummed tangibly through his body.

"What happened?"

His face was granite and she knew at once he'd sold his soul once more. Fury seeped through her, sharp and searing. She struggled for calm, waiting to hear what he would say, even though a deep sense of betrayal filled her.

"I will gain a title. An estate. Everything you desire."

"And in exchange?"

"Information."

"And?" She crossed her hands over her chest as if the movement could contain her fury. "You've never shrunk from the bald truth before. Whom do they want you to kill?"

"I cannot tell you."

"Of course you can't. Just as you could not tell me Powell was in up to his ears in corrupt activity. But you think I will marry you. A man who will have no standing in society other than some newly created title." She wanted to cry. How close she had been to being willing to give everything up for him, even if he didn't succeed. But here was proof he had not changed, had resorted to what he knew best in order to solve the problems their love posed. He wanted a new life, one not tinged by darkness, but how could either of them have it if it was built on death, on servitude to a cause in which he didn't believe?

"My brother…"

"Lord Templeton? Who married his mistress… Yes,

certainly he will help you."

"Jane, it is unimportant."

She threaded her fingers through her hair and clasped her head in her hands in disbelief. "A life is unimportant? As mine was in Vienna to that man? How can you say such a thing?" Her head ached. Her heart ached. "How can you give up everything you are on merely the chance of a future with me? I didn't fall in love with that man who would risk everything."

"Didn't you?"

She swallowed hard.

"Come here, Jane." He reached for her, drew her in close. She longed for this, missed his scent, his taste, missed the way she felt when their bodies entwined.

It would be so easy to let him seduce her into compliance. However, to live with her on the terms she had set, he intended to not only act the assassin, but to risk his life. Risk the soul she had thought yearned for redemption and renewal. The way she yearned for something more than everything she had ever known.

She pulled away from him. "I don't want the hands of a killer on me," she whispered, knowing it was cruel.

He let her go. She lowered her lashes against the naked agony in his eyes. Her heart twisted in her chest. She didn't know how to save him and how to save herself.

"You did in Vienna." She shuddered at the hoarse rasp of his voice.

Naked body against naked body standing in the inn on the outskirts of the city, coming to him freely. She remembered those moments with such strong force that she nearly lived it again. She had felt free, had believed in him, had known he would fight for her. It had been a dream, and he was here now, and he was about to risk his life. But what could she say that would stop him?

"That was out of pity. That was good-bye."

His jaw worked, then relaxed and his lips tilted up into a devastating smile. He stepped forward, every bit as dangerous as he had been that first day she had looked up at the angel of death.

He curled his hand around her bare neck, pulled her close. Light dimmed. His scent and heat filled the space between them. She wanted nothing more than to press herself against him, be with him in the way they could never truly be, not unless she was willing to run away.

"Your pity is a wondrous thing. Say good-bye to me once more."

His lips on hers were the beginning of a promise that she felt in every fiber of her body. He saw through her words. He would not let her go.

She reveled in that promise, accepted it as if it were the truth. Later, she could return to reason, but for now she was happy to give in to his will once more, to luxuriate in his touch and the way warmth trailed like honey everywhere his fingers skimmed.

His lips coaxed hers, and she threaded her arms around him, under his coat, and drew him closer, pressed against him to feel the hard lines of his body. His arousal, too, was hard and she shifted against him as desire settled sharp and spicy low in her belly. She knew how he felt, how he tasted, and it made the anticipation so much sweeter.

"Jane." Her name was an exhale, a sigh against her skin. "I've missed you."

She had missed him too. Not just this, the energy that raced through her, but his conversation, the way he looked at her, the way he listened to her. He had become, against all odds, her friend. But not like any friend she had had before with whom she still needed to hide parts of herself.

With Gerard, she wanted to open up more, give more, unite her body with his until there was nothing between them but pure understanding. She wanted the physical and the cerebral transcendence. But she didn't want to put any of it into words. She simply wanted to—

Touch him. Her hands explored the curls of his hair around his neck, the skin beneath smooth and warm. She wanted to press her mouth to that skin, to feel his pulse beneath her lips. Once she'd bridged the barrier of space, desire bloomed, turned into a living ravenous thing that demanded control. She gave in to that need.

Her mouth was everything and his body her world. A dizzy heat consumed her. Her fingertips tingled as they ran over the texture of his skin, and the hair that lightly covered his arms, his chest, and his legs, nestling that part of him that even the thought of pierced her with sharp pleasure. But too much cloth separated her thoughts from her desire. She pushed his coat off his shoulders, left the cloth bunched up halfway down, trapping his arms for moments that allowed her to explore. She ran her hands over his shoulders again, now only separated from his skin by the cloth of his shirt.

He moved his arms and she felt the muscle flex under her hands, a taut strength that thrilled her. She knew what he could do, and what he felt like above her and inside her. She knew he could lift her effortlessly, that his strength was both tender and fierce.

"Gerard," she said on a breath, drawing out the syllables.

Her voice broke whatever spell had kept him complacent, letting her take the lead. Instead, he pulled his arms out of his jacket and wrapped them around her, one hand burying in her hair as he drew her mouth to his, claimed it with his lips, his tongue, his breath. Claimed her with his heat and his will.

His other hand slid lower, grasping her bottom, urging her against him. Sensations were sharp and yet she melted into his mouth, exploring, teasing, pushing and pulling. She was so thirsty for him, and at the same time the thirst was unquenchable. She pulled at his shirt, releasing it from under his trousers so that she could slide her hands under, feel the bare skin of his stomach, taught and textured.

His hand on the bare skin of her thigh was a shock, her night rail bunched up against her back. Then he let go of her, the cloth falling, and he grabbed her again at her hips, lifting her. The world tilted and she clung to him, dizzy and disoriented, until the soft cushion of the high-backed chair was beneath her. He knelt down in front of her, pushing her nightgown up, running his hands over the bare skin of her knees, up her thighs, thumbs catching just at the apex of her thighs as his hands wrapped around.

She watched him across the expanse of her body and he looked up, met her gaze.

"You are so beautiful," he whispered. There was only her one candle flickering in the dark, and the thin moonlight through the window. His gaze seared her, his expression intense yet full of wonder. He was the one who was beautiful, but he made her *feel* beautiful. Made her aware of the preciousness of the night and the fragility of their created space.

He bent his head and she reached out to caress his dark curls, hand falling to the side as his lips touched her skin. She sucked in her breath and watched—felt—as he made his progress up her thigh, lips warm, tongue wet. His hot breath feathered across her center, and then his lips followed. At the sweet contact of his mouth on her, she sighed and her head dropped back against the leather chair, feeling the strangest sense of peace, of having come home.

An instant later, peace was gone and her hips were writhing as the sensation grew. He was licking, stroking, torturing her with his mouth and she loved it all, wanted more, wanted that explosion she knew would come. And then she was there, shuddering, moaning, reaching for him. He slid her down until she straddled his hips where he knelt on the floor, and kissed her. He tasted foreign but she knew that foreignness was her own scent.

"The floor," he said, his voice guttural, strained. She went where he urged, lying down on the thick carpet she had never thought of before as anything other than a decorative element or warmth for bare feet on a late night. Now the earthy smell of wool surrounded her a moment before Gerard covered her with his body.

She was languid with spent pleasure as he slid inside her, stretching her with his hard length, but desire rose again, sharp and compelling. She met his thrusts with her hips, with her hands on his back, her thighs clutching him.

"Jane, Jane," he murmured, kissing her neck frantically, her cheek, clutching at her as he searched for his own release. Then he surged inside her and he buried his head against her shoulder, his low moan vibrating against her skin as he thrust and thrust into her until the tension eased from his body and lay upon her, his chest rising and falling against hers, his breath against her ear. They lay there in silence and she shifted slightly, tightening her thighs around him to keep him there, joined to her.

At length he rose up on his forearms and looked down at her.

"Jane," he said, his voice dark, devoid of passion. "*Trust* me. I am doing this for us."

She tightened her hold even more on him, drew him back down to her chest. He was doing this for them, for her, but not for him. As they had traveled along the Rhine, the stories they had shared, the love that had blossomed, had been of two people shaping their lives and finding that they wanted more. Gerard did not want darkness but he would delve back in in the hopes of a bright future. But how could that life be built on more death?

"Do not do this thing, not for me. Not for anyone."

He pushed up, breaking free of her arms, sliding from her body. Cool air swept in where he had been. He fastened the falls of his pantaloons as he stood, and she sat up slowly, watching him stalk to the window, stare out into the night.

"Do you fear for my immortal soul?" he said at last, mockingly.

"Yes." She stood, strode over to him and pulled on his shoulder until he turned to her. "Yes!"

"You need not. I destroyed whatever there might have been years ago." His voice was flat.

"Gerard."

"Jane," he said, imitating her. Then he let out a deep breath, ran a hand through his hair and the frozen facade cracked. "What do you suggest then? I love you. I cannot accept that you live your life and I live mine and that life is not the same."

His scent still wrapped around her, she tried to imagine never seeing him again. When she had left him in Frankfurt, she had thought that the last. Then again, when he left Vienna… No. That was a lie. She had known from the first that their lives were inextricably tied. All these weeks the practical Jane had been taken over by some emotional creature she hardly recognized. She clung to the last shards of herself, to the woman who would live life on her own terms, who would only compromise if it were reasonable.

"I don't know," she said helplessly. It was too much to tell him she would have him as he was, an outsider, a shadow, that she was willing to leave her own life behind.

"Then it shall be this way, and you will *trust* me, Jane." He took her face in his hands, demanded her acquiescence.

She closed her eyes, rested her cheek into his palm, her heart aching.

"I'd better go."

Her eyes flew open. His hands dropped and he slipped past her to where his coat lay upon the floor. His *coat.*

She followed him about the room, down the hall and to the kitchen door. She wanted to throw herself into his arms and make him stay.

"When?" she choked.

He shook his head. "There is planning to be done. Do not ask me for more, Jane. You know how this works."

She laughed bitterly. "Yes. I know. And how may I find you?"

"I have rooms…I have had for years," he said. "Do you

intend to visit me?" His raised eyebrow and amused smile irritated her, as if he were the only one who could sneak into buildings and bedrooms. Not that she had ever tried before. Or perhaps she would risk her reputation and show up someday at his doorstep.

"Perhaps or perhaps not," she said. "But I find my mind eased by knowing that the man who wishes to make me his wife is not simply a figment of my imagination who disappears with the next breeze off the Thames."

He laughed. "A very vivid imagination that would be."

She smiled tightly and watched him step out into the night. Her chest tightened, stomach roiling and she called out quickly, "Gerard…"

He turned back, eyebrow raised in question.

"I'll trust you." She took a deep breath. "I'll trust you to be a better man."

A better man. Emptiness hollowed him out as he left her. She doubted him. He had made light of her concern, but perhaps she was right. Perhaps he was trying to create gold from base metal when all it would ever be was base metal. He returned to his rooms exhausted. The highs and lows of emotion were new to him and stole clarity of mind. He lay down on his bed—a narrow thing that had been intended for a valet but as he didn't currently have one and Thomas had infested the main bedroom, he was making do— and stared up at the ceiling. Contemplated his immortal soul and the actions that might compromise that dubious thing.

In his possession was a file on a man who had managed

to slip through the British government's hands time and time again. Smuggling, sedition, treason even. Yet Arnold Vesper had become something of a folk hero, ignoring the government and war to benefit the poor. Then he'd stopped suddenly, six months before Napoleon was caught. Gone to ground so completely that he might very well have died. Or left the country.

They wanted him dead or alive. Dead preferably, as no one wanted to risk the chance the people would riot if it were found he'd been brought in. The death needed to look like a common brawl, or something natural. If Gerard could find and kill this ghost, he could have his title, have Jane.

This job was another Szabo, another one he was obligated to take regardless of what he discovered about the mark when he did his own investigations. Even if he found Vesper innocent, a hero in truth, Gerard could not turn this work down and still gain his heart's desire. But the cold, calculating approach to work felt foreign to him now, and donning it was like donning a mask. There was a man he could be, a man who was decent and honorable and who did not walk alone.

Surely he could still be that man even after this last job. It was a mission for the country he intended to adopt as his own. That was a form of patriotism, was it not? If the action had the full sanction of the government, how could it be a blot on his soul any more than the lives a soldier claimed in wartime? He clung to that thought as he gave way to sleep. He clung to that thought as he woke, more tired than he had been the night before. And he held on to it tightly as he began the work of tracking down a ghost. He didn't expect it to be overly hard. After all, like recognized like.

Chapter Seventeen

"This is a foolish thing you do." Bohm chided her for the fifth time as Jane handed him her cloak. "Let me go to him. He will come to you."

"I am here now safely. You may return home, if you like," Jane said, ignoring him.

The only reason—well, one of two reasons—that Jane crept through the dark with the intention of climbing a wall and entering Gerard's apartments was to prove to him that he was not the only one who could have the element of surprise. In some way, to prove she had power, too, of the sort he so seemed to value.

The other reason was that they had parted on difficult terms. He had not said he would call on her. There was no appointment to meet at a future date. He might very well conduct his mission and die trying and no one would think to inform her.

She wanted to see him again, convince him this time that

his actions were misguided, though she had not managed to think of a solution of her own. But there would be another option, she was certain of it. She needed Gerard to agree to wait.

Bohm huffed in the dark. "I will be here when you descend, but you will pay me more. If you don't break your neck."

She covered her mouth to stifle the sound of her laugh even as she agreed. "Give me a lift?"

Grudgingly, he hoisted her up until she could grab on to the lowest windowsill. She held her breath, hoping no one was a light sleeper, as the last thing she needed was for any of his neighbors to wake up and look out their windows at the strange woman climbing up.

From there, she pulled herself up, inch by inch, searching for hand and footholds. The undertaking was far more difficult than she had imagined. She should have realized. She had climbed trees and follies on her father's estate in her childhood. As an adult, she was an avid sportswoman, proficient at archery, competitive at pall-mall, a strong swimmer. None of that made her necessarily capable of holding up her own weight plus that of her winter clothes as she scaled a wall.

The window that was cracked open was a stroke of luck, and Jane tiptoed her way across the narrow ledge, holding desperately on to the fingerholds in the wall. If anyone saw her, her reputation would be gone completely, but this was not Mayfair, it was a respectable neighborhood populated by merchants and solicitors, and apparently assassins. If his neighbors only knew...

Her arms screaming, she lifted herself up, her stomach tight as she pulled over the windowsill and, as silently as possible, into the dark room.

"Who the hell are you?"

The voice that challenged her was not that of Gerard. The sound of the bed creaking and the scrape of something metallic made her freeze in place. She should hide. What if she had entered the wrong apartment? Wrongly deduced which window would be his based on Bohm's description? The scent of brimstone filled the air and a candle illuminated the room.

In a long white nightshirt was a boy of maybe fourteen, with light brown hair and dark eyes. The angles of his face bore a striking resemblance to Gerard's. His son? The thought disturbed her, but surely he would have mentioned such a thing? More likely was that this was a brother, although he had not mentioned one in England. But there was a resemblance to Templeton, as well.

"Who are *you*?"

"Considering you are the one invading my bedroom, I really think you should answer my question first. You don't look like a thief or a murderer."

She laughed. "I am here for Gerard."

Tension lined his youthful form. "Then you've found the right rooms and I think it best we find him. Are you armed?"

"Would a murderer tell you if she was?"

A grudging smile lifted his lips and he inched his way toward the door, never turning his back to her.

"He knows me," she finally said with some exasperation. The last thing she needed was for this boy to sound an alarm and make this daring excursion into a scandal. "And I'm no danger to him, but I'm not about to give you my name because my reputation is at risk. You are his brother?"

He flung open the door. "Gerard!" he called and Jane winced at the loud sound.

A door opened. Feet stomped down the hall. "Thom—"

Gerard was barefoot and bare-chested and a slow heat gathered within her.

"Jane."

"Is this your mistress? Why doesn't she use the front door?"

"She's not my mistress but that is an excellent question. Jane?"

"I was curious about the ivy. It's an unusual variety."

Gerard snorted.

"Thomas, meet Lady Jane Langley, your future sister-in-law. Jane, my rapscallion brother, Thomas."

Despite the urge to deny Gerard's claim, Jane held her tongue. Arguing with him on the point of marriage would only confuse the issue and draw out this farcical scene longer.

"So I gathered," she murmured instead.

"You're getting married?" The accusatory tone in Thomas's voice made Jane tense.

"Yes, but you aren't to say a word of it to anyone."

"You're eloping?"

"It's a…secret engagement," Jane said helpfully.

"You do realize that's the first time you've said yes." Gerard's expression was filled with delight.

"I…"

"Say nothing. Let me enjoy the moment."

"You're being ridiculous."

"This way," Gerard said roughly, directing her out of the room. "And where is Bohm? How could he let you do something so stupid? How could *you* let yourself do something so stupid?"

She laughed as she let him forcibly direct her down a short hall and into another, much smaller, room. "It is rather stupid of me, isn't it? That's what love does apparently. Eats away at reason. I never understood Shakespeare before, or Austen even. People were so dramatic and unreasonable, but now I know. And Bohm is waiting for me."

Gerard shook his head. "I'll be right back."

In his absence, she looked around the small room. It was sparse, bare of much but a washbasin, set of drawers and a bed, and Gerard's familiar valise. His boots, too, were standing in the corner as if they were still molded to the man's calves. She walked to the window, looked out to the street. This room faced the other way, toward the mews.

She felt Gerard's presence before she heard him.

"I sent Bohm home. I'll make certain you return safely."

She turned to him and nodded in acknowledgment, then gestured to the room. "The servant's quarters?"

Gerard shook his head with a rueful smile. "Yes, indeed. I've been ousted by my brother. But be serious, why are you here?"

She threw herself into his arms, clung to him. "What I said this afternoon still stands, Gerard. I don't want you to mistake what I said in front of your brother, but I could think of nothing but you all day, because if you are to do this thing, then this may truly be a good-bye. I cannot wait powerlessly for you to call on me again, or to never do so again. I want you, I want to hear your cries of pleasure, feel you deep inside of me. I want to have that moment when we are joined so close we might as well be one being, nothing separating us. I want to commune with you in the most physical and spiritual way possible and I wish it to be every night that we may. This is all we have, is it not?"

The little speech cut through Gerard like a dull knife, nothing clean, nothing easily patched up.

"Jane, my love." He took her face in his hands, stared into her pleading eyes. "This is only the beginning of us. I am done with this life. There is only this one thing left to do and then no more shadows. No more darkness and servitude."

Her eyes were luminous with unshed tears and it tore at him.

She raised one hand and laid it over his. "I want to believe you." She looked as if she wanted to say more but she bit her lower lip, her lashes sweeping down over her eyes. Blocking him out.

He wanted to demand she look at him, that she believe him. But how could he make a promise he couldn't keep? He ran a thumb over her lips, freeing the lower one from the prison of her teeth. She sighed, and he leaned forward to catch the softness of her mouth beneath his. He teased her lips with his tongue, coaxed them open until she was kissing him back, lifting up to press herself against him. Her hand dropped, and he moved his as well, one tangling in her hair, loosening the pins that kept the mass high on her head. The strands came tumbling down, caressing his skin, releasing the scent of her rose-scented bathwater.

He breathed it in. Breathed *her* in.

"In the dark of night," he whispered. "I've wondered why I love a woman who so rejects my desire to be with her forever. I've wondered if I'm fooling myself, if you are right, after all. Love is not enough. That no matter what I do, no matter which way I turn, we cannot be together. I wonder if I am clinging to what you represent, a life that's brighter than the one I've lived."

She was utterly still in his arms, her arms and body stiff. "And…at what answer do you arrive?"

"You are here, are you not? Seeking me out? Returning to me again? You say one thing but then you come to me. I think perhaps you know as well as I why I keep going, because we can reason away the love if we wish, and yet it is still there, vibrant and true. We both still want something more, something that we've only glimpsed in our few moments together.

"But what I wonder most of all," he said, "is how you can love me. Yet I don't doubt in any way that you do."

"I wonder it, too."

Jane, ever honest, and yet the words cut deep. She wanted him to reject Anche's request, presented him with an impossible situation, one in which he could never have her. Trade a life for his title and lose her. Forego the title and never have her. At least titled he could still convince her.

"Tonight," she said softly, "we are still Jane and Gerard. Gerard and Jane. Simple people. This room could be one that we stayed in on the banks of the Rhine as we fell in love in our own world."

The memories were bittersweet. He had been full of hope. This night, on the cusp of gaining what she had said she wanted, he felt further than ever from achieving the peace he desired.

"I don't want to think about it," she said suddenly, and stepped away from him. She unfastened her dress and he watched her shed the first layer, then the rest. As she began to pull off her chemise, he joined her, pulling his loose shirt over his head, his trousers down. When they were both naked, she went to him, placed her hand on his chest and he stared down into her wide-open eyes.

"This thing between us… You are right. It isn't reasonable. It isn't safe. But tonight, I want it and I want you and tonight, I don't care what tomorrow brings."

He clung to her words as he clung to her. Again and again, she returned to him. A lifetime could be strung together from such moments. A lifetime.

He laid her down on the narrow bed, covered her body with his. He kissed her face as he parted her thighs, as he joined himself to her, needing that connection above all else. Once there, buried inside her warmth, surrounded by her life, melded together, pulse and flesh, he stayed there until the mere throbbing of their pulse grew into a restless desire. Until their limbs intertwined as they arched and writhed. He savored each gasp and moan that escaped her. Urged her with his body to her pleasure, and when she found it, she brought him with her, his release overtaking him until he lost himself inside her, closed his eyes and slept.

When he woke, it was still dark outside. Beneath him, Jane was asleep. He lifted up on his arms and stared down at her.

Elope with me.

But he didn't say it. Instead, he slipped from her body and went to the washbasin. Cleaned himself with the cool water, dressed. As he did he felt the weight of her regard. She still lay there on the bed, naked where he had left her, legs parted. He could go back to her, slide again into her warmth, pray for the night to last forever. Except, it was time to take her back before light illuminated their actions. Despite the daring stupidity of scaling this building, Jane would not wish to be ruined publically.

He picked her chemise up from the ground and brought it over to her. She rolled to her side and sat up. Just as silently as she had undressed, he helped her to dress, then he took her home, to her father's home. The next time he saw her he would claim her as his own.

Or—

He had always thought through every situation, contemplated and planned for every eventuality, but this possibility he no longer wished to imagine. The rear door was not open but locks and closed doors had never been a problem for Gerard. He saw her safely back inside and with a kiss as silent as their voices, slipped away. He returned to his rooms. Changed his clothes, his appearance, went back out into the world.

The last known place that Arnold Vesper had lived was in Cornwall, but that had been years ago when the man's crimes had been primarily limited to smuggling champagne and other goods. A relatively minor crime considering it had been wartime and a man might have loyalty to his country, but needed to eat above all else.

But then Vesper had been charged with sedition, a pamphlet of drawings that spoke of the King's madness, the Regent's gluttony, and other sins with the suggestion that the monarchy should be ended.

Sometimes returning to a mark's childhood and early days was useful to gain insight into the way the man thought, where he might choose to hide. But though he was not English, Gerard knew enough of small rural towns to understand that any questions a stranger asked would find its way to Vesper.

In London, a palm could be crossed with silver or gold with far better results. There were several dozen Evas here, women and men who gathered and sold information.

As he stepped out of the Billingsley, the sun was breaking through the sky in fiery lines. He walked down the street but knew before he turned the corner that he was being followed. Skillfully followed, but nonetheless, Gerard had rarely not been aware when he was being trailed, and at this hour of the day, when the street was near empty, detection was easier.

He kept going, set his trap. And then pounced—upon Herr Bohm who gasped and held up a hand for Gerard to release him. With a disgusted twist of his arm, Gerard did. Bohm coughed and bent over.

"Why are you following me?"

"I told her it was a matter between lovers, but she insisted. Wanted to make certain you were safe. Promised she'd take two footmen everywhere she goes. And I agreed because I was curious. I thought you were giving up the game."

"I am, I have, but there is one more detail to attend to. Your job is to protect her."

Bohm shook his head. "I retired, briefly, from intrigue when I met Julia. Returned after her death. Few women want a man who disappears in the middle of the night, or for days at a time, unable to discuss their work, living a life steeped in lies."

"Many women marry soldiers who go off to war for years."

Bohm looked him straight in the eye, his gaze full of admonition. "We are not soldiers. Don't fool yourself for even an instant."

Gerard ran his hand through his hair again, a habit he tried to break and managed to avoid when he was at work, but he was tired. Bone-deep tired. "I don't."

He could repeat the plan, explain that Jane would have him no other way, and yet she would not have him this way, but that was not a confession he wished to share with Bohm. Despite the older man's attempt at romantic advice, Gerard did not want it. If he sat down with a drink, he might be able to tell it all to himself in any event.

"Do you intend to continue following me?" he asked in frustration, ready to continue before the sky lightened to daylight. "Will I have to disable you to throw you off?"

"Perhaps you need a second pair of hands for a while," Bohm said.

"I work alone."

Bohm laughed. "Not if you marry, my friend. Not for very much longer at all."

Chapter Eighteen

Jane had only ever called on Lord Landsdowne alone once before. Then, as now, she waited in the large, dimly lit sitting room with its portraits of the Landsdowne family. Men and women who resembled Gerard, but there was not, nor would there ever be, an image of him here or in the portrait gallery on the above floor.

"I often imagined that if I had had a daughter, or a granddaughter even, she would have been like you."

She had expected to hear the creak of Lord Landsdowne's Bath chair but instead he appeared nearly silently, his cane held in his hand but unused. With each year that he grew older, he continued to surprise her. The man could be feeble and weak when it served him, but show strength when that was his intent, as it apparently was today. Why? She struggled to work through all the possible iterations. The man was Machiavellian. He did nothing without reason.

"I'm not certain I take that as a compliment, my lord."

He nodded with the faintest smile, one that reminded her sharply of Gerard. "It is a testament to the respect I have for your intellect. Your father always underestimated you because of your sex." Her stomach clenched and she was torn between repeating Landsdowne's compliment in her mind and buckling under the raw hurt at the truth of his words. Her father still did not respect her the way Gerard did, the way Lord Landsdowne did.

The earl moved farther into the room, now using his cane, the polished wood tapping heavily upon the floor with each step. He gestured to a chair and she sat, realizing he could not do so politely until she had. He lowered himself into the wingback chair across from her and continued. "When you came to me six years ago and asked me to ruin a man, I was confirmed in my suspicions."

She flushed. Although she had shared this story of the music tutor with Gerard, he did not know it was his own grandfather who had aided her. But how could she have told him that then and revealed how much she knew? He would never have let her go for reasons entirely different than love.

"We said we would never speak of that again," she said quickly.

He waved a hand in the air, dismissing her concern even as he spoke. "My apologies. In any event, now you surprise me."

Irritation started to build. She stared at him and waited for his reason.

"I did try to push Marcus in your direction. I would have been quite happy to unite the Langley and Landsdowne fortunes."

"Marcus was never a match for me." Though she had

always known marrying well was important, she refused to put herself into the care of a man she could not admire.

"No, but I hoped you would help mold him. Gerard is no match for you either."

Even as she realized his warning revealed that Gerard had spoken to his grandfather of Jane, everything in her rejected Landsdowne's statement. Gerard who had tended to her, made love to her, trusted her, was more a match for Jane than anyone she had ever met. He was a man struggling to master the world around him yet held back by one crucial detail outside his control. As was Jane.

"Only because of his birth."

"An accident of birth is the phrase, but it changes everything."

"He is determined to overcome that." It was odd to be defending Gerard when she herself doubted his actions, believed his quest fruitless.

"It won't be enough."

She knew that, too, of course. Just as Marcus's wife nee mistress, the new Lady Templeton, would not be welcomed everywhere, any title Gerard gained would do him little good in society. There would be whispers. And Jane, in turn, would be their recipient. She had never intended to be the champion of outcasts. Nor did Gerard need her to be his champion. He could find a way to achieve his every goal, except for one.

A hollow darkness coursed through her chest, making her ache. Still, she longed for him.

"You know this, Jane." Landsdowne's voice was surprisingly gentle as he spoke to her reason, to the part of her that did know, that looked askance at her tumultuous emotions. "You are not a fool."

"Of course not," she said instantly, hiding the despair that was tearing her apart inside. But this was not the time for unchecked emotion. It was the time to gain answers, to determine where Gerard was and what he intended to do to achieve his aims.

"And you know I refused to help him."

"Yes. And *you* know that he went to Anche, to trade secrets. Money would have been enough with your backing, but your fear and your need to control everything is likely resulting in exactly what you did not want."

Landsdowne looked away, a rare sign of weakness. She had always admired and respected the earl, known that he was a man who understood subtleties. She had never doubted that he would help her when she approached him about the music teacher.

"You can still help. You can support Gerard, petition for a title. Make it so that he does not have to trade his soul."

"Imagine if all of England's nobility were to seek titles for their by-blows. Beyond that, Gerard was raised in France and Italy. His tutor was a Catholic but his mother was a Jewess."

A Jew, like the much admired Fanny von Arnstein in Vienna, or like the Rothschilds who had funded her in Frankfurt. Did they know Gerard?

"I see you did not know."

She shook her head. There was more to the earl's refusal. "What of it, my lord? You have had far lesser men dine at your table." Landsdowne's grudging smile admitted her point. It was not Gerard's heritage that held him back. "He is taking your secrets to Anche, in any event."

Landsdowne sighed. "I am old, Jane. A man has only a certain amount of power. This you know. What I have amassed, the leverage I have, will be spent the moment I support Gerard."

As if he were saving for some greater need, some other scheme that furthered his own goals, whether personal or for England, at the expense of his family. "He is still your blood, and he's served you all of these years out of familial loyalty. I do not think you need be jealous of your power."

"Says the woman who demands a title in exchange for her hand. You are not without a choice, Jane. You could elope with my illegitimate grandson who has acted as a spy and mercenary these last twenty years."

She was asking him to do what she herself would not—to compromise and risk stepping into the abyss. Gerard was only doing this for her. If Jane would not compromise, then Gerard would compromise a life devoid of shadows. The weight of the last few weeks, of the choice she had resisted again and again, crashed down on her, turning the edges of her vision to black. Her chest ached. If she loved Gerard, then she could not stand by, vacillating stupidly at every turn.

"I have to go." She didn't wait for Landsdowne's response. She had to find Gerard as quickly as possible, before he traded his life for hers.

W hen the carriage pulled to a stop, the door was flung open and Bohm's furious face met her gaze.

"I was hired to protect you. You hired me to protect you. How am I supposed to do such a thing if you leave without me? If I don't know you are safe at home? Gerard tells me his woman is intelligent, a match for him. I do not see this woman! For this I leave my life in Vienna where I am beloved."

She didn't speak as she descended from the carriage, accepting his solid arm even as he raged at her. He was right. She did not know if the matter with Szabo was resolved, or if Gerard's presence in her life would introduce new dangers. Beyond that, despite her wish to save Gerard from himself, she had forced his hand, propelled him into a situation where he could not escape the darkness of his upbringing.

She had laughed that night in Germany when he had told her the story of Lord Templeton interfering in Gerard's work, had called Marcus a fool. But she, so quick to judge, had been no less. Had been much worse, in fact, because she knew very well she loved Gerard, and yet it had taken Landsdowne's obstinacy to make her own all too clear. Eventually Bohm fell quiet too. They entered the house in silence. In the hall, she didn't know if she should leave him there or if she should wait. Her maid took her coat and her gloves and then Jane dismissed her.

And waited.

"My wife," Bohm said finally. "Szabo killed her."

Jane looked at him. He was looking down at his hands, flexing them and straightening them.

"He'd had a bet on my opponent. I was the favorite. He wanted me to throw the match. Rather, he took Julia. I'd done some work for him here and there, little jobs, much as Badeau does. That is how I know him. I was good friends in my youth with Francois Badeau."

"Did you do it?"

Bohm's lips curled and he looked straight at her. "For Julia, anything. And then I went to collect her. She was furious with me. She had never cared that I was half criminal, but she believed in a sportsman's honor. I told her it was a ridiculous distinction."

Jane swallowed hard. She had never told Bohm the details, what Gerard intended to do, why she needed to follow him. Perhaps by now Bohm had gathered that Gerard had believed he needed to kill that man in the warehouse to fulfill his quest.

"How—" She wet her mouth and tried again. "How did she die?"

The carriage had stopped but she didn't rap for the coachman to open. Instead, she waited for Bohm's answer, for a confession that could not leave this place.

"Szabo asked me to throw another match, now that he believed me to be his man. I said no, that it did not matter what he threatened, I would not. I came home one day to find that Julia had jumped from the window of our apartment and had broken her neck. Suicide was the official word, but many people saw a man enter our rooms, heard a fight. There was a broken vase and signs of a struggle."

"I'm so sorry." Useless words, but they weren't just for Bohm. They were for Gerard, for Jane, for that man who by now likely lay dead somewhere.

He took a deep breath. "If I am not here, you wait for me."

She nodded. "Did you find Gerard?"

"Yes."

"Did he…"

"He knew I was following him. Apparently, I am no longer as stealthy as I once was."

Jane laughed with him but neither of them was filled

with mirth. Bohm had chosen to leave that life behind and he clearly understood just what was at stake for Gerard.

"He doesn't know that it doesn't matter to me," she said, placing her hand on the door. Then she stopped and looked at Bohm once more. "Do you think Szabo will still come after me? After Gerard?"

Bohm's dark eyes were unflinching. "I do not know."

She nodded. "I hope…I hope you'll stay until everything is sorted out. If it is sorted out." It was entirely possible it would never be, that Jane would never again be able to take her own safety for granted. "You are right. I've been reckless and foolish but my world changed when I met Gerard. I…I am no longer confident in my choices and my judgment."

He laughed, the sound quiet and bitter, but then nodded.

Jane took a deep breath. To say her world had changed was such an understatement. It had tilted and crashed and then had been picked back up and placed on the axis inside out and upside down. Everything was unrecognizable. And now the center of that world, she had broken that too.

Gerard tracked down Vesper by suppertime. He peered into the window of the man's home and watched the very domestic scene of him trying to make his chubby baby laugh. Vesper was known as Evans these days, worked as a clerk in a textile shop, lived modestly and below notice despite the bank account that proved he had profited well from his life as a smuggler.

But all signs pointed to Vesper having given his old life up fully, much the way Gerard hoped to. His stomach churned and his chest felt weighted down. Even if Vesper had not given up the work, Gerard had not uncovered any crimes darker than those Anche's file had claimed. Perhaps an Englishman born and bred might find the charges reason enough but Gerard had no such loyalty to a nation.

Vesper was likable, which was what had made him beloved and protected by his community, made him inaccessible to the British government. When he had gone to the ground, he had done so wisely, new identity, new look, not a word to his old friends. Yet there were always people who knew, who could sniff out the person who didn't belong, who was hiding something, people who gathered information while it was still fresh and held it in waiting for the day it might be of use.

Gerard had made it of use.

Except— He stared at Vesper's wife's young face, her joy as he handed the baby back to her, the kiss they shared over the baby's head. It was a damn near idyllic scene. Sickening in its sweetness. Except Gerard craved that sweetness.

He wasn't judge and jury. It wouldn't matter even if he had uncovered darker crimes in this man's past. His own past was not unblemished and perhaps someday the gun would be trained on him. Some man would be sent to assassinate Gerard Badeau, the new Baron Alandale.

He needed to find another way forward, to convince Jane to be his whether or not he met her demands. Or…he could watch Vesper just a little bit longer, hope that the man did something that made Gerard able to live with Vesper's blood on his hands. He hated even the thought.

Movement made him pay attention again. Vesper pulled on his boots and then slipped into his heavy coat. He'd only been trailing the man for less than a day. He'd follow him to wherever Vesper was going and then leave. Move on with his life, whatever it would be.

It was a long walk through the frigid night, and the wind picked up as they reached the Thames. The waterfront was still full of life, the tavern windows bright, noise and inebriated humans spilling out.

Down an alley, he followed Vesper, until the other man stopped in the shadows of a heap of garbage. Gerard studied the street. Ahead of them was a warehouse, a wooden structure with one door set inside. A guard kept watch in front of the door.

Vesper pulled something round and metallic out of his pocket. It looked like a watch. Another man came around the far corner of the alley, stopped by the guard, patted him on the shoulder. The sound of their voices carried but the words were indistinguishable with the wind. However, they were walking away from the warehouse together now, and that was unmistakable.

Break for supper? Was that guard really so predictable in his routine, and so careless as to leave his post unmanned? As soon as the two men were out of sight, Vesper ran to the door, slid a key into the lock, and slipped inside. Gerard waited a moment before following. The door was locked again, but that was a small matter and less than a minute later Gerard was inside as well, blinking into the darkness as he waited for his eyes to adjust. None of Vesper's actions thus far were those of an innocent man.

The sound of flint and metal struck Gerard an instant before he spied the small flame enclosed in a lantern. Gerard bent down, hid behind the large piles of...cloth?

Did this warehouse belong to the textile merchant for

whom he worked? If so, what sort of work did Vesper do here at night? If Gerard were a man who gambled, he would bet that Vesper intended to steal from his employer. Why? Why not simply keep to himself, live a quiet life with his family? Was he impossibly drawn to the thrill of the illicit? Or perhaps there was some other reason.

Nonetheless, Gerard was going to let Vesper live. Even if he found out that tonight's actions were part of some grander plan to kill the King of England, it was not for Gerard to stop him. Not anymore. Would Vesper even listen if Gerard warned him? Told him to go home to his wife, give up the game? Would Gerard listen if someone were to say such a thing to him? Jane had. Bohm had. Yet here Gerard was.

And he was going to make a different choice. But he didn't move, words pressing against his closed lips. A warning. One thing more he could do for this man.

"Vesper," Gerard said, hearing his own voice with a stab of shock.

Vesper froze in his tracks and looked around wildly. "Who's there?"

"People want you dead. If you've gone to ground, given up the life, stay that way. Leave the country, even. You can afford to do that. Whatever you are doing here…don't do it."

"I don't know what you are talking about," Vesper repeated, his voice low and controlled but seething.

"I've warned you. You're a marked man. If I found you, others can as well."

The man was trembling now, looking around him. Gerard followed his gaze, to the iron pipe. Vesper was searching for a weapon, not that such a thing mattered. By the time Vesper reached it, Gerard would be gone.

Chapter Nineteen

*T*he next time he saw her he would claim her as his own.
Gerard stood outside the Langley townhouse and stared at the fortress. It was easy to scale, to storm, to steal into or to gain access to in any myriad of ways. All but the metaphorical.

Gerard had never pretended to be an honorable man. Honor among thieves, perhaps, or in his case, assassins. The word still rankled. He had never considered himself such, that work claiming only a small fraction of his deeds, but nonetheless death's shadow had been large in his life. No longer. He had put it aside that night in Frankfurt. He had promised himself reborn.

His action tonight was the right one, the one for which even Jane had hoped, and the one that made the social chasm between them much wider. The one that had him standing outside in the dark of night instead of slipping into her bed and...*claiming her as his own*.

He ran his hand through his hair. He was so tired, and thoughts jumbled in his head, words and images, sounds and emotions. Gerard had found the work of information collecting and spying to be mentally engaging, but he was no longer the man who was ruled by pure reason. He had started to crack, to need more than endless traveling, more than impersonal rooms and no true sense of self. Then he had met Jane. *Needed* Jane.

He couldn't go to her yet, and he could not claim her. If he stayed away, then there was always a chance something would change, some new opportunity would present itself, or that he would forge a new solution.

He returned to his rooms and found Thomas awake and sitting in the parlor holding an unopened letter in his hand. The boy looked both guilty and belligerent, and thus the letter must belong to Gerard. He narrowed his eyes. The wide, slanting scrawl looked familiar.

"I suppose I should be thankful that you do not take the further step of actually opening my letters."

Thomas's cheeks stained red.

"I saw Giana's name. That is our sister, is it not? You never told me she writes to you."

Gerard took a deep breath and sat down in the chair opposite Thomas. He was exhausted but his brother had as deep a desire for a family as Gerard did. Even a motley one that spanned borders.

"You will have a chance to meet her very soon," he said. "I intend to bring her to England."

Thomas frowned. "And what about you? Where will you be?"

"In England as well." As long as the next interview with

Anche went well. He rubbed the bridge of his nose.

"So you are staying? Because you are getting married? And Giana and I…we are to live with you and your new wife, who likes to climb buildings and sneak into men's bedrooms."

His new wife. The word pained him because for the first time he was aware that he might not achieve his aim. Short of abducting Jane, he could not force her to choose him.

"I have a brother who runs away from his school and a sister of an age to marry. I think those are excellent reasons to settle down for a while."

Thomas was quiet.

"Hopefully Jane will not mind the burden of two siblings," Gerard said into the silence, even though that burden was the least of his worries.

"Why are you doing this?" Thomas said. "You owe me nothing."

Why? The great question. And the answer? An amorphous desire for something more, something meaningful, something beyond the days and nights that were all the same, that held nothing of lasting value. No one would remember Gerard when he was gone.

But he had a family of sorts. And…somehow, he would still have Jane.

The next morning the sun was wincingly bright and Horse Guards was bustling and noisy. The contrast to the storm within Gerard made the dull ache in his head throb. He needed all of his wits about him as he was about to break a contract for the first time, one with far greater stakes than ever before.

Inside the sparsely decorated office Anche greeted him almost jovially, standing up and coming around from behind his desk to take Gerard by the hands.

"Good morning, Mr. Badeau. I hardly expected the deed to be accomplished so soon but I was pleasantly surprised by your request for an interview. Now I truly understand Lord Landsdowne's ability to know so much. Perhaps you will rethink working for me."

"I did indeed find Vesper," Gerard said.

Anche's smile faded. "Your demeanor is rather cool for one about to become the new Baron Alandale."

"I let the man live. If you wish his death, you will need to find someone else to do the job, but I feel comfortable saying he is no longer a threat to the government."

"So you believe yourself capable of assessing who and what is a threat to England?" Anche said harshly. "Rather arrogant of you."

Gerard shrugged. Whatever Anche wished to call it, Gerard's assessment remained the same.

"I could have you arrested."

Gerard's jaw clenched. It was a bluff on Anche's part, but that did not mean Anche was not a danger to him. "You have no reason to."

"Easy enough to create one, Mr. Badeau. You should have thought of that when you agreed to a bargain you did not intend to keep. You are now a liability to the British government."

Gerard had known this risk, but if he intended to stay in England, he needed to settle this matter with Anche now.

"I do not wish to be an assassin, not even one sanctioned by you and King George. The secrets I offer you are more than enough in trade for what I want."

Anche stared at him. Gerard waited, knowing that there were calculations happening inside the man's head, just as there were in Gerard's. This was the moment of bargaining, where he needed to hold back all he was in fact willing to do.

"You should have thought of that before you accepted the task. Now you are a threat."

"Hold your enemies close."

Anche laughed. "You *are* arrogant."

"Call it what you will, Anche. I value my immortal soul more than I fear your threats." Inside Gerard felt buoyant, as if the weight of years had been lifted off him. As if the world were full of possibility. As if a man truly could craft his world for himself.

"The barony is off the table."

"So be it."

Despite Gerard's words, he needed to know that Anche would not pursue his threats. He did not want to make his home in England only to have to watch over his shoulder the rest of his life. Giana and Thomas had no true stake in life in England. He could easily move them all elsewhere. Except Jane... He could not predict Jane.

But just as Anche needed to bluff, so did Gerard. He strode to the door and opened it. He looked back at Anche. "I would say it has been a pleasure..."

Footsteps sounded in the hall and Gerard tensed even though he knew it was unlikely to be some attempt on Anche's part at physical coercion. After all, the man had not known a mere ten minutes ago that their agreement had been voided.

"You expect I will just let you walk out of here?"

Anche's words were so like Gerard's thoughts that he merely shook his head with a laugh.

"If you intend to threaten my grandson, I shall have to invoke some consequences of my own."

Gerard laughed again as he turned to the open space where the Earl of Landsdowne stood, leaning ever so slightly on his cane. At long last, the old man had decided to acknowledge Gerard as his blood.

He had no doubt his grandfather's appearance was due to some strategic decision instead of loyalty. However, he had learned long ago that one did not turn down payment out of pride. It was time to see just how much power his grandfather had.

Chapter Twenty

Jane waited for Gerard to come to her. He loved her, she told herself. And she made plans. They would go to America, or Canada, or Paraguay. They would create a life for themselves in which no one knew them and there were no old expectations to meet. No ridiculous quests for titles and wealth.

All of those assumed he hadn't yet achieved that goal. She wasn't certain what she would do, what he would do, if he had. Or if in the attempt, something had happened to him. But the last was a possibility difficult to fathom. He was so capable and strong, an army in the form of one man.

Her heart ached and she wondered if she could die of heartache. There were so many strands of the tapestry of life at play that she could not be certain what was the reality she was living, what would make a future for them that would not end in misery. And did it really matter if it did end in misery if at least they were together?

The night had been endless, and throughout the day every minute that passed felt like an eternity. Now that she understood how much she loved Gerard, how much she was willing to give up in exchange for a life with him, the not knowing, the inability to take any action, was torture. Sometime in those countless hours, she ripped her Lady Justice necklace from her neck, breaking its fragile clasp, and stuffed it in a box where it would no longer mock her.

She stayed in her room, as if doing so until he came to her could hold back time.

Then, in the early hours of the afternoon, Silvie barged into the bedroom. Jane stared at her cousin, but didn't move from under the covers.

"The maids tell me it is like a deathbed in here," Silvie said, pulling open the curtains, "and yet they have no idea what ails you other than a 'headache.'"

"Go away."

"But a certain gentleman has not crept into your townhouse in a few days," Silvie said, settling herself down on the edge of Jane's bed, clearly with no intention of doing as Jane requested "and you were here last night, so I surmise that the reason lack of such goings on coincides with a mysterious illness is that there has been a lovers' spat."

Jane burst into tears. It was stupid to do so. She didn't feel any more or less melancholia than she had a moment earlier. And it wasn't as if Gerard and she had actually fought. Yet, simply Sylvie mentioning that there had been a lovers' spat sent Jane's eyes watering.

"That bad? I don't like this Badeau. You are not yourself anymore. It is one thing to fall in love but it has changed you completely."

"I fell in love and lost my mind," Jane said with a laugh, sitting up and wiping at her eyes. "But that is hardly his fault."

"I am not certain about that. Nonetheless, moping about does nothing. Either go to him and reunite or move on. We have been in London for long enough that people will think us rude for not accepting invitations. You *do* have a duty as my hostess."

The mere thought of having to exchange niceties and meaningless conversation exhausted Jane. "I don't want to see any people," she said, flopping back on the bed. But that wasn't entirely true. Silvie's presence had broken the spell of despair. There was still a world outside her imagination, outside this room. She looked to her cousin. "I really don't know who I am anymore, Silvie. I do things I wouldn't normally do. I am here in London when I had looked forward to assisting my father in Vienna. I...I am willing to elope with a man whose greatest claim is that he is the illegitimate grandson of an earl."

A man who was an assassin, who might have added one more soul to his accomplishments.

"I think it best that we have the maid draw you a bath, and then perhaps stroll about in the park. And it is not too late to accept an invitation for the evening, I am sure. As I told you, I loved that soldier because he saw the world. But once I saw it for myself, I didn't need that love anymore." Silvie slid off the bed and pulled the rope for Jane's maid. "Perhaps you need to discover who Jane is now."

It was an idea that didn't depend on Gerard. For the first time in days, Jane smiled. The very idea felt hopeful, like a breeze of fresh spring air. Perhaps her old life would no longer satisfy her but there were other interests she had never fully pursued, such as music and art, and she was determined to do so now. She agreed to attend a soiree that evening, a small one that she was certain would be populated with people she liked better than most, and Silvie rushed off to pen their acceptance with excitement.

That evening, wearing one of her new dresses from Vienna, with Silvie at her side and a glass of wine in her hand, she stood in the drawing room of Lord Parrington and his sister, Lady Alinora Aubrey. Lord Parrington was a war hero and bore the scars of his service. But aside from a white line that now perpetually twisted his lips and the bald, disfigured patch on his scalp, he looked every inch the part of a noble hero. Jane had always thought him handsome in an unrefined, purely masculine sort of way. His sister, by contrast, was the epitome of femininity, petite and delicately beautiful, with dark hair and dark eyes. Interestingly, the siblings had hosted Lord Templeton's wedding last year at their country seat.

Lord Templeton, Gerard's brother-in-law.

With an imaginary swat of her head, Jane forced away any thought of Gerard. She was here tonight to rediscover herself and her place in society without him.

"Lady Jane, it's a pleasure to see you back in London."

A genuine warmth filled her chest at the familiar voice and she turned to greet Lord Carslyle. Though he had a reputation of being nearly as brooding as that ridiculous poet, Lord Byron, he wore a rare smile.

"I'm happy to see you as well, my lord. And yes, I did see your card but I've been indisposed. I hope you'll forgive me for not responding promptly."

"Jane, I'd forgive you anything."

She let out a breath she hadn't realized she was holding. It was good to see him. Carslyle was the closest thing to a friend she had other than Silvie. More of an older brother, actually. His presence made her feel almost…as if everything were the way it usually was.

She turned to introduce him to Silvie, but her cousin was a few steps away talking with Lady Alinora.

"Stroll with me." Carslyle took her arm and made it clear the words were more of a command than a request. Tension thrummed inside her again. He knew Landsdowne as well as Jane if not better considering he was one of the earl's inner circle, the "Group of Eight." Was some new scheme being hatched? Had Landsdowne said anything to him?

She rested her hand on his forearm and they slowly navigated the room, moving toward the less populated corners.

"What is on your mind?" she asked.

"I heard, of course, about your ordeal," Carslyle said.

Jane laughed. "No one else tonight has yet mentioned it. I did wonder at the silence. In Vienna, for a week it was all anyone would speak of to me. Surely Lord Powell's death has been noted in the last month? His heir notified…"

"Lord Powell was mourned, but I know nothing of his heir. I am more concerned about you. You look well and yet…not what I expected."

She laughed again. "What did you expect?"

"The indefatigable Lady Jane, who would regale us all of her adventures with the same pragmatism and wit she always has. Instead I see a woman who looks…lovesick."

She stopped and stared at him, and then realized that doing so would make others notice them and so she started walking again, as did he.

"Perhaps I am wrong. Perhaps it is too forward of me to say such, but I have known you for nearly fifteen years and…having suffered the malady, I believe I recognize its signs."

First Silvie, then Bohm and now Carslyle, as if opening herself up to emotions opened new facets of the people around her.

She took a deep breath. "You are not wrong, but please tell me I do not wear the symptoms of this illness so clearly for all to see. If so, perhaps it is better I go home and stay there until I am well again."

Carslyle laughed, and he shook his head. "Oh Jane. I think it is perhaps obvious that you are…changed. But not the cause. Who is he? Some Russian princeling? An Austrian count?"

Her heart ached, the past months flashing through her like lightning, illuminating everything, teasing at places in her mind that were not fully awakened and places in her soul that had been sealed shut.

"He is…Lord Templeton's brother."

Carslyle frowned, and she knew he was confused because Marcus Templeton had no legitimate brothers.

She waved her hand. "The wrong side of the blanket."

His eyes narrowed. "You met him when Landsdowne asked you to shepherd Lady Templeton into society?"

She shook her head. "That would make sense, I suppose, but no. I met him in Vienna. He is here in London now. I wish he were as suitable as a prince or count. But enough of me," she said. "You've never told me about this secret love affair. Who was she? When was it?"

"She chose someone else, but that is an old story. What does Landsdowne say of this?"

The very question angered her. Landsdowne was just one man, one very old man who liked to have his hands in everything. She was grateful to him for the assistance he had afforded her, but she did not wish to be beholden to him forever. Or to think that his opinion mattered more than her own.

"The problem is not Landsdowne, it is not even Gerard. The problem is me, Carslyle. I thought I was that pragmatic girl you knew and instead I've discovered that I am far more... I chose you, Silvie, Landsdowne, all of society over him and I regret it more every second."

Having said as much to Carslyle, her own feelings were clarified and she no longer forced herself to stop thinking of Gerard. Instead, she gave in to the memories and the worries. Awake in her bed for hours in the middle of the night, she wondered how he was, what he was doing, if he had killed someone in order to gain what he thought Jane demanded and if, in doing so, he would even receive the title, as she wouldn't put it past Anche to rescind a promise on some technicality. And, although it had been less than forty-eight hours since she had seen him last, the question plagued her: did he still love her?

She still loved him.

In the darkness of the night, that was the revelation that stunned her the most. It did not matter if she were the old Lady Jane Langley or the new. If she was strong or weak, prompted by reason or love, beset by guilt, anger or shame. It did not matter that he might have already done something she abhorred instinctually, that would likely haunt him longer than anything in his past. She still loved him, still wanted to see him and spend her days with him. To discover all the parts that had not yet been revealed. To help him bear the pain.

She rolled out of bed and changed her clothes, choosing a dress she could easily fasten herself. Yes, it was foolish to an extent to go to see him again at his rooms, but it was more foolish to wait for him to come to her. Someone had to bridge this chasm between them, to bring them both to their senses.

She woke Bohm up. He grunted at her and she left, waiting for him at the bottom of the servants' stairs.

"Where to now?"

"To the Billingsley."

"I do not know the finer points of English mores but...I believe it is not the usual to call on a man at his residence."

Jane crossed her arms and stared at him, as if anything that had occurred in the last months had been usual in her life.

"I shall go and bring him back."

She couldn't abide having to wait a moment more and yet, Bohm was right.

"Go then," she said, and wrapped her arms more tightly around herself. "Bring him back."

Chapter Twenty-One

"Jane."

Jane awakened all at once, and blinked at the glaringly bright morning light. Late morning from the look of it. Then she scanned the room for the man whose voice had ripped her from her sleep.

He was sitting at the foot of her bed, unshaven and tired-looking, that dark hair rumpled, his clothes rumpled as well, as if he had slept in them or perhaps not slept at all.

"You are here," she said, relief flooding through her. She pushed at her night covers and crawled toward him. He reached for her. "Bohm found you?"

He nodded. "But I would have come, in any event. It was the first moment I could."

She swallowed hard and clung to him, savoring the strength of his body beneath her hands, that he was there and real. That the long night and waiting was over.

"Jane."

"No, don't speak. Let me."

Gerard frowned.

"It took me too long to realize what was important and what was not." Her confession, her plea for absolution was jumbled. All the thoughts she had had these last weeks disordered as they left her mouth. "Perhaps it is too late." How awful for him if she were to tell him now she would run away with him only to discover he had already committed the deed. He would resent her. "Gerard—" She bit her lip, unable to say any more, too full of confusion and pain.

"Let *me* speak then," he said. "I want to know what a peaceful life with you would be, in which I can enjoy your intellect and your humor, your view of the world. One in which there are no intrigues endangering you or us."

He sounded so sad, as if he thought that desire impossible.

"You asked me to run away with you," she whispered. "In Vienna. I should have said yes. If I could go back in time, I would."

Gerard was silent and the silence ripped through Jane's throat, her chest, bared her open.

"I know I hurt you," she said. "I know I was stupid. Incredibly so."

"Ah, Jane," he said on a sigh, She pressed her cheek against his chest and breathed him in. His words vibrated against her hair, against her skin. "You were in an impossible situation. And you were right. I have acted as the tool of men who wield political power. The greatest power I have is the ability to disappear."

"Disappear." Her stomach lurched and nausea rose up into her throat. What had he done? What had she done that he was at the point of giving up not only on them both but on himself?

"At every turn, you followed me," she whispered. "Came to me. You said you would not let me go and you meant it. Tell me you still mean it, because this time I intend to follow you. I won't let you go. I won't let you disappear."

G erard leaned back, took her cheeks in his hands and searched her eyes. He wasn't certain what she thought he would do but he was holding tight her words in his heart. If she could go back in time, she would have run away with him. She didn't need a title or position in society. They could create their own world somewhere else, far away.

Twenty-four hours ago when he had stood outside her house at both the highest and lowest point of his life, he had despaired of this. She met his gaze, her eyes luminous, shining with that inner light that was so a part of her. He could burn in that light and accept his fate happily.

"I am done hiding from my heart." She inhaled sharply and then threw herself against him, pressing her mouth to the curve where his neck met his shoulder, where his pulse throbbed and his skin was soft. "I love you. *Gerard*…I love *you*. I am yours, my heart, my soul, my body. Everything."

Her soul. It was a word that meant so much more to him now than it ever had before. He was no longer an empty shell of a man longing for a family, loving a woman he hoped would help him heal the void inside. Instead, he could come to Jane now as her equal.

"I don't intend to disappear. In fact, for the first time in my life, in no small part due to you, I can. Jane, I told Anche no."

She made a small noise and then trembled against him. He took her face in his hands once more and drew her gaze to his. Tears brimmed on her lashes and the twisting of her face as she tried not to cry tore at his heart. Of course, she had imagined the worst, and she had known that it would have destroyed him. And them. He laughed, even though he wanted to cry too, and wiped at the wet trail a tear left on her cheek.

"So I am rather glad you would have me as I am, because he was not best pleased." She looked worried now, and he spoke quickly to alleviate the new fear. "But luckily, we shall not have to go to such an extreme to live our life together."

"Gerard…"

"My grandfather, as you know, is a formidable man. And if I wish, if *we* wish, the barony may still be mine." He held his breath for her answer. He would do whatever she wanted. She had saved his life, his soul, and made him whole in a way he had never been before. She loved him, an impossible thing to believe, but she had said it, and despite everything she was there in his arms. Warm, alive, vibrant.

Jane felt like a ship battered in a storm. So many emotions had filled and destroyed her these last few minutes that she barely knew what to say or what to think. But Gerard was holding her, and he had chosen himself over pursuit of her. He had…he had finally let her go, and in doing so…

Tears spilled again as her heart burst. She had doubted him. His past, the intensity of his desire for her, all of it had terrified her. But he had chosen a different life.

He had said she had saved his life but she could see now that he had also saved their love. Perhaps she had been willing to run away with him, but she had settled for a love that pained her even as she could not live without it but now…now she was learning that there was a love even greater, that her admiration for him was even greater.

"Jane, what say you?" His voice was warm and deep, caressing her with each syllable.

"I love you."

He bent his head and captured her lips. She gave in to the touch with a sigh of pleasure, of love, of coming home. But then there was cool air where he had been.

"I love you too, but the barony. Is it what you want? Landsdowne will make it so, if it is."

Landsdowne. His very name was a weight upon her. The way Anche had been. So he had recognized Gerard as his own. Perhaps it was an acknowledgment of his debt to his grandson, but acquiring a title for Gerard would be more than that, another debt to repay. She shook her head.

"No," she said. "No. Let us start our life without any intrigue and darkness. Just…just Jane and Gerard, as we were in that inn in Vienna. But forever."

His beautiful smile made her heart lift to meet it. "I love you, Jane. You are wise and perfect and…"

"I am neither of those things, but what of Szabo? Will we ever truly be free of the intrigue?"

He took a deep breath and then shook his head. "I do not know. Though Szabo does not know my…this name, he knows yours. And though I am confident in the safeguards I used to conceal my identity, to ensure I had an identity I could return to, I don't wish to mislead you."

She nodded. "Then perhaps England is not the place for us? Perhaps we need a new home altogether, one where Lady Jane Langley is merely Jane Badeau. Or Jane... whatever name we choose."

"Is that what you wish?"

She shook her head. "No. I would do it if it were the only way to be with you but I think..." She laughed. "Perhaps Herr Bohm would consider staying. Perhaps we need a half dozen Herr Bohms."

His smile was tight.

"We will figure it out," she said with a shrug. It was morning and he was here in her room, holding her. There would be time enough for the practicalities. "Gerard, I love you."

His eyes brightened. "I cannot hear that enough. Say it again."

She laughed. "I love you."

He wrapped her close in his arms again, mouth meeting hers. She had a million questions to ask him and there was so much more to discuss. About Anche, about his grandfather, about his childhood and about Szabo, but all of that could wait. What mattered at that very moment were his lips on hers, on the fact that *he* was hers. His hands that held her tight as if he'd never let go.

And he wouldn't.

Neither would she.

Chapter Twenty-Two

Jane had never seen Lord Landsdowne in a more domestic situation. Sitting next to Thomas and Mr. Brown, Thomas's tutor, a crackling fire in the background, he was surrounded by the greenery and mistletoe that decorated the sitting room for the Christmas season. Of course, he *was* arguing with Mr. Brown about Kant's *Critique of Pure Reason*, but still.

In fact, Jane was bemused by the entire situation, the room that was filled with people visiting the estate until after Twelfth Night. Lord and Lady Templeton were present, with their daughter. Her father, Lord Langley, was there as well. *That* had been a surprise. Silvie was there, too, and Herr Bohm, of course, who had become more of the family than a bodyguard.

And then there was the newest addition, Katherine, who rested in her father's arms despite the nurse who hovered nearby. Katherine was why Jane's father was there, why the

Templetons had come as well, a baby being sufficient reason to bring this rather motley family together.

The only one still missing was Giana, Gerard's plans to retrieve her during a post-wedding trip to the Italian peninsula postponed by Napoleon's escape from Elba and the renewal of conflict on the continent. Traveling alone, he could easily have avoided the battlefields, but he had wished neither to leave a pregnant Jane nor to endanger his sister. After Twelfth Night, now that Jane, Katherine and Thomas were settled at the new estate, and with Silvie staying until his return, he would go.

"My turn, Alandale," Langley said, reaching for Katherine. Her father took great pleasure in calling Gerard by his new title, as if it were balm for having to earlier accept a match he felt was beneath the family.

The new title was a significant source of Jane's bemusement, as well. Not only because she and Gerard had decided not to pursue the barony, but also because she had only just begun to accustom herself to the name Mrs. Badeau when she had had to adjust to answering to Lady Alandale. Nonetheless, Lady Alandale she now was. Only two weeks after marrying and beginning to settle down at Gerard's newly purchased estate, Anche had arrived, a dour look upon his face. With Napoleon escaped, he was desperate for information, and Gerard just happened to have some of use, as well as contacts with whom he could put Anche in touch. Eight months later the barony had been awarded.

Had Landsdowne been involved behind the scenes, pulling strings he had been reluctant to pull before? Jane couldn't say. All she knew was that ever since changing his mind about assisting Gerard, Landsdowne had taken a great deal of interest in his grandson, insisting on introducing him to his closest friends.

While some acquaintances had remained sticklers and Jane had received fewer invitations for a while, Landsdowne's approval had certainly helped ease the awkward transition into a somewhat scandalous married life. At the same time, being married had afforded Jane a freedom to pursue intellectual interests she had not previously. Those circles, the ones she most valued, were even more welcoming than before.

"Careful," Gerard said as he gently transferred the bundled infant.

Langley shot him a baleful look before he turned his doting eye back on his granddaughter. "What a pretty Kate you are. With any luck you'll grow up to be as intelligent as your mother, as well."

Jane stiffened at the words, the overheard compliment that her father had never given to her directly. She hated that she felt some small pleasure at them. After all this time, she should hardly care what her father thought. Yet, she still did.

"Come, Jane," Gerard said softly, stretching a hand out to her. "Let's take a stroll out on the balcony and look at the stars."

She pulled her thick cashmere shawl tightly around her shoulders and followed him outside into the cold December night. He pulled her into his side, his arm around her waist, and they stood close together, breath frosty in the air. The moon was a sliver and she could barely discern the outline of trees that delineated the garden from the woods beyond.

"Did you ever imagine—" She stopped, because of

course he hadn't. How could either of them have imagined such a gathering as the one tonight? His grip tightened. He turned her and she looked up into his face. The moonlight reflected on his eyes and she studied them, marveling at the change a year had wrought, the lack of shadows in his gaze.

"For once I agree with your father. You are beautiful and intelligent, and now the mother of our child." He broke off and she thought his eyes glistened. "Thank you," he whispered. "For Kate, for your love, for life."

Tears stung her eyes, and her heart was too full to speak. Instead, she lifted her face to his. Her lips to his, to the kiss that was everything she needed and more. To the love she had never truly imagined possible but now was theirs.

OTHER BOOKS BY SABRINA DARBY

Lord of Regrets

About the Author

Sabrina Darby has been reading romance novels since the age of seven and learned her best vocabulary (dulcet, diaphanous, and turgid) from them. She started writing romance the day after her wedding when she woke up with an idea for a Regency. She resides in Southern California with her husband and son. She can be reached on Facebook, Twitter, and her website www.sabrinadarby.com. To learn about new releases, join Sabrina Darby's New Release List.